THE PARTISAN

OTHER BOOKS BY BENJAMIN CHEEVER

The Plagiarist, 1992

The Partisan

BENJAMIN CHEEVER

Atheneum NEW YORK
Maxwell Macmillan Canada TORONTO
Maxwell Macmillan International
NEW YORK OXFORD SINGAPORE SYDNEY

Copyright © 1993 by Benjamin Cheever

Atheneum   Maxwell Macmillan Canada, Inc.
Macmillan Publishing Company   1200 Eglinton Avenue East
866 Third Avenue   Suite 200
New York, NY 10022   Don Mills, Ontario M3C 3N1

Macmillan Publishing Company is part of the Maxwell Communication Group of Companies.

Library of Congress Cataloging-in-Publication Data
Cheever, Benjamin, 1948–
    The partisan/Benjamin Cheever.
        p.   cm.
    ISBN 0-689-12174-1
    1. Authors and publishers—United States—Fiction.   I. Title.
PS3553.H34865P37   1993   93-13445
813'.54—dc20   CIP

Macmillan books are available at special discounts for bulk purchases for sales promotions, premiums, fund-raising, or educational use. For details, contact:

        Special Sales Director
        Macmillan Publishing Company
        866 Third Avenue
        New York, NY 10022

10 9 8 7 6 5 4 3 2 1

Printed in the United States of America

For Jezebel

This is the excellent foppery of the world, that when we are sick in fortune—often the surfeit of our own behavior—we make guilty of our disasters the sun, the moon and the stars: as if we were villains by necessity, fools by heavenly compulsion . . . Tut, I should have been that I am, had the maidenliest star in the firmament twinkled on my bastardizing.

—Lear

THE PARTISAN

1

That was the summer I worked for the *Westchester Commons*. I was in love with Amy Snodgrass Rose. Amy was in love with David Hitchens. David was in love with Gloria Thomas. I was in Westchester. Amy was in Washington State. David was in Montreal. Gloria had gone to Paris. The sex was very safe.

And I was very lonely.

I sent a postcard every day. "Nonsmoking film major seeks statuesque redhead to share his dreams. Correction: N S F M seeks to support redhead's dreams. Correction: N S F M dreams of redhead. Oh, you know what I mean. Anything but smoking." I always signed it: "Desperately."

The messages weren't all that witty. I didn't think a sense of humor was what Amy wanted in Mr. Right.

I had a box of fifty copies of the same card. She wouldn't have to read the message to know it was me. The picture was of Geronimo. It had been taken by De Lancy Gill in 1905, four years before the old chief's death. So the sachem is in his late seventies but still looks like he'd rip out your white heart for a peppermint Lifesaver. He made Gill pay him two dollars before he'd pose. His was a good face for the cards I sent to Amy Rose. The Apache looked like I felt: beaten but resolute, humbled but still proud.

I'd learned not to count on the U.S. Postal Service for precision, but I guessed that if I sent a card every day she'd think of me often. Who said that showing up is eighty percent of the job?

And Amy was a job I wanted, although I liked the job I had. You've probably seen the *Westchester Commons* or something like it. It's a weekly giveaway, a shopper, a book of advertisements.

Locals find it in the mailbox, and we try to have a pile out at the newsstands for people who are just passing through and might want to enroll in the basic handgun course, visit a garage sale, or purchase a bedroom set, like new.

My family had always gotten the county shopper at home. First I read the personals. I thought I'd learn about sex. I didn't. In fact, the classifieds made real-life sex seem even less a possibility. Everybody who wasn't a "sensitive MD" was a "financially secure nonsmoking white Christian professional who loves to cha cha cha."

If I couldn't buy love, I thought maybe I could buy something else, and I began to read the ads for merchandise. In order to get a bargain out of the *Commons*, you have to go to some person's house.

I tried it once. I meant to buy a parlor bicycle for Uncle's sixty-sixth birthday. The seller was in Griswold. Griswold is fifteen minutes away on the Saw Mill River Parkway.

She sounded Italian. Maria something-or-other. I found the house at about 7 P.M. We were alone. Maria was a good-looking young woman, slender and without a wedding band. The front hall smelled of meat sauce.

The bicycle was in the laundry room. There was a black lace brassiere hanging over the seat. The cup was large. We talked for a while. Maria was shy, embarrassed. This too seemed propitious. What I couldn't figure out was how she would have known who would answer the ad. It was like something out of a fairy tale or Joseph Campbell: Place a notice for a piece of exercise equipment. Marry the first man who comes to see it.

I asked if she would accept a personal check. She would. We kept talking, and then, more to have something to do with my hands than anything else, I picked up the brassiere. The seat cover was badly torn.

I couldn't buy a bicycle with a torn seat. Not as a gift for Uncle. The symbolism would have been too obvious.

I haven't gone out on an ad since then, but I did still enjoy seeing them. Most of our copy was written by civilians. We called them "reader ads." People expose themselves when they write:

BUDGET BRIDE: New, full-length wedding gown. Two bridesmaid's dresses. Never been worn. $1,000 or B.O. Call 890-2550, ask for Josie. I'm in the back.

I was glad to be at the source of all this self-expression. Most of the walk-ins were pretty easy to take. Sometimes I'd pitch in with the wording. Then they'd write a check. Usually it wouldn't bounce.

There were the exceptions: people who managed to bring a high level of unpleasantness to the simplest interaction. I always wonder how these types survive. Who feeds them? I just barely get enough love to live on, and for that I have to debase myself. I send postcards. I shop for stationary bicycles. I chop wood. I scrape the dinner dishes.

But there are men and women out there who wouldn't cross the street for anybody else. And there are other men and women who love them. Which puts the first type, the unpleasant type, way ahead of me. Or that's how I see it.

Some people are eaten alive by their desire for money or fame. Not me. I just want whatever magic it is these creeps have. I want the sort of love you don't have to earn.

One incident comes immediately to mind. The guy wasn't just smug, he also had class. Wasp was the word he brought to mind. Not Wasp as in white Anglo-Saxon Protestant; Wasp as in bankrolled, with a talent for outdoor sports, an enthusiasm for gin, and a stinger where the tongue ought to be.

Adonis was wearing a blue blazer with no crest, a blue Brooks Brothers shirt, no pocket, a pair of chinos with no belt, Bass Weejuns without socks.

The frames of his glasses were that off-red that has to be special ordered. The lenses were not thick. These were the sort of glasses the costume people put on a movie star with 20/20 vision when they want to show the audience that he's serious-minded but they still want him to be a heartthrob.

We had a bell there on the counter. I was standing about two feet away from this bell. He came in, looked me in the eye. Then he hit the bell.

I jumped.

"I wonder if you can help me?"

"Yup," I said, and tried for a smile. The customer is always right. Obnoxious sometimes, but always right.

He was carrying a leather briefcase, shabby, but clearly it had once been ridiculously expensive. From this upper-class artifact he removed a single piece of stationery.

I asked if I could read it.

"Absolutely," he said. "That's why I'm here. I want people to read it."

So I did:

> *Halt!!!* For Sale Now. Police dog. Sexually intact. Takes commands in German. Has traveled widely. Answers to Rilke.

"None of my business," I said. "But I don't think this gives all the necessary information."

"Of course not. I could write a book about the dog. In fact, J. R. Ackerley wrote a marvelous book about his German shepherd: *My Dog Tulip*. But you must have read it?"

I hadn't.

"Well, you must. I could certainly produce a book about Rilke, but I'm not going to. Not and pay for it by the word."

"It's fourteen dollars for fifteen words," I said, "and thirty-five cents for each additional word." I stopped and counted. "You've got eighteen words, so that's $16.40. But I think we could do more for less."

Then I got THE SMILE. I couldn't tell yet what it meant. I hope that even then, I didn't think it was friendly. But this may be hindsight.

"What about shots?" I asked. "What about biting? How much will you settle for?"

"What about shots?"

"Has he had them?"

"Certainly he's had his shots."

"Biting?"

"Rilke would never bite anybody who didn't deserve it."

I swallowed. "Is he purebred?" I asked. "AKC?"

Now the stranger seemed bored. He was examining his finger-nails.

"What do you think?" he asked, without looking up.

I nodded. "All right." I reached under the counter and came up with a blank form. We kept a box of cheap ballpoints in a box behind the counter. I took one of those.

"How much do you want?"

The stranger ran his right hand through his golden hair. He had a very deliberate way of moving, as if there were a camera somewhere and it had a crush on him. "Money is the last consideration. The right people can have the dog for free."

I leaned over the counter and wrote. "Here we go," I said, attempting the manner of a much older man, and pushed the completed form back in his direction. "It's twelve words." And then, as he read, I recited:

> Free to good home. AKC German shepherd. All shots.
> Gentle with children.

The handsome stranger looked at me and smiled. Or at least his lips smiled. "I don't know how to thank you," he said.

I shrugged. "It's my job," I said, shyly.

"And you're good at it," he said. "A sort of Maxwell Perkins of the classifieds."

"I wouldn't go that far."

"You undervalue yourself."

I shrugged. By now I was intensely uncomfortable.

"How much is this going to cost?"

"It's less than fifteen words," I said. "It'll run you fourteen dollars for a week."

"And how much for mine?"

"Yours is eighteen words. That's fourteen dollars for fifteen words and thirty-five cents for each word after fifteen. I think it comes to $16.40."

"Are you sure?"

"I think so."

He took a huge black fountain pen out of his jacket pocket, did some figuring on the sheet of paper I'd given him, and then turned it back to face me. He put the cap on his pen, put the pen back in his pocket. "I come up with $15.05," he said.

I looked at his figures, shrugged apologetically. "You're right. I can never remember if it's fourteen dollars for fifteen words, or fifteen dollars for fourteen words. I jumble it up. I'm one of those right-brain people. Sorry."

"*Non se preoccupare*," he said.

"I'll need a phone number," I said, "and a name."

He pointed to the top of his piece of stationery. "John J. Gilbert, M.D.," it read, and there was a Maryland address.

He took out his enormous pen, uncapped it, and wrote in a local phone number. The pen went back into his jacket pocket, and a wallet came out. Dr. Gilbert produced a ten and a five. He fished five pennies out of his chinos. I got THE SMILE again. "Humor me, Max," he said, sliding the coins out onto the counter. "Let's go for broke this time. Run the original."

2

But now I've gotten ahead of myself. The story really begins with a newspaper article more than a year before my summer at the *Commons*. That was in the spring of 1990. And up until then, our odd little family grouping had enjoyed, or at least tolerated, a cloistered existence. Not that I minded. My sister minded enough for both of us.

"If Nelson murders somebody and I grow up to be a Tenth Avenue whore," she once complained, "it will be boredom, not wickedness, drove us to it. No television; there's not a decent novel in the house." The place was crammed with texts, of course, but these were mostly third rate. If a piece of fiction or history was found to have merit, Jonas would lend it out. Better still, he'd give it away.

Jonas Aldous Collingwood had written eighteen gloomy novels. The critics were impressed with his eye for the telling detail. The public hadn't noticed. Then the *International Herald Tribune* ran that article. It said that his last effort—*My Life as a Woman* (Brindle Publications, 1989)—was not fiction at all, but rather a "thinly disguised memoir" of the years its author spent with the resistance in Italy during the war.

First the reporters came in a trickle. They read each other's stories, and the trickle became a drove. Uncle was a great subject: the novelist who had shot men. The Hemingway of Westchester, they called him. Never mind that no two men or prose styles could have been less alike. Jonas did have a beard. He and The Papa both spoke Italian. I don't know if Hemingway ever developed a riff for visitors, but Uncle certainly had.

"I like to imagine myself," he told interviewers, "at the end of my life, standing buck naked at the door of my now-empty house, pressing the final volume of the complete works of Francis Parkman into unwilling hands. An Avon lady or a Jehovah's Witness collecting names for Armageddon," he'd say, and chuckle merrily, as if he had just thought up the line in their honor. The living room rang with laughter when strangers came, and there was touching. The sense was always one of privileged familiarity.

I used to be afraid that two of these people would get together afterward and compare notes. But they never did, which—when you consider the clannishness of American journalists—is a lucky thing. I guess they all thought the experience too intimate to share.

The guests arrived right after lunch and left before dinner. Not one of them ever stayed to eat. My sister, Narcissus, said it was a fear of poison.

Aunt Elspeth responded to this accusation with some heat. "Nobody was ever killed by the meals served in this house," she said. And I rose to her defense: "Besides, how could a stranger know about Aunt's cooking? These people aren't frightened, they're coy. They don't want to be tamed."

Not that food was necessary. Uncle always managed to get some sort of salt on their tails. Whenever possible, he dosed them with alcohol. Otherwise he'd just dose them. He'd interview his interviewers: "So tell me, because I am curious, what *do* the best young people think of Dickens these days?" There was never even a whiff of the brimstone that was his characteristic smell. "And where did you grow up to be so smart?" he'd ask, without irony. For those of us who knew him, the performance was astonishing, like watching a rattlesnake pick up eggs.

It didn't take long before he had the guests shifting about on the sofa. "I want to get you in the right light," he'd explain, with apparent embarrassment, "so as to be certain of the color of your eyes." Nar swore she could see their pupils dilate. "Have you ever considered serious fiction?" he'd ask them, seriously.

The visitors never stayed for the lamb chops and brussels sprouts. They also wouldn't leave until the table was set. Then they'd reel back across the lawn to the drive clutching some dog-eared classic, touched and sometimes greatly cheered. I recall one blonde stringer, a teetotaler so drugged with flattery that she forgot to use her rearview mirror and crumpled the bumper of her rented Ford Escort on our stone retaining wall.

Even the dullest of them sensed that they had been admired, and not solely because of their association with the *New York Times* or the *Des Moines Register*. They were right about this. Uncle didn't just like them for the luster they would give to his myth, he liked them for what they were; he liked them for being alive. Jonas himself found life to be an almost impossible job. He was genuinely curious about how other people managed.

What the guests didn't know—had no way of knowing—was that this admiration was frequently coupled with a murderous disdain, that the dusty copy of *Man's Fate*, plucked by their host from his personal collection, might well have been purchased the week before at Mount Pleasant Library's annual sale. Aunt Elspeth was on the board.

Some of the reporters were canny enough to try and refuse the books. Uncle simply wouldn't allow it. "If I can't even give the great novels away," he would say, smiling wanly, "then I must truly be in a bankrupt profession."

The only way they could safely attack him after having walked off with his copy of *Little Dorrit* or *Our Mutual Friend* was to first acknowledge having taken the gift and then somehow repudiate the gesture. None of the malicious ones was adroit enough to do so. Besides, most of them liked Jonas. He was precisely the sort of writer they did like: polite, talented, and dirt poor. His full beard was gray. There was an uneven jerk to his stride. They were reporters and had probably noticed the cane in the umbrella stand. So his admirers were not vexed by envy. They all thought that if they *really* wanted to, they could grow up to be him. I never thought that, but then *I* stayed for dinner.

Uncle was well aware of what he was doing. "Setting the hook," he called it when he gave the books away. And yet when somebody thought to reverse the trick, he fell like a stone.

The first sign of trouble—the apple in our particular Garden of Eden—was a Smithfield Ham. United Parcel delivered it two days before Thanksgiving.

I lugged the package into the kitchen, cut its bonds with a steak knife. Jonas was tickled. "I don't believe I've ever had a piece of meat with instructions before," he said.

I don't remember now if I laughed. I certainly shouldn't have. Because looking back now, it's clear that that moment was a tragic one, the breach in the citadel, the beginning of the end.

In December Uncle got twenty-five pounds of white pistachio nuts. Aunt Elspeth received a fruitcake and a chickadee pin in sterling silver.

We celebrated the virgin birth by getting into uncomfortable clothes, listening to classical music, and eating too much.Uncle had written a novel in which the heroine, the beautiful Assunta Gonfiare, consumes so much *bistecca al forno* on Christmas Day that she bursts and dies, "thus leaving the world by the same portal through which the shade of our Savior was entering it, and on the same day." He called this the Piñata school of spirituality: "You must bludgeon the body in order to free the hidden treasures of the soul." I think he was joking when he said this. He was smiling. But you could never be certain with Uncle when a thing was screamingly funny and when it was not funny at all.

On Christmas morning we would present each other with colorful boxes stuffed with uncomfortable clothes. Usually there would be a toy. One year Nar spent some of the money she'd earned as a counselor at the Pocantico Hills Day Camp on a set of powerful miniature binoculars for Uncle. The December after I turned thirteen, Jonas gave me a single-shot, bolt-action 22-caliber rifle. We were not rich, and so the presents we gave each other were meant to be practical, something to cover our nakedness. We wore our gifts at dinner with the tags still on, in case exchange or refund was indicated.

This was the first Christmas in my lifetime at which Elspeth's beautiful "baby" sister, Lily, did not make an appearance. Even after moving to San Francisco, she had always flown back in December, staying in the Tarrytown Hilton for at least a week. Her absence was felt on many counts. She was a great admirer of the novels and kept her host quite pink with praise of his work. She was enough of a stranger to make Nar sit up straight, and to keep my elbows off the table. Also, she gave the best presents.

Not only did Lily fail to appear in 1990, she didn't even send gifts. Or rather she enrolled the entire family in a Fruit-of-the-Month Club, which pleased Jonas mildly and left the rest of us quite bitter.

Under the tree that year, Uncle found a red woolen turtleneck (from Nar) that, in his words, "would have taken the skin off a rhinoceros." Over this, he sported a heavy shooting jacket (from Elspeth) in which he claimed to have discovered cardboard shoulder pads.

"No, no," he said, when Elspeth offered with some asperity to take the jacket right back. "Paper products are of great utility in the construction of certain articles of clothing." He took a gulp from his large, celebratory glass of scotch. "Probably it's recycled newsprint. I'll wear it with pride."

I had gotten into a dress shirt that was supposed to iron itself (a gift from Jonas). Wrinkle-Pruff was the trademarked brand name, and indeed it seemed as though the creases would have stopped bullets. I had on baggy flannel trousers (Elspeth 1988). Under my red crew-neck sweater (also from Aunt), I wore a necktie with reindeer (Nar 1989) and paisley suspenders (also Nar). "I know this is a disappointment," she'd said as I unwrapped them, "since all you want for Christmas is Amy Snodgrass Rose. I would have given her to you, but I couldn't find a box in the shape of an hourglass."

"Even if you'd found such a box," I said, "I doubt you could have gotten her into it."

"I think you're wrong," said Nar. "Besides, you won't know until you've asked."

"I've asked."

"There's asking, and there's asking. You've never known how," Nar said, laughing as if it didn't matter. " 'And I say unto you, Ask, and it shall be given you; seek, and ye shall find; knock, and it shall be opened unto you.' "

I shook my head. "I do think that ours may be the only household in the lower Hudson Valley in which the Gospels are still quoted as advice for singles. But you are mistaken. I have asked, I have sought, and I have knocked."

Nar shrugged. "It's all in the tone of voice."

"It's got nothing to do with my voice," I said. "She lives in Briarcliff. I don't have a car. Not even a howler monkey could make love at that distance."

"You have feet," said Jonas. "You could walk."

"Sure," I said. "I'll phone her now: 'Hi, Amy, this is Nelson. How about a movie? Good. Listen, if we want to make the four o'clock show at the Multiplex, we'd better leave your house at around two. Oh, and wear sensible shoes.' Probably she's never strolled on the shoulder of Route 9A south. She'll love it: the thunder of the tractor-trailers, the grit in her eyes, the colorful litter."

Nar was shaking her head. "I knew I should have bought you the Ferrari Testarosa. I wasn't sure of the color."

"Red," I said.

"To match your eyes?" said Nar.

Elspeth broke in. "Nelson has beautiful eyes," she said. "China blue eyes."

I pretended not to hear this. "With black upholstery," I said.

Sister had on one of my new self-ironing shirts and the blue suede skirt that was her big gift from Jonas. This cut her painfully at the waist. On her narrow feet she wore the outsized pair of fleece-lined slippers that I'd found for $6.50 at an Odd Job outlet store in Manhattan.

Elspeth's skirt (Jonas) fit around her narrow middle. It was so long, however, that it not only reached the floor but actually followed behind her like a bridal train. It was only because of her extraordinary agility—Aunt had been a dancer—that she was able to walk about at all. Above the skirt she wore a gray silk blouse, with a tie (Jonas 1989) and the aforementioned chickadee (source as yet undetermined).

I remember December of 1990 as being unseasonably warm. I'm not entirely convinced that it has to do with the buildup of automobile exhaust in the atmosphere, but there is no denying that winters in lower New York State are not as consistently wintery as they once were. Joe of Joe's 24-Hour Mobil remembers that his great-uncle raced horses on the thick ice that used to form across the Hudson's widest point. "You couldn't race sparrows on it today," he says.

Uncle says tradition must always rely in some part on a failure to recognize obvious change. So, despite the balmy weather and the excess of clothing, there was a fire smoking ominously in the Collingwood hearth. I'd been sent out by Aunt the day before to buy wood at the 7-Eleven. The five logs (1 cubic foot) were shrink wrapped, cost $3.98, and had a yellow plastic handle and a slogan: "A bundle of warmth worth taking home." Nar says all the best writers are in advertising. I suppose they are. But so are all the worst writers. The contents of *le plastic bundle* were identified as "Mixed Hardwood: 80% Oak/10% Hickory/10% Other." I wondered what the copywriter meant by "Other." Pine? Poison ivy?

"Dear Lord," said Jonas when we had settled at the table, "we take great pleasure in the loving presence of those tied to us by long association and financial dependence." He paused here to glance at my sister, and then at myself. "But we do also thank you for the surprising, for the miraculous kindness of strangers."

"Amen," we said.

"Amen," said he.

"Next you'll get the English Wax Jack and the NordicTrack video," I said, picking up my fork.

Elspeth wanted to know what a Wax Jack was.

"It's like a candle," I said. "They used to have them in England."

"Where would you have heard of a Wax Jack?" Elspeth asked.

"Same place our miraculous stranger got the ham," I said. "The display ads in the *New Yorker*."

Aunt smiled weakly. Uncle seemed not to be listening. This was no surprise. When alone with his best beloveds, he made an art of not listening to—or at least not acknowledging—what was said around him.

I looked to Narcissus. She was my audience. But she wasn't interested either. She was the beauty in our household, and I guess she thought—quite rightly—that any material expressions of yearning should be aimed in her direction.

The subject didn't surface again until the gift fruitcake was freed from its brightly colored tin. By this time the fire had gone out. Uncle's cardboard jacket was on the back of his chair. Nar had undone the top button of her skirt. Jonas, Elspeth, and I had all eaten to excess. I'm not sure Nar had eaten any dinner. I saw, actually saw her consume a couple of celery stalks before we sat down. She moved her potatoes around, she cut her meat. Celery was all I saw her eat.

The cake tin had an illustration of a London street scene: snow falling; jolly, alcoholic faces peering from the windows of a coach-and-four. "Come on, Daddy, who is this mail-order Lothario?" Nar asked. She insisted on calling Uncle "Daddy," although he wasn't even a proper uncle, which is to say there was no known consanguinity. (We were both adopted, but that's another story. Or rather it's this story, later on.) In any case, the false intimacy had the desired result: It gave Uncle color. Nar is the sort of girl who likes to make men blush. (Just sixteen that September, my sister was physically and emotionally precocious.)

"He's a writer," said Jonas. "Please pass the ice cream."

"Oh, my God," said Nar, pressing her right hand to her bosom and rolling her eyes in mock passion. "Beware of geeks bearing gifts."

Uncle was staring thoughtfully into the half-empty pint of Ben & Jerry's French Vanilla. He poked around in the cardboard cylinder with a large, slightly tarnished silver serving spoon. "There are writers who have also been men of parts," he said. "Churchill, of course, supported himself with the pen. Admiral Nelson's letters fill seven volumes. Milton not only was a great poet, he was also a great revolutionary; served as Cromwell's Latin secretary throughout the Protectorate."

"Dead, all dead," said Narcissus. "Churchill was an antique even when he was alive. Milton wouldn't have time for poetry today any more than he'd have time for God. Lord Nelson would use the ship-to-shore: 'Emma, this is Victory One. Do you read me?' "

"Now, now, Narcissus," said Elspeth, getting up to clear. "Certainly your PSAT verbals were a disappointment, but there's no cause for bitterness."

Nar stood, fastened her skirt, and straightened it with a dramatic sweep of her right hand. "Make it a personal attack if you must," she said, "but I'll bet three of these goddamned factory fruitcakes that he has horn-rimmed glasses, slender ankles, and the backbone of a chocolate eclair."

"You have no idea how it would please me if we could go from grace to dessert without your violating at least one of the Ten Commandments," Jonas said quietly, putting the ice-cream container down on a brass trivet.

"Honor thy father and thy mother," I said. "No reference to uncles."

"Thou shalt not take the name of the Lord thy God in vain; for the Lord will not hold him guiltless that taketh his name in vain," said Jonas.

"What about her?" asked Nar. "Will he hold her guiltless?"

Uncle didn't seem to have heard this either.

"I'm still dying of curiosity," said Nar, accepting his deafness on the second subject and returning to the first. "Who is this literary supplicant? Somebody who wants to get into your root cellar and look around? Write up his impressions for the *Sewanee Review*? I know how hard it can be to break into the academic world."

Jonas took a bite of cake, chewed, and swallowed before bringing his famous blue eyes to bear. "Delft blue" they'd been in a recent interview with the *Christian Science Monitor*.

"I suppose it is one of the charms of youth that its judgments are made before its research is fairly begun," he said, pausing to brush his lips with a white linen napkin. "Still, you might be interested to know that the young man in question is a medical doctor. And a Harvard graduate."

"I thought he was a writer," I said.

"That's so," said Jonas. "He's written a full-dress biography of John Dos Passos." Then, as if to change the subject, he shifted his attention to me and asked, "How old are you?"

"Nineteen."

"That's what I thought. By the time he was your age, he'd already done the Cheever bibliography. He found and indexed stories nobody else even knew existed. Since then he's written essays on O'Hara and Updike."

"Let me guess," I said. "His name is John?"

My sister didn't notice this one either.

Uncle's eyes flickered, but he said nothing.

"Well, is it?" I asked.

Still no answer. Slowly, deliberately, Jonas cut himself another small piece of cake.

"I don't care what his name is," Nar said. "I'm still certain I could take him in a fair fight."

"And what's a fair fight?" I asked, picking up my fork and running a thumb down the tines. "Did you give Cameron a fair fight?"

Nar didn't seem to hear this. She stood up, came around behind Jonas, and picked up my dessert plate. It was almost as if she were going to help clear.

"Well," I said, "did you?"

"I loved Cameron," Nar said haughtily. "I'm still broken-hearted."

"Maybe so," said Jonas, scratching at his beard, "but it was Cameron who had to leave a perfectly good teaching job and move out of the county."

"Not my fault that we live in the twelfth century," said Nar, still standing directly behind me at the table, holding my plate at an angle. Ice cream began to drip onto the left shoulder of the red sweater Aunt had ordered for me out of the Christmas issue of the L. L. Bean catalog: *For the outdoors inside each of us.*

I turned, took the plate from her hand, and put it back in its place. "Maybe it's not your fault," said Jonas. "But it did work to your advantage."

"How so?" asked Nar.

"If our school board had been any less benighted, they might not have assumed that any fifteen-year-old girl was the victim, or any twenty-eight-year-old man the predator."

I stood, picked up some empty glasses, and headed for the kitchen.

As I walked away, Nar took my seat, and I could hear her beginning to cry. My sister cries with great facility. She's genuinely sad, the shoulders quake, the little face gets wet, and then it's over, like a summer squall. Afterward she's fine; afterward the rest of us are a wreck.

By the time I got back from the kitchen, she had composed herself. "You're ganging up again," she said, dabbing the pretty face with her napkin. Actually it was my napkin. "Why must any attack on literature be apostasy? We all know that the novels written today are artifacts, like bows and arrows were after the invention of the repeating carbine."

Jonas cleared his throat in a way that was supposed to be menacing.

Nar shrugged unhappily. "The people who do read books are old ladies who got the habit a hundred years ago, or else they can't afford a TV."

I picked up two dessert dishes. Nar hadn't had ice cream. Her cake was untouched. "Everybody can afford a TV," I said. "Appalachia is a forest of antennae. They watch situation comedies on death row. Outside of the hardcore Amish, this is probably the only family in America without a television set. We should be— what do you call it? Hallmarked."

"I believe landmarked is the word you're searching for," said Jonas.

"Locked up is what we should be," said Nar. "Or put on display in the Museum of Natural History. Right between the woolly mammoth and the diorama of the Hunters and Gatherers. They could put our living room in a glass case: The Readers."

"That sounds splendid," said Elspeth, "providing, of course, we had access to a good library."

"It is true," I said, "that a lot of the people I know don't have time for books. Or that's what they tell me."

"It's not because they don't have the time," said Narcissus. "It's because they have better ways to spend it. Books don't matter anymore. And I mean novels in particular. Novels don't even have any information in them. And this is the age of information."

Jonas coughed. "Nelson's choice of companions has always been a source of bewilderment to the rest of us. Remember he was once in love with that Grafton girl?

"And I applaud your taste for modernity," he said, turning to Nar, "but ideas are as potent now as they were at the time of Gutenberg."

Aunt Elspeth came back into the room, took the plate from in front of Jonas in one hand, the cake tin in the other, and moved away with a swish of her long skirt.

"Television is an idea," said Narcissus. "Movies are an idea. Nintendo is an idea. The VCR was a good idea. So was penicillin. You don't have to read to take penicillin."

When I got into the kitchen, I found Aunt Elspeth with her hands submerged in the sink. We had a dishwasher, but Elspeth rarely used it. Something about phosphates. I could hear the debate escalating in the dining room. "Isn't it an honor to scrape the plates of greatness?" I said, pushing fruitcake into the small aluminum garbage pail that stood beside the refrigerator. This was the compost-heap pail.

Nar's voice came through the doorway. She was talking about me. "You come down awful hard on Nelson. But you wouldn't hire a private tutor for him when his chemistry teacher specifically asked you to. I bet your generous doctor friend had multiple tutors. I bet a hundred dollars he attended private schools."

Jonas didn't answer. Or if he did, it was in a hiss so low that I couldn't hear it in the next room.

"Well," said Nar, "which was it? Choate? Groton?"

Aunt took one hand out of the sink and drew a finger across her forehead. She smiled weakly. "Would you rescue the ice cream before it melts?" she asked.

When I got back into the dining room, Jonas was looking pale. "Don't give me that tripe about nature and nurture," he said, bitterly. "Your brother was named after a man who went to sea when he was twelve. The weakling son of an impecunious Norfolk parson. Catherine Nelson died in 1767, before the boy was ten. His father couldn't afford to feed him, much less hire a raft of private tutors." Uncle folded his soiled napkin, put it back under the fork. "Men are not born or made," he spat. "Each and every one of us is his own creation. And his own responsibility."

"Amen," I said, picking up the ice cream. I'd heard the speech before. Many times.

"Right," said Nar. "And isn't it fascinating how well all those Rockefellers have done? Year after year, generation after generation. Quite a coincidence of brilliancies."

"If it were not for the generosity of that much-maligned family," said Jonas, "you and your darling brother would almost certainly have been placed in a New Jersey orphanage."

"You've told us all about it," said Nar. "Raised like laboratory monkeys, with a clock and a hot-water bottle for a mother. Good story. Dickens would have liked it. But Dickens has been dead for a long, long time."

"Well," said Jonas tartly, "I hope all this knowledge of English literature translates into an improvement in your test results.

Because right now it looks as if your college choices will be extremely limited. Assuming, of course, that I'll be in a position to pay the tuition. Since a scholarship is right out of the question."

Nar got up, threw down her napkin—actually it was my napkin—and stood there trembling.

"Maybe I don't care about college," she said.

"Good," said Jonas. "You can go to the Empire State School of Cosmetology. And then you can go to work."

"That's what I hate about you," said Nar. "I'm sure there are plenty of good people in cosmetology."

"Your point," said Jonas. "There's no law that says a genius can't go into cosmetology."

Narcissus was furious. I'd never seen her so angry. She was almost screaming. "That's right," she said. "And this may come as a shock to a man of the people like yourself, but there's also no law that says an asshole can't be graduated from Harvard."

Jonas stood, his back ramrod straight with rage. "Young lady," he said, "this is still my house, and you will kindly watch your tongue."

"Asshole," said Nar. "Merry Christmas, asshole!" She kicked off her outlet slippers, strode around the corner and down the hall to her bedroom. A door slammed. Opened and slammed again.

Jonas flashed his eyes in my direction. I guess I was smiling, or at least I did not look sufficiently censorious, because when Uncle saw my face, he frowned deeply. "I suppose you think she's right?" he said.

Despite an international reputation for noticing details, he often used to run us together. He even called me Nar now and again, as in "Oh Nar, do you know where my reading glasses are?" or "Nar, dear, have you seen my wallet?"

I shrugged. "No," I said. "I'm the other one. I'm the one with the dishpan hands. She's the one with opinions."

3

"If I had seven daughters, I would give them all the names of flowers." That's what Jonas used to say when people asked where "Narcissus" came from. The name was precious to him. Part of the reason must have been that it was the only thing he was able to give his de facto daughter that she accepted in good grace and without question.

He and the little flower fought constantly and with the passion and acuity of lovers. The Christmas, or Harvard, squabble, which I have recorded, was followed by a few days of peace. Then we went into the camisole battle, or the war of the shoulders.

The occasion was Brindle's annual New Year's party. To the extent that Uncle had an employer, Brindle Publications was it. He was old-world enough so that we always attended. I understood this. Elspeth understood. Nar didn't understand.

"If you have to pull your forelock," she said, "can't you do it on the phone? Why must your entire family get dressed up and eat a hotel dinner in order to demonstrate your obvious thankfulness?"

Tradition had it that we wore our Christmas clothes, although certain small alterations were permitted. This was not a religious occasion, and the premium on discomfort was therefore not so high. Nar, for instance, had moved the button on the waistband of her gift skirt. I had put one of my new shirts through the washing machine so many times that it was thoroughly wrinkled, if not yet comfortable. I washed it without soap, so as to spare the environment.

The party was to be held at 1 P.M. at an establishment not twenty minutes from our house. Uncle was notoriously prompt. Elspeth, Jonas, and I were dressed and ready at 11:50 A.M. Uncle had on a new bow tie. This was another gift from our mysterious stranger.

Nar appeared at 12:20 P.M. She was wearing the lavender camisole that had been bought for Elspeth in California by Lily the year before. My sister's hair was black, her shoulders were white, her lipstick was red, her eyes were cornflower blue. I thought she looked terrific.

Jonas wanted to know what Nar was doing in mother's pajamas.

Nar blushed. "Going to lunch."

"Not with me, you're not," said Jonas. "Not to a party held by my publishing house."

"But Daddy, it's so comfortable," said Nar. "Besides, you see people wearing these to dinner parties all the time now. Look at Madonna. She wore a black camisole to the film festival at Cannes."

"And handcuffs," I said.

"I think," said Jonas deliberately, "that Madonna is a whore. But not even Madonna would wear that sort of contraption to a dinner sponsored and attended by people whose primary interest is in farm equipment. These are businessmen, engineers. They'll want to know what's holding it up." He turned to Elspeth. "You explain," he said.

Elspeth put a hand on Nar's arm. "Certainly it's fetching, honey," she said, "but we will all have to walk in from the parking lot. With your shoulders bare like that, you'll catch your death of cold."

Then Nar looked at me. "Tell them," she said. "You were young once."

I shrugged. "Catch a cold," I said. "Catch pneumonia. Die. I don't care."

Nar marched off to her room. When she returned, twenty minutes later, she was wearing a raincoat tightly belted at the waist. Now if I had been in Uncle's place, I would have called for an inspection, but I was not in Uncle's place, and Jonas was a proud man.

Brindle Publications had had offices in midtown. They'd been in the Fred French Building on Fifth Avenue. This was a distinguished location. *American Heritage* used to be there, too. In any case, when Brindle was still in the city, the annual gala had been held at the Plaza Hotel on the last weekday before the holiday.

Then, early in 1990, the company relocated to a recently completed and subsequently bankrupt complex near our rented house in Westchester. Blenheim Park is in Tarrytown. The Blenheim part of it comprised three big boxes faced with a material reminiscent of mirrored sunglasses. The park part of it was mostly parking lot, although there were some sections of cedar-bark mulch in which a few dwarfish hemlocks had been placed to die.

As a consequence of this move, the venue of the party was also changed. Brindle engaged the Washington Irving Dining Room in a hotel and convention complex that overlooked the Hudson River in Tarrytown.

Blenheim was certainly a peg below the Fred French Building, and we didn't expect the Half Moon Convention Center to compete with the Plaza. But even Uncle was surprised when the invitation—which arrived in November—suggested that we each select our main course when we RSVPed. The choices were chicken provençal and prime rib.

"It *is* convenient," Elspeth said, searching, as always, for the silver lining. "Grand Central can be so overpowering. Now we won't have to take the train."

"That's right," said Nar. "Daddy can drive, and we can all die a horrible holiday death."

Uncle owned a cream-colored Ford old enough to excite the interest of car buffs. This was a Falcon, and Jonas often referred to it as Robert McNamara, as in "after dinner we can all go out for a Carvel, if we can just get Robert McNamara to turn over." I liked the way this sounded, but I'd had no idea what it meant until we studied Vietnam at Briarcliff High School and I learned that McNamara had been secretary of defense during that inglorious conflict. And that before he took the post, he'd been president of Ford, the man responsible for the Falcon.

We kept the battery wrapped in burlap in an old aluminum milk bottle box, which was kept in the outsize bottom drawer of a tallboy that Uncle had inherited from his parents.

"It's not much of a piece," he used to say, "but it's the only thing left from my childhood that doesn't fill me with shame."

Its bottom drawers were large enough to hold the milk bottle box, and a warm battery is a happy battery. Still, I always took it out twenty-four hours before important family outings and hooked it up to the trickle charger.

After Nar's reappearance, Elspeth checked to make sure that the invitation was in her pocketbook. I carried the Die Hard to the car. Jonas followed with a crescent wrench. His leg had been acting up recently, so he used his cane. The cane was in his left hand; he had a rag and the car keys in his right. He carried the small crescent wrench in his teeth. That was one of the qualities that made Jonas so hard to dismiss. Even in his old age, he would carry things in his mouth if he had to.

I took the rag from Uncle's hand and the wrench from between his lips. Nar and Elspeth got into the back seat. I bolted the battery onto its rusted platform, and Jonas connected the cables. We both wiped our hands on the rag.

The Falcon fired on the second try. Jonas put the car into reverse and started down the long, winding drive to Route 448.

Some stranger, presumably a sightseer or hiker, had parked in the little patch of ground that had been cleared for use as a turnaround. Uncle was forced to come out of the end of our driveway in reverse. He did this slowly, with his neck craned and his ears cocked.

The stretch of asphalt for which he was headed is almost as deadly as it is scenic. Route 448, also called Bedford Road and sometimes Route 117, runs south from Phelps Way, splitting the 3,600-acre Rockefeller estate like a crystal geode into two bucolic vistas. There are hills on one side, low-lying meadows on the other. There are stands of giant beech, green fields, stone walls, cows, even horses. The farmland, which would not be out of place upstate, stands out in stunning contrast to the density of southern Westchester. People pull onto the shoulder and get out of their cars to gape or hold children up to the fence. Motorists in no particular hurry will stay on the roadway but slow to a crawl. The motorists who *are* in a particular hurry fly into a fury. Some of these content themselves with making a racket on the horn. Others hit the accelerator and swing out into oncoming traffic.

The road is just two lanes wide, and since the shoulders are often lined with gawkers, the danger of a crash is considerable. People heading in the opposite direction are sitting ducks. John D. Rockefeller III was killed this way in 1978. He was seventy years old at the time, young for a Rockefeller.

Our driveway debouches onto Route 448 about an eighth of a mile north of where John Rockefeller was killed. The highway is straight as an arrow's flight for fifty feet before our driveway. Plenty of room to reach a murderous speed.

I wasn't happy with Uncle's decision to back out without stopping, nor was I surprised to hear the squeal of tires. I braced myself for the impact, but there was none. Instead, a horn blared once. Then a bright blue Miata roared by. Jonas cranked down the window of the Falcon and thrust the middle finger of his left hand out into the winter air.

Nar cheered.

"I wish you wouldn't do that," said Elspeth, in her most pained and motherly tone of voice. "You never know if one of these people is going to be a hooligan."

Uncle smiled faintly as he worked the shift. (The Falcon was a standard, three forward gears on the steering column.) "Hooligans almost never drive Japanese cars," he said.

"Hooligans or not," I said, "tossing strangers the bird is unseemly conduct in a Brindle author."

"Since there are only three Brindle authors extant," said Jonas, "and since I am one of them, it seems to me that I can act as I damn well please."

Brindle Publications took ninety-five percent of its revenues from the sale of catalogs of farm equipment. Over thirty years there had been brief excursions into other areas of publishing. The most spectacular of George Brindle, Jr.'s many moderate failures was a periodical for farmers called *Sun to Sun*. This effort had had a few minutes in the limelight because of the unfortunate title of a piece on crop enrichment. But by the time "Soiling Yourself" made *Esquire*'s Dubious Achievement Awards, the monthly had ceased publication.

Even a broken clock is right twice a day, and when Brindle pulled back from its mainstream efforts it was with two profitable ventures. These were Uncle's novels and a line of cookbooks that was working its way around the globe under titles that always began with the adjectives Hale & Hearty.

And so the Collingwoods were invariably seated with the two middle-aged men—Nathan Smith and Peter Godwin—best known for the richness and variety of their sauces. Jonas used to call them Hale & Hearty, "because of their books and because they aren't." This made Elspeth extremely uncomfortable. She was afraid "one of the children will slip up and call dear old Mr. Smith 'Hale.' And then where will we be?"

"Good question," said Jonas. "Where will we be?"

A large white banner suspended over the convention center's front desk informed us that the management supported our troops in the Gulf. There were also signs directing us to the "Brindle Celebration." We took a series of thickly carpeted tunnels to the Washington Irving Room. Elspeth proffered our invitation, and our names were checked off a list by a young blonde in a blue double-breasted suit. I couldn't even catch her eye.

Elspeth traded our invitation for name tags and a table assignment. Jonas took the stack of paper badges from his wife, tore them in half, and put them in the white sand of one of the two ashtrays that flanked the door to the dining room.

"I do hope Mr. Godwin has recovered," said Elspeth. Smith had attended last year's party alone, saying that his partner was suffering from gout.

Hale & Hearty were not at Table 11. Their places had been taken by a couple of younger and much less distinguished men. Both suits were blue, both ties were power red, both heads of hair were dark brown. And both had been blow-dried. One of the strangers was fat and pale, the other thin and quite pale. They had left one empty seat between them. Nar took this. She still had her raincoat on. The fat one offered her a Rolaids.

Then he passed the package around the table, telling us his name as he did so. He mumbled and I didn't get it. Nobody took a mint. Two waiters dressed as minutemen arrived with an enormous platter, and we were each given a peach half on a piece of iceberg lettuce.

Nar leaned forward and sniffed her peach. "Mmmmmmm," she said. "If I'm not very much mistaken this is fresh out of the can."

Then the thin young man stood up. I thought that he might have to go to the bathroom, but no, he just wanted to introduce himself.

"Allen Crenshaw," he said, as if addressing an auditorium, "Allen like the wrench. Crenshaw like the melon." Then he sat down and pointed at Uncle.

"Jonas Collingwood," said Jonas.

"Salesman?" asked Allen.

Jonas pretended not to hear.

"Uncle's a writer," I said.

"Congratulations," said Allen. "Catalogs?"

"No," I said. "Books."

"Oh," said Crenshaw. "I just read a wonderful book."

"And I suppose it changed your life," said Nar, smiling as she took the blue napkin out of her cut-glass water goblet and spread it on her lap.

"That's right," said Crenshaw without irony. "It's an old book, but maybe your father has heard of it. The man who wrote it had a name like a library."

"Carnegie?" asked Jonas, who seemed to have recovered his hearing.

"That's right," said Crenshaw.

"He started out as a bobbin boy," said Jonas. "Got to be one of the richest men in the world. And by the time he died in 1919, he'd given away nine-tenths of his fortune."

"I didn't know that," said Crenshaw.

"He wrote a lot about responsibility," said Jonas. "What exactly have you read?"

"Just one book," said Crenshaw. "The one he's known for."

"*Triumphant Democracy*?" asked Jonas.

"No."

"*Gospel of Wealth and Other Timely Essays*?"

"No," said Crenshaw, "the book that put him on the map."

Jonas looked bewildered, so I chimed in. "*How to Win Friends and Influence People*?"

"Bull's-eye," said Crenshaw. He looked at Jonas. "Do you write that kind of book?"

The hearing seemed to have gone again. Uncle stared blankly ahead.

"Are your books inspirational?" asked Crenshaw, more loudly this time.

"I hope so," said Jonas, standing and turning to Elspeth. "*Vorrei un whiskey,*" he said. "Something for the bride?"

Elspeth shrugged. "*Un bicchiere di vino.*"

"What about me?" asked Nar. "I want a whiskey sour."

"You're under age," said Jonas. "Besides, I only have two hands. Ask your brother."

So I got up as well. I was taller than Uncle, had been since my fifteenth birthday. Still, I was always surprised to see it. Jonas was a little man, 5 feet 5 inches, and he almost never stood fully erect. Uncle had long arms, wore his hair short, and under the beard there was an enormous chin. Nar had once observed—during an afternoon walk—that he cast the shadow of a chimpanzee. I have always thought it an obvious if unimportant refutation of the theory of evolution that many of the world's most intelligent men have looked exactly like monkeys. Lincoln was a gorilla with tuberculosis, Churchill was a depilated orangutan, Einstein a gibbon. Darwin himself was caricatured as an ape in a much-reproduced picture that ran in the *Hornet* in 1871.

Jonas got his double shot of J&B, and the wine. The wine was free; the double shot of brand-name scotch cost $7.50. We stood together while the bartender poured Nar's whiskey sour out of a can and squirted me a Diet Coke.

I saw Brindle first. He was a big, square man with gray hair cut as if he were in basic training, or just getting over an infestation of lice. He had one of those heads that I've always associated with the Roman Senate. His blunt, regular features were just slightly more pronounced than was common and seemed to carry the promise of violence, or at least of temper. He would have looked good on a gatepost. Or a pike. His suit was dark blue with a thin stripe. It was new without being the least bit becoming. He came up behind Jonas and put an arm on one shoulder. "Happy happy happy New Year!!!," he boomed, smiling.

"Same to you," said Jonas, weakly. "This is my son, Nelson. I believe you've met."

The Chairman and I shook hands.

"What happened to your shirt?" he asked.

"Nothing," I said. "I just washed it a lot."

"Oh," said Brindle, but he didn't look as if his curiosity had been entirely satisfied. He turned back to Jonas. "We've liked your books so much," he said.

Uncle coughed into his hand. "I'm glad to hear that," he said.

There followed an awkward silence, which I finally tried to fill. "Any particular book?" I asked.

"No," said Brindle.

"Well," I said, "which did you like best?"

Brindle colored slightly. "You put me in an awkward position," he said. "I don't consider myself qualified to be a judge of literature."

I shrugged. "You know what you like."

Brindle nodded.

"So which did you like?"

"Well," said Brindle, "I don't know which I liked, because, well, because I haven't actually read your father's books."

Now it was Uncle's turn to blush. Brindle reached out and patted him on the back. "Excuse me," he said, with genuine embarrassment. "What I meant to say was that we like your books as a product. Besides," he said, with forced cheerfulness, "I don't have to read you as long as some people do."

Uncle shrugged. "I suppose that's right," he said.

"You're damn straight it's right," said Brindle. "You know how many inches we publish each year on cotter pins?"

Uncle didn't know.

"Hundreds. It's been years since I've laid eyes on a cotter pin."

There was another painful silence, so I jumped in again. "Where are Smith and Godwin?" I asked.

"Who?"

"You publish them," I said. "The cookbook writers."

"You mean Hale & Hearty?"

"That's right."

"They've gone to Random House," Brindle said. "Unhappy about the sale."

"What sale?" Jonas asked.

Now Brindle looked bewildered. "Don't tell me you weren't contacted?"

It was at this moment that Mrs. Brindle came up to the bar. She too was large and square. She looked a great deal like her husband. In fact the features were so similar that she could have been the other gatepost. Her hair was longer, although it might have been a wig, and her suit, cut in approximately the same style as her husband's, had a skirt instead of trousers. "George," she said, in mock anger. "You are so rude. I sent you up here five minutes ago to get Angie some juice to stop her hiccups. I suppose you've been alienating your customers."

"He's not a customer," said Brindle, smiling calmly.

"Well," said Mrs. Brindle. "Then you should stop wasting your time."

The Chairman turned back to Uncle. "Excuse me," he said. "I have to go now. But I suppose I should tell you that we're gone. Brindle is no longer. Swallowed up," he said. "I'm out of work."

"You're also a rich man," said Mrs. Brindle.

The Chairman smiled. "I have been compensated," he said. "Adequately compensated. But you'll do fine. The people at Classic are thrilled to have you. They're talking about bringing all your books back into print. Some sort of trade paperback," he said, and then moved away.

We collected our drinks and headed back to the table. As we drew near, I could feel Jonas stiffen at my side. The main course had arrived. It looked dreadful, but Uncle wasn't thinking of his chicken. He was looking at his daughter. Nar had stripped down to the pajamas.

"Oh, Daddy," she cooed, looking across my arm to Jonas as I passed her the drink, "this is much better than the Plaza."

Elspeth stood and took the glass of wine from her husband's hand. "The chicken does seem to have been thoroughly cooked," she said.

"It certainly should be," said Jonas, sitting. "They had a month."

Crenshaw heard this and broke into giggles.

Nar put a hand on his forearm. "You have a great laugh," she said. The Melon colored noticeably. I remember thinking that Dale Carnegie wasn't going to be able to help him now. He had pulled his chair out so that he could get a better view of my sister. And the cast of his eyes was so hangdog, so adoring, that I was embarrassed on his behalf.

I ate a forkful of chicken.

Jonas was sitting at my right. "It's not very good," I said.

"No," he said. "It's not meant to be."

"Has the Chairman always been like that?"

"If you mean not reading, then the answer is yes. He hates even to look at print. When they write the annual report, he hires a young man to follow him around on the golf course declaiming the drafts."

"Is he illiterate? Can he read?"

"I think so. He'd just prefer not to. He's out of the habit. If we had a fire, I don't believe he'd read the exit signs. I'm just another cotter pin," Jonas said, and smiled.

"If you had to be a pin," I said, "you'd be a tie pin, or a collar pin."

Jonas picked up his roll, looked at it, and put it back on his bread plate. "Hemingway would be a brass barometer," he said.

"Walt Whitman a feather duster," I said.

"No," said Jonas, "you're confusing biography with art." He was already losing interest in the conversation.

Crenshaw had tucked his napkin up under his chin. He'd eaten most of the meat off his rib. He was talking earnestly to my sister.

And she was listening, just as earnestly.

"What's the first principle?" he asked her.

"I don't know," said Nar. "I know the First Commandment: 'Thou shalt love the Lord thy God with all thy heart and with all thy soul and with all thy mind.' "

"Nope," said Crenshaw. "Not commandment, principle. The first principle is: 'Don't criticize, condemn, or complain.' "

"Oh," said Nar.

"It's all about putting yourself in the other guy's head," Crenshaw explained.

"I've heard of that," said Nar.

"Confidence is also essential," said Crenshaw. "Confidence in others, but also confidence in yourself. Let's take you," he said.

"All right," said Nar, and I swear she fluttered her eyelids.

Crenshaw paused for a moment but then continued the lecture. "You probably think of yourself as somebody ordinary, a young person without anything in particular to contribute. That's what most people think." He picked up the bone of his prime rib and gnawed thoughtfully. "That's what I used to think about myself," he said. He put the bone back down and wagged his head at the enormity of such an error. "But I was mistaken. And so, young lady, are you."

"Oh," said Nar, leaning forward as she spoke. "Am I really such a fool?"

Crenshaw smiled broadly. His chin was shiny with juice. "This may come as a great surprise," he said, "but you are quite a beautiful woman."

Nar reached out with her napkin and dabbed his chin. She hadn't just caught the Melon, she'd also netted Rolaids. He wouldn't talk with Elspeth. He couldn't even eat. And he looked like a man who, under ordinary circumstances, might have wielded a very heavy fork.

By the time we got up to leave, one of the minutemen had appeared at the far end of the dining room with a vacuum cleaner. Rolaids managed to insert himself between my sister and the Melon for long enough to help Nar on with her raincoat. I suspect he considered this a victory. Putting on clothes, taking off clothes. What's the difference? Crenshaw certainly didn't like it. He made a great point of taking down Nar's phone number. And not sharing it.

When we got to the parking lot, the light was almost gone. A warm battery is a happy battery. A cold battery is a dead one. The car wouldn't start. "I'm freezing," said Nar.

I went back into the building and called Joe at Joe's 24-Hour Mobil.

We didn't get to the house until well after dark. We hadn't thought to leave the outside lights on. Coming in from the drive, Nar tripped. I heard her cry out in pain and surprise. She'd turned her ankle badly.

"It's the ice on the slate," said Elspeth. But it wasn't ice. Nar had lost her footing when she stepped on a brown cardboard box that had been left on the path by United Parcel. Jonas and I carried her across the threshold.

I learned later that this was a package of Georgia fatwood. I think it must have come from Uncle's beloved stranger. Jonas wouldn't say, nor would he let me read the return address. I did glance at it, though, as I walked backward toward the kitchen door with my sister's legs in my arms. It looked to me like Doctor Literature lived somewhere in Maryland.

4

After the hullabaloo, no one will remember the little virtues: that Jonas was witty, that he was generous. "I've long felt," he used to say, "that there are three taps at the pantry sink: one for hot water, one for cold, and the third for cash."

When he sold a book, the trash man got fifty dollars. When Jonas went into town and took a cab, the tip would often exceed the fare.

If Uncle's philanthropy did not make much of an impression on the world at large, this is probably because he had no money.

"Life in Pocantico Hills is expensive," he used to say. "With children it's prohibitive."

I think he felt that he'd been tricked into fatherhood.

"You should have seen your aunt dance," he once told me ruefully. "When I met her, she was living in a rat hole in Greenwich Village, subsisting on cigarettes and coffee. It would have taken a man with more discernment than I could muster to see that what she really wanted was to spend her life making macaroni-and-cheese casseroles, attending library meetings, and wiping runny noses."

I guess a lot of men are surprised and dismayed by the claims of domesticity. Jonas had a case. We were not even his real children.

He joked about the "fire-sale babies," but I think he found our problems sobering enough.

"Nelson was trouble from the get-go," he used to say. I didn't walk by one, nor did I talk by two. And there were the rubber sheets. We had a grandfather clock (this was an expensive antique and had come with the house). I'd lie awake listening to the chimes and imagining how pleased everybody would be when I appeared at breakfast, tired but dry. Then I'd fall asleep and dream that I was out running across the hayfield that lies between our house and the road below. It was always dawn, the birds raucous with joy, the sky a pearly gray. I'd stop, check to make sure nobody was looking, and take a long, gratifying pee in the hay.

The family pediatrician suggested an electronic gadget that would fire off bells, "give shocks whenever the boy begins to micturate, and condition him out of it." Aunt thought the idea too cruel for words.

And I started off as a bad student, spent two years in the first grade. By the time I learned how to read and graduated out of rubber sheets, I'd developed a new and even more alarming tendency. I got into fights. But these weren't your regular schoolyard tussles. I never lost. The child I had my little misunderstanding with was often seriously hurt.

These sociopathic instincts were kept from having more serious consequences by the fact that I had made myself, as Uncle used to put it, "an honorary proletarian." The Pocantico Public School had its share of Rockefeller descendants, and there were the brilliant offspring of distinguished doctors, artists, and social activists whom that family had lured to the area. There were also, however, the sons and daughters of the people who drove the Rockefeller lawn mowers and operated the Rockefeller backhoes. These were my friends.

Uncle used to say that my social instincts were "highly democratic," but really, he didn't approve. I remember overhearing him quarreling with Elspeth about it one night when I was thought to be asleep.

"I suppose we might be thankful," he said. "At least when the boy goes to jail, he'll speak the language. He may even know his roommate."

Because of my frequent fights, I was taken to a psychiatrist, diagnosed as dyslexic. The prescribed eye exercises diminished my reading problem. My grades rose. Unfortunately, this created a rift between me and the people who had been my friends.

So I became a semisolitary. The spring I turned nine, the plans for a big birthday party had to be scrapped. There was nobody to invite.

Nar looked at first to be the good child. She did walk at one and talk at two; she never repeated a grade. The longer she stayed in school, however, the less interested she became. By the time she hit junior high, most of her passing grades were earned by personality rather than by any application to academics. Personality was Nar's talent, and her undoing.

"I thought it so winning," Jonas said, "when she was three years old and would sit in anybody's lap. But when she got to be thirteen and kept right on doing it, I began to worry."

5

I don't know if the gifts stopped or if Jonas just stopped sharing them. I was in Manhattan at NYU that winter and only visited the country on weekends and days off. Still, I'm sure I would have heard about it if there had been packages openly received. I came home for Easter, and there was nothing on the dinner table that I could attribute to the kindness of strangers. My sister—recently off her crutches—teased Uncle mercilessly. "No sugar eggs with Henry James inside?" she asked. "No bonnet for Auntie?" Jonas pretended not to know what she was talking about.

I actually felt a little sorry for the old man. He was trying to begin what his new publisher had already touted as his "break-out book," a nonfiction memoir of Italy during the war.

Brindle Publications had been purchased in December of 1990 by the German conglomerate Ich Spreche Nicht Viel Deutsch. This group, best known for the manufacture of common household tranquilizers, also owned several magazines and Classic, a large if largely unprofitable American trade publisher. Brindle's top officers were parachuted out; the business was folded into Classic. Jonas would certainly have been informed of the transaction immediately, if Jonas had gotten his mail. But Uncle almost never got his mail.

Pocantico is a hamlet and therefore exists in municipal never-never land. Going south on Route 448 through the Rockefeller meadows, one passes tennis courts and then a Tudor-style school on the left. Down and to the right there's a cluster of old houses around a sort of common. This is the hamlet's center. The residences are sightly and well ordered in a way that is quite out of place in this part of the country.

"Oh, honey," the wife says as the Buick full of sightseers slows to a crawl, "I hope we're not lost. This is beginning to look like Vermont." And if the geometric tranquility excites suspicion, that suspicion is well justified. These houses didn't settle here, naturally, around the square. They were torn from their original foundations, carefully laid out.

There are at least three ways of defining the hamlet. The first is to accept the area served by the school district, but this—because of its excellence—has been expanded over the years and now takes students from Elmsford and North Tarrytown. If one thinks of Pocantico as the Rockefeller park and the lands immediately contiguous, we would also be included. Our house is dab smack in the park.

However you rule on this point, there was no question that we are not in Pleasantville. Pleasantville is an incorporated village whose clearly drawn boundaries we live comfortably beyond.

"If I don't literally reside in a village with a saccharine name," Uncle said, "then I'm damned if I'll get my mail there." So he didn't get his mail at all.

The house was on a named and numbered road. United Parcel and Federal Express—both relatively new to the mail delivery game—could find us with ease. But the U.S. Postal Service, with its years of experience, would not. When I was having trouble sleeping, I used to like to imagine squads of uniformed clerks sitting or standing in those giant buildings in which the mail is sorted, making sure that none of ours got through. *We Deliver! We Deliver!*

Jonas didn't mind. "There's something heartening about the obduracy of the human spirit," he said, "the triumph of passion over rationality. It was precisely this sort of pigheadedness that made it so much safer for the Jews in Italy during the war than it was for their brethren in Germany."

"The truth is," said Nar, "that Uncle doesn't really want letters." We got the junk because that came addressed to "Resident, Pleasantville." It was only the personal mail that didn't make the cut. Once in a great while, somebody was smart enough to figure the riddle out, to ignore Uncle's explicit instructions and write to him in Pleasantville. I always suspected that when this happened, Jonas himself would throw the letter away. There were exceptions. Communications from Lily he kept. She had always written to us in Pleasantville. But then Lily seemed to exist above or at least apart from the law.

Brindle's correspondence had been handed over in person by Uncle's editor, a single woman who lived in Ardsley and professed herself "delighted to make that pretty drive."

When Christabel came by, Uncle would fish my .22 and a box of bullets out of the hall closet. Ms. Gordon had been in Spain for the civil war and was quite a good shot. Editor and writer took turns firing at the empty cans that I used to set up on the retaining wall. Christabel could shoot standing. If Uncle was going to hit anything, he had to lie on his stomach. "I'm just exactly like an old whore," he once said, "useless out of the prone position."

"Supine," I said.

"That's right," said Nar. "Whores lie on their backs."

Christabel had quit on the day her employer was engulfed by the German firm, and so the several messages mailed to inform Uncle of the corporate mating were returned to sender.

After the New Year's party, Brindle himself must have passed on the word of Uncle's confusion to the people he had sold his company to, because from that day forward, the publisher employed Federal Express.

Once the lines of communication were opened, the process was lightning fast; within weeks, Jonas had been signed up for a $225,000 advance. I suppose that people knowledgeable about the publishing business will say that he should have used a literary representative, but Uncle's beloved agent, George Smalls, had died in 1985, and the business had been taken over by the widow. Jonas couldn't abide Mrs. Smalls.

Cameron had gone to work for a big literary agency in the city. Nar, his former student and intimate, had wanted Uncle to have Cameron negotiate.

"I thought you liked Cammy," she said.

"I do," said Jonas. "I like him a lot. But what would Donna Smalls conclude? Besides, there must be some limit to my avarice. I'm already getting more than five times as much as they've ever paid for a novel."

So he handled the negotiations himself, or rather he had me handle them, telling me precisely who to call and what to say.

Classic celebrated the signing with a half-page ad in *Publishers Weekly*. This was—to my certain knowledge—the first time cash money had ever been spent to promote Uncle's work. The display featured a drawing of what Jonas might have looked like fifty years ago. The artist's imagination caught him at dusk moving in a half crouch out from under a stand of tall pines. He looked feral in a way that was familiar and warlike in a way that seemed entirely out of character. He was wearing a beret cocked jauntily to one side and carrying an M1 Garand.

"Jonas Collingwood will give the best account of the good war since Irwin Shaw's *Young Lions*," said the ad copy. "It is as if Marcel Proust had taken up arms. Freed at last from the constraints of polite fiction, this writer of European best-sellers" —Uncle had once made the list in Finland—"will mingle politics and esthetics in a triumphant marriage of literature and journalism."

But Jonas didn't act like a man who had been freed from anything. I suppose the metaphor is too obvious to be fully believable, but he seemed instead to have been trapped in the foreground of that artist's sketch, wearing somebody else's hat and carrying a large and unfamiliar firearm.

He never had talked to me about his work. His trouble didn't change this. But even as an occasional visitor I could see how badly the writing was going.

The signs of distress were clearly visible. It was as if someone had opened a valve in his big toe and then begun slowly, deliberately, to inflate the old man with a bicycle pump. His features thickened. Elspeth had to bring his chinos to the Korean dry cleaner to have the waist let out. But that wasn't the worst of it. The worst of it was that he stopped typing.

Uncle worked in a room that was just off the pantry. He called it the root cellar. And it did run into the side of a hill, in which it was partly buried.

"They weren't putting in root cellars when this cottage was built," said Elspeth. "Besides, the floor is made of wood. It was probably a tack room." There were brass hooks on the wall. Uncle kept his blue blazer on one of these. He wrote in chinos and a button-down business shirt, which he wore open at the throat. The shirt was usually Brooks, white or blue. When company was expected, he put on a bow tie. He used to put the blazer on whenever anyone came to the door. Uncle was always the one to answer the door. And he always put his jacket on. He put the blazer on for the *New York Times.* He also put it on for Maue Oil.

Whatever its origins, his adopted office was spare and dark. He wrote on a folding aluminum table he'd borrowed from a friend who had since died of a heart attack. He sat at this on a dining room chair with a cane seat that shed fearfully.

The table held his typewriter, several piles of manuscript, and a large clay ashtray that I had made for him in shop class. There was also a photo of one of Lord Nelson's letters. This was the first one the great seaman sent after having lost his right arm at Tenerife. It was to Lord St. Vincent and was written with his left hand: "I am become a burthen to my friends and useless to my country. . . ."

There was a pewter frame with a black and white likeness of Aunt and Lily. The picture had been taken right before the two were sent to a private boarding school in Switzerland. They were both wearing long white dresses and black Mary Janes. The sisters sat together on a concrete bench, under a dogwood tree. Neither girl was smiling.

This was the only photo of Elspeth in the house, and I remember wondering why Uncle would want to excite such an unflattering comparison. Even then, even when the girls were in their teens, Lily was a beauty and Elspeth was not.

There were always books piled on the floor, and these recently had included a number of memoirs about Italy during the war. Since signing the contract Jonas had read *And No Birds Sang* by Farley Mowat, *Naples '44* by Norman Lewis, *Family Sayings* by Natalia Ginzburg, and *The Impossible Victory* by Brian Harpur.

It was quite uncharacteristic of my guardian to make a study of the subject he was working on. Also, he seemed to have become a good deal less discriminating in his choice of reading matter. I remember being shocked to find a hardcover copy of *Partisans* by Alistair MacLean. The tail of the letter "r" in the title swooped down to make a circle that held two men with tousled hair, a mountain with tousled snow, a torpedo boat, and a brunette with come-hither eyes. This was not the sort of cover art that usually caused Jonas Aldous Collingwood to dive for his wallet. But then nonfiction was uncharted territory.

Aside from table, chair, and piles of books, the root cellar office was equipped with three file cabinets purchased by Aunt from a defunct insurance agent. These were in battleship gray. The drawers were labeled: Prospects, Life, Auto, Fire, Flood, and Personal Injury. I believe that many of them still contained old Mr. Claxon's papers. The only drawer I ever saw my Uncle use was the one marked Personal Injury, and the only thing I ever saw him put in it was a citation he'd been given by the Westchester Association of Bookstore Owners.

There was a wood-burning stove, and while the windows were small, there were enough of them so that a prisoner who knew the season and the geographic region could have guessed the time of day.

The fire was pleasant enough, and Uncle was commonly enthusiastic about his work, but I still don't quite understand why that gloomy room was such a draw for the rest of us. When Mrs. Picone came on Tuesdays to clean, she'd get the vacuum going and then make a beeline for the typewriter. It usually took her about five minutes to flush her author. Jonas would wander around the rest of the house in great irritation until she was done. Elspeth wasn't quite so bold, but she did seem to be in there emptying the ashtray whenever Jonas wasn't in there filling it. The dogs, when we had dogs, always napped under the table. We even had a cat once, a coal black stray whom we named Flood, because he made a nest in the file drawer with that label.

When we were tiny, first I and then Nar used to like to play on the floor around our guardian's feet while he wrote. Elspeth would leave us in there when she needed to go to the market or for a permanent at Rose's World of Beauty. Most of the time he didn't mind. Most of the time he didn't notice. We were banished, of course, when we learned to speak.

"It's a little like a monk's cell," I once told Nar.

"Provided the monk smoked Marlboros," she said. "The Marlboro monk: Chastity, piety, poverty, silence, and lung cancer."

"Nothing in the Bible about nicotine," I said.

But there was something about the love of money. And Uncle seemed to have caught it, or rather it had caught him. Maybe it wasn't money at all. I can never decide if we in this country care too much about money, or if we're only pretending about money when what really matters is sex or power or the fear of death.

But I'm not being fair. The first check, one for $75,000, arrived in February. The envelope with the check in it sat on the kitchen counter for a week and then went into the scissors drawer. It was not taken to the bank.

Nar was exasperated. "He's a mobster who's just made the heist of the century; he doesn't want to buy anything that might arouse suspicion. You'd think all that money would be burning a hole in his pocket."

I shrugged. "Well, I can see whose pocket it's burning a hole in."

"It's crazy, me not having a horse," she said at dinner the day af-ter the check arrived. "I could stable it at Fox Hill. It's practically a waste of money for me not to have a horse."

Uncle had a way of pulling down his glasses and looking over them when he wanted to give the impression of age and authority. That's what he did now.

"I know that a great many intelligent men and women have de-voted the prime of their lives to convincing you of the opposite," he said, "but it is not possible to waste money without spending it."

"Oh, come on," said Nar. "We live right in the center of the county's best system of trails. Sally Winder has a horse, and I can outride Sally any day of the week."

"Thou shalt not covet thy neighbor's horse," I said.

"I don't want *her* horse," said Nar disdainfully. "I wouldn't ride Colonel Moseby on a bet. I want a jumper."

Uncle didn't say anything. The money, or promise of money, seemed to have lodged like a musket ball near the base of his spine. He was paralyzed. Not that he couldn't walk. He could walk all right. Walking wasn't what mattered to Uncle. Writing was, and he couldn't write.

He was still hunkered over his old black Royal manual, but there was no sound. He looked like a writer, he smelled like a writer, but he didn't write. He'd just sit there smoking. In the mornings he had coffee. In the afternoons he drank water from the tap. "Adam's Ale," he called it, but if it had ever had the power to intoxicate, that power was now gone. When the sun went below the yardarm and he broke out the half gallon of Old Smuggler, scotch whiskey didn't seem to help either.

In the afternoons, when I was around, we always used to do yard work together. "Manly chores," Nar called them, and snick-ered, but I think actually she was sore about being excluded. Jonas and I would split wood for kindling, or turn over the soil in El-speth's vegetable garden. When we had a lot of time, and particu-larly if the sky was overcast, there was often a little bow to culture. He'd ask me, "How long has it been since you've gone to the Mu-seum of Modern Art?"

"Not for a while."

Jonas would shake his head. "Just seeing Rousseau's *Dream* is as good as a week's vacation," he would say. "Did you know that the painting was a gift from Nelson Rockefeller?"

"Yes," I would say. "You told me."

I'd learned to pretend to take these offerings seriously. I'd also learned that this was a charade. We weren't going to take a train to see any water lilies. We were going to stay home, roll up our sleeves, and perform the sort of tasks for which people without green cards are commonly paid a good deal less than the minimum wage.

But now, with this new trouble, he wouldn't take the afternoon off. He said he had to write. He wasn't writing.

"There's a bomb in the root cellar," Nar said, when I aired my worries to her. "If it goes off, we're all going to be very sorry."

"Maybe it's just a great book," I said. "His break-out book."

"Possible," said Nar. "But I doubt it. This sounds macabre, but I think the very best we can hope for is a mild stroke."

"Aren't you the cheerful one."

"I'm also the one who lives at home," she said. "He sits in there all day and does nothing. He doesn't read. He doesn't take a nap. He never speaks on the phone. Remember that old familiar clackety-clack?"

I nodded.

"He typed all day and snored all night. You knew right where he was. He's usually in there where he's always been. But I don't know that. I'm afraid he might sneak up on me anytime. Catch me on the toilet, in the tub, on the phone with the Melon."

"Why do you suppose he's having such trouble?"

"I don't know," Nar said, shrugging. "Maybe he's got some dreadful secret. Something he doesn't want to come to grips with. Not even for $225,000." Then she smiled. "Maybe he collaborated with the Germans."

"What about the wound?" Uncle's leg was supposed to have been badly broken by the explosion from a German Nebelwerfer.

"You can't know about an old scar," said Nar. "Maybe he was a Fascist. Maybe he got shot by some young Italian girl fighting for every true value."

46

"So instead of being the Ernest Hemingway of Westchester, he might be the Klaus Barbie?"

Nar nodded. "Nazi on the Hudson. He'd look good skulking toward the camera with his hands cuffed and his hat pulled down over his eyes."

"He never wears a hat. Nobody with his sort of pretensions has worn a hat since Kennedy."

"You know what I mean. He skulks well enough. You and I could go on the news and say what a kindly old gent he really is."

"That's right," I said. "Wouldn't hit a fly."

"He might insult a fly," said Nar. "He might be sarcastic with a fly, but he'd never hit one. Too obvious."

"I like the idea of his being a collaborator," I said.

"It would be a gas to be on 'Oprah,' " said Nar. "I could give out his recipe for schnitzel."

"Too good to be true," I said. "Probably he's just afraid he can't write badly enough for Classic."

The publisher sent an editor out to our house for tea. I don't remember the exact date. The ground war in Iraq had begun and ended. Most of the yellow ribbons were still up. It must have been early spring. Probably it was sometime in April, although it wasn't April 1. That I would remember.

Paul Whitfield was Classic's executive editor. May still be, for all I know. He brought a shopping bag full of scones and muffins from some pricey Manhattan deli.

He arrived in a black Saab convertible. Jonas was there. I was there. Elspeth was there. Narcissus was not there. We all went out to meet the car. It had its top down and its bra on.

There was a lot of talk from us about what a fine car it was, and a lot of talk from Whitfield about what a great house we had. "And the location."

Then we went into the living room, and Jonas and his new editor spoke about Operation Desert Storm. Elspeth brewed the Hukwah tea and put the muffins on a Canton platter. I was relieved to see that nothing homemade had been produced.

Aunt is a brilliant cook. I have seen her make a nourishing meal out of two old eggs, a chunk of moldy cheese, and three pieces of stale bread. Nar and I used to joke that if Aunt had been present at the miracle of the loaves and the fishes, no miracle would have been necessary. But if Aunt is upset or angry—and I thought she might not like Whitfield—her food can make a person quite sick.

Take the iced tea. We have iced tea all year long. She keeps it in a one-quart jar of pebbled glass that has "Cookies" written on the side in yellow block letters. When there's mint in the garden, there's mint in the tea. Compared to soda, or even juice, it's a relatively economical drink. Uncle approves of the fact that it is traditional and unprocessed. Elspeth actually boils the water and uses tea bags, never what she calls "that dreadful sugary dust."

Sweet tea is generally a good sign, although a tea that has been sweetened to excess may indicate a mild sense of anomie. It can also go the other way. When the Challenger went down in 1986, for instance, there was no sugar in the tea for a week. And while I wasn't old enough to notice, Jonas claims that Elspeth got so angry when Ford pardoned Nixon in September of 1974 that there wasn't even any tea in the tea. Just a quart of water with a sprig of brown mint.

In any case, I was glad that Whitfield had come with his own provisions. My designs on Uncle's money were not as passionate or as tightly focused as those of my sister, but I didn't particularly want us to lose $225,000 because of a batch of horribly burned cookies or a spoiled pâté de foie gras.

There was a distinct possibility that Jonas himself would blow the deal, without benefit of poison. Uncle was always gracious but rarely diplomatic.

Whitfield was talking enthusiastically about the commercial possibilities of an H. Norman Schwarzkopf memoir. "There's a tremendous appetite out there for information about that man."

"Really?" said Jonas. "The only thing I want from him is the name and address of his tailor."

We had a little silence after that one.

"I'm a patriot, of course," Jonas said, finally, "but I don't like to be lied to."

"Do you really think he lied?"

"Those people can't tell a lie from the truth anymore," said Jonas. "They aren't soldiers, they're politicians. They call it the Defense Department. We haven't been properly invaded since 1812. It's the War Department. That's what we used to call it. That's what it is. When you start off lying, there's very little temptation to reverse the trend."

Whitfield shrugged. "My reaction isn't as harsh as yours seems to be. Nobody can survive these days without being aware of the importance of public opinion. I think the cameras had as much to do with our defeat in Vietnam as did the men in black pajamas. You couldn't be romantic about a war that was on the evening news. If they'd had live video from the beach on D Day, Eisenhower would have been relieved of his command within the week. He might actually have been tried and shot."

"I think you're wrong there," said Jonas, "but I take your point."

Whitfield was a tight little item in his early fifties. His brown hair, speckled with gray, was neatly trimmed. The suit was dark and flattering. The tie had pictures of stirrups. He wore leather hiking boots with a thick tread. He had deep blue eyes, and when he looked at you, he didn't blink.

"I came up through business," he explained. "Sales, actually. But I've always loved books."

Jonas lit a cigarette, nodded.

"Ever read Lee Iacocca's autobiography?" asked Whitfield.

Jonas hadn't.

I said, "I read it. He writes that his family was so close it was like a single person with four parts."

Whitfield didn't seem to be frightfully interested in my literary opinions. "It may not be for posterity," he told Jonas, "but it's a helluva good book."

Uncle scratched his nose. "There are many good books I haven't read," he said.

"This is one you shouldn't miss," said Whitfield. "I'll send you a copy."

"Thank you," said Jonas, and he inhaled.

"Now, Iacocca needed somebody to help him," said Whitfield. "He needed a writer in order to tell the story of his life. Did you know that William Novak wrote Iacocca's life for a flat $50,000 fee?"

"No," said Jonas.

"He did," said Whitfield, nodding. "People who'd never bought a book in their lives bought that one. The sucker sold and sold and sold." He smiled around at us when he said "sucker." I guessed the word was supposed to show what a right guy he was. I guessed that was also why he'd worn the boots, so that he could use a word like "sucker" without getting his socks wet.

"Of course, Novak's a lot more expensive now," he continued.

"I'm sure he is," said Elspeth, beaming painfully at her guest.

"In the case of your husband," said Whitfield, brightening, "we already have the writer. He's a two-banger. He's got both the story and the talent to present it."

"Thank you," said Jonas, but he didn't look particularly grateful.

Elspeth asked if Mr. Whitfield desired more tea.

"If it's not too much trouble," he said. Elspeth went out to the kitchen to put the kettle back on.

"We'd like to bring you out in the spring," said Whitfield. "We're all very excited about this book."

"When would you need the manuscript in order to publish in the spring?" Jonas asked.

"September at the very latest. We'd want to show it to the book clubs. The movie people."

Jonas looked uncomfortable. "It always takes me a couple of years to write a novel. That's after I get up a head of steam."

"You must have a head of steam by now?"

I could hear the kettle whistle. Uncle smiled faintly. "No. I haven't yet been able to write anything I'm sure of."

Whitfield sighed. "This isn't a novel. You've already written the novel. Just take it out of the woman's mind, switch the focus to the man, and move the setting from Rome to the coast."

Jonas didn't say anything. Whitfield let the silence last for a good ten beats. Then he started up again, still cheerful. "You won't have to make anything up. Just tell it as it happened."

Jonas cleared his throat noisily. "I don't wish to sound immodest," he said, "but I do have a style. I cannot be expected to function as a sort of prose videocam."

"We're aware of your reputation," said Whitfield. "Didn't somebody once call you the Jane Eyre of late twentieth-century Westchester?"

I didn't say anything. A cloud passed across Uncle's face, but he didn't say anything either.

Elspeth began to make another pass with the food. "I think it's Brontë," she said, smiling. "Eyre's the character, Brontë's the writer. Besides, if there is a Jane Eyre role in this household, I'd like to think it's mine."

Whitfield shrugged, picked up one of the carrot muffins he had purchased in Manhattan, and inspected it, while Elspeth stood in front of him holding the plate. Then he put it back.

"I'm glad the subject came up," he said. "Because we don't want this book to be WRITTEN. We just want it written. Even with William Novak, Iacocca does not turn into a poet. What he had was a great story. He'd climbed almost to the top at Ford. He was Mr. Mustang. You remember the Mustang?"

"Yes," said Jonas. "John Rockefeller was killed in one. It happened less than a mile from here."

"In any case," said Whitfield, "Iacocca was right up there. He'd eaten in the private dining room for Ford executives with the waiters in white jackets. The hamburgers were made out of ground steak. The coffee was served from silver pots. Then Ford took his title away. The company set him up in this nowhere office. I think the coffee actually came out of a machine. Can you imagine that, Lee Iacocca drinking coffee out of a machine?"

Jonas nodded. "Yes," he said. But if he meant this to be biting, Whitfield didn't notice.

"You have a terrific narrative as well," the editor continued. "You've got this young man, an American. He's living in Italy. You've got the war. There's a big castle up on the hill."

Uncle put out his cigarette.

"There's a small force of German soldiers staying in the town. At some sort of boarding house. One of them's a bully. His name is Eric. Am I right?"

Uncle was scratching at his ear.

"You've got this girlfriend. She's a beauty. The German is also in love with her. We've had this all through the mind of the girl, the sister in Rome. Cut her. That's clearly the way to go. Don't you agree? I mean, for dramatic purposes?"

Uncle nodded. "For dramatic purposes," he said.

It was at this point that the doorbell rang. Elspeth went to get it. The rest of us stayed in the living room. It was my least favorite of the Enablers. The name is actually Grafton. We just call them the Enablers. I think Jonas must have started it, but we all do it, all of us except Elspeth. They are the family whose television we watch. They live in a clapboard house on the common, about a mile from us. We go there for the Olympics, general elections, and national tragedies. They always seem glad to see us.

I could hear the inquiring bass of the Enabler at the kitchen door. Then I could hear Elspeth's tremolo: "No, Bill, dear, I'm afraid she isn't home." The kitchen door closed.

Whitfield looked annoyed. "Back to the story," he said. "The protagonist has a girlfriend."

"She's not his girlfriend exactly," said Jonas. "He's infatuated with her, and they spend time together. They make love once. Quite late in the book."

Whitfield smiled. "Actually, that's better. Expectation is nine-tenths of the fuck," he said, and laughed. The boots again.

Jonas didn't laugh. Neither did Elspeth. I laughed, but then I'm the one who's interested in advertising.

"You write a long letter to your sister with a description of the girl on the beach in her *costume da bagno*. Incidentally, I liked that a lot. It's summer, she's tanned. She's got masses of long, dark hair and this terrific body. I love where she wades in up to her waist; she's carrying her shoes."

Uncle smiled. "It's difficult for an American to understand how

52

valuable such things were in that time and place. If she'd left a pair of good leather shoes on the beach, they almost certainly would have been stolen."

Whitfield was nodding, smiling. "That's right. The shoes are English. Boots that lace way up the ankle, too small for a man, too large for a child. They're a gift from the German officer."

Jonas nodded. "Eric is handsome in a strapping, unreflective sort of way. His Italian is very bad, so she has no way of gauging the depths of his stupidity."

Whitfield grinned. "I hope you don't mind me asking this, Mr. Collingwood," he said, moving forward to demonstrate earnestness, "but how fast do you type?"

"Oh, he types very fast," Elspeth said warmly.

Whitfield ignored this. "Indulge me," he said to Jonas. "How many words a minute?"

Uncle bristled. "I wasn't aware that I was applying for a secretarial job," he said.

"We don't want writing with a capital W," said Whitfield. "If it's too well distilled, people are going to think you made it up."

He leaned forward, put down his teacup. "You were in the war," he said. "Use it. I mean, you *were* in the war, weren't you?"

Jonas leaned forward, picked a cigarette out of the package that lay open on the coffee table, and lit it. He did not meet the editor's eye.

"You were part of a group that killed people? Shot German soldiers?"

"Boys, really," Jonas said, inhaling deeply. "We were all children."

Elspeth, Jonas, and I escorted the editor out to his car, then stood by while he checked the straps on its bra. He backed out of the drive. He didn't use the turnaround. He didn't even pause to listen, just roared out across both lanes of the main road, shifted gears, and headed south to Manhattan.

By the time I lost sight of the Saab, Jonas and Elspeth were already halfway to the house. They were walking arm in arm. I hadn't seen them touch each other since we all went to the funeral for Lily's husband. They hardly ever touched, and when they did it seemed almost to be an expression of grief.

6

I've always been mystified by the interest adult adopted children take in their biological parents. They appear on TV. They write books. They are careful to explain that they have wonderful adoptive parents, but still they want to track down the *real* ones. What in God's name are these people looking for? Don't they know that by the time they're twenty-one, they've had the only childhood they're entitled to? There's something ridiculous about the search, those big, sad faces yearning for a missing babyhood. They should get drunk instead, or hit somebody, or cry.

Bloodlines have always seemed to me to be entirely beside the point. Love is a choice. Families are made, not found. Those pivotal connections are forged by some mysterious alchemy of tenderness and cruelty, not by the matching of genetic fingerprints.

What is this mania for *real* parents? Your real parents are the ones you have. Romulus and Remus were suckled by a wolf. They founded Rome. Winston Churchill was brought up by a nanny. He hardly ever saw his biologicals. Once you're raised, you're raised.

Don't some Gestalt therapists claim that it's never too late for a happy childhood? Nonsense.

It's conceivable that the victim of a disastrous upbringing can become a happy or at least a successful adult. But he'll never become a happy child. Not unless you drop him on his head.

Still, I suppose I should take the time to explain how it was that sister and I came to be raised by strangers.

I'm not as interested in this as the viewers of "60 Minutes" are presumed to be, but here it is: We were both adopted by Elspeth's sister, Lily, and by her husband, Hamilton Ballard. The Ballards lived across the Hudson in Montvale, New Jersey. They were childless. Hamilton, a lawyer, was deeply involved in school politics. When a bright young girl whom he had been counseling got pregnant, he was the first one she told. She was then a senior at the local high school with a full scholarship to a distinguished college. The father was said to have been an auto mechanic. The unborn child threatened to ruin her life. The Ballards sent Ms. X to a lodge in New Hampshire, and—in the fullness of time—they adopted the baby boy. That was 1971. I was that baby.

Then Hamilton got sick the first time. Leukemia. Lily devoted so much energy to nursing her husband that she found herself neglecting the infant. Meantime, Lily's sister, Elspeth, had given up on her career as a dancer, moved out of Greenwich Village, and married Jonas. The Collingwoods were childless and had set up housekeeping in the middle of a park, in the middle of one of the best school districts in the state. I was shipped to Pocantico. Nobody knew at first how long I'd stay. But by the time Hamilton got better, or seemed to get better, I had taken root.

This same smart girl, now an Ivy League sophomore, and the

same guy, still an auto mechanic, got drunk together. Ms. X called Hamilton. Back to the lodge in New Hampshire. Hamilton and Lily arranged a second adoption. Brought the baby home. Then Hamilton got sick again, like clockwork. Nar came to Pocantico.

Sister and I used to joke that there was nothing wrong with Hamilton's blood, he was just allergic to children. Allergic to us: the toxic babies.

At least we've never been blamed for his death. This may be because nobody much liked Hamilton.

Periodically, he'd get drunk and lash out at his nearest and dearest. In particular, he used to go after Elspeth. I think it was her goodness that made him wild. Also, he was a coward and she never bit back.

Once, in a drunken ramble, he pointed out that his wife's sister had the head of a plow horse.

It was quite the scene. "Neigh, neigh, clop, clop," he said, then reared and galloped around his armchair three times before collapsing onto the floor. It was a holiday. We were at home. Bing Crosby used to sing it: There's no place like home for the holidays. Maybe I'm just bitter, but I can't help but wonder if Der Bingle ever gave the Ramada a try.

We were all disgusted with Hamilton, but he did have a point. Elspeth has outsize brown eyes, and her teeth are too big. I suppose it's disloyal of me to notice, but when she's feeling shy— which is a regular occurrence—my beloved Aunt has been known to stamp the ground and nicker.

I remember asking her once what was the matter with Hamilton, and she just shrugged. "*Cornuti*," she said.

Jonas couldn't abide his wife's sister's husband. Called him "the lawyer doll."

Hamilton's downward trajectory was probably inevitable, but the marriage to Lily didn't help. His parents were so offended that they disinherited their youngest son. The senior Ballards were the sort of upper-class New England stalwarts who make a virtue of conventionality.

Lily was half Italian, older than her husband, and had been raised as a Catholic. Hamilton's parents thought their son was doomed. And as is often the case with the judgments of cold-hearted and unimaginative people, they were dead right.

It was not a happy union. Sister and I were lucky to escape to Pocantico, although the move was not official and the adoption papers were never altered. Jonas has no patience for red tape. Elspeth didn't press it. The process would have highlighted her brother-in-law's misfortune. So, legally, Sister and I are both Ballards. Emotionally we're Collingwoods. Biologically we pick it up as we go along.

Jonas was in the habit of introducing me as his boy. The situation was far too complicated to explain to strangers. But he treated me like a son on probation. Whenever I failed, I sensed his withdrawal. If you asked him about this, he'd say that judgment is one of a father's responsibilities. I used to wonder, though, if he could have maintained so much objectivity with a blood relative.

Elspeth I didn't worry about. If I were justly convicted of a brutal murder—and, given my nature, this was a possibility—I could count on Aunt to bake a rasp file into a cake and try and smuggle it into my cell. Jonas wouldn't visit at all. He might even help with the prosecution.

7

I didn't think the Waspy Adonis had made that much of an impression, but he must have done. When I came home from work one evening and saw that blazer draped over a chair in our kitchen, two weeks had passed since our meeting, but I still reacted like a well-trained dog to a rolled-up newspaper.

This was on a Tuesday evening, June 18 of 1991. I know the date because it was exactly one month before the anniversary of the Battle of Waterloo. Laura Grafton had driven me home from work. I came into the house in a sort of trance. I used to spend a lot of time daydreaming. I imagined that I was in advertising. In this particular reverie, I was making a pitch to the people who manufacture Preparation H.

I pictured myself at a podium, addressing a group of six or seven large businessmen in dark suits. If this had been a Disney film, my fairy godmother would certainly have created this group of executives by waving her wand over a flock of crows.

"I don't know if you gentlemen are superstitious," I said, looking into their inscrutable faces, "but I think it is more than coincidence that we should meet on the exact day of the month on which Napoleon was defeated. As doubtless you recall, that battle was fought on July 18, 1815. Did you know that hemorrhoids may have had as much to do with the outcome as did the fact that the Guards advanced in column?"

They did not know. It's always surprising to me how little the modern businessman knows of his own business. I put up both hands, palms forward. "No, no," I said. "I'm not inventing anything. This is historical fact. The emperor was in such pain that he couldn't sit on a horse. They had to carry him around in an armchair." I took a dainty sip from the water glass on my podium.

"I suppose it was felt that the sight of Napoleon in an armchair would have given the wrong message to men who might at any moment be cut down by musket fire. So as the day progressed, he couldn't appear before his troops. And you know, of course, that when they did catch a glimpse of him on the field of battle, they always used to fight like devils."

The assembled executives still didn't see what I was getting at. A small one in the back stretched his wings. The crow in the center dipped his beak into his water glass, tipped his head back to swallow: "So?"

"Simple," I said. "Get the rights to the painting by Jacques-Louis David: *Napoleon Crossing the Alps*. He's in the saddle, looking good enough to eat. Cognac's been using that picture for years. Only for us the text reads, 'He lost his empire. You needn't. Use doctor-recommended . . .'"

I was dreaming along, kind of humming the "Marseillaise," when I caught that glimpse of navy blue, just out of the corner of my eye. I jumped before I knew I was jumping. I jumped even before I knew I'd seen a jacket, or whose jacket it was. It looked liked Uncle's, of course, but it was much larger, and not frayed.

I collected myself. I was at home. I was in the kitchen of the house I'd grown up in. I had been named after England's greatest naval hero. Horatio Nelson had lost his arm, he'd lost his eye, and he'd lost his life with almost perfect equanimity. I shouldn't be undone by the sight of a blue blazer, especially one that didn't have anybody in it.

There were two bottles of red wine on the counter beside the stove. We never bought wine. Having lived in Italy during the war, Uncle claimed he couldn't bear the idea of paying five dollars a bottle for the same beverage Tuscan farmhands used to drink with their bread and olives. Besides, on our budget and with his patriarchal thirst, scotch by the half gallon was strongly indicated.

Then I heard the voices. There's a rectangle of slate out behind the house with some canvas chairs, one glass table, and a rusted hibachi. This was called the back terrace. It was not called the patio. It was never called the patio.

I could now hear the pleasant sound of muffled laughter. Somebody coughed. I guessed it was Uncle preparing to read. He often read to us from his works in progress. He had a great, rich voice. Years of scotch rocks and cigarettes. The passage sounded familiar:

"Whether I shall turn out to be the hero of my own life, or whether that station will be held by anybody else, these pages must show. To begin my life with the beginning of my life, I record that I was born (as I have been informed and believe) on a Friday, at twelve o'clock at night. It was remarked that the clock began to strike and I began to cry, simultaneously."

It's a game we play with the first and last paragraphs of well-known books. The reader covers the spine with a misleading dust jacket. Contestants get ten points for the title, seven points for the author, two points for guessing if the writer is a man or a woman.

There is no way to go directly from the kitchen to the terrace, so I went back out the door I'd just entered and came around the corner of the house. The two men were sitting across from each other. On the table was a pile of books. Among these were many of Uncle's early novels. This surprised me. I didn't know he had copies. There were also two heavy crystal glasses. This was no surprise.

"*David Copperfield,*" I said.

The guest turned. I could feel my bowels tighten. "How's Rilke?" I asked.

"Fine," he said. "How's Maxwell Perkins?"

"In school," I said. "Still learning."

"Nelson," said Jonas with false heartiness, as he got to his feet. "Welcome home. Meet Dr. John Gilbert." He waved an arm at his guest, who had also risen. "Let me introduce my nephew, Nelson. He's a student of film."

"We've met," said Gilbert. "In fact he's fiddled with my prose."

"Or tried to," I said. "And if I'm not very much mistaken, I've also eaten your smoked ham."

"Well," said Jonas, pulling thoughtfully on his beard. "So you two are old friends." He sat back down. I took a seat.

"Since you're friends," said Jonas, "I suppose you'll be pleased to know that I've asked Dr. Gilbert to stay for dinner. He brought two wonderful bottles of Chianti. Nar should be home in an hour or so. We can eat then. I thought in the meantime we'd go for a walk."

The doctor smiled. He was in almost exactly the same outfit that he'd had on at the *Commons* two weeks before, except that the jacket was now being worn by the kitchen chair. And something else was different. Socks, he was wearing socks. "I've been admiring the countryside," he said.

The house does have quite a view from the terrace. There's a great open field the Rockefellers grow hay on, and down at the bottom there are two giant beech trees, and then Route 448. Across the road the ground dips into another expanse of meadow, on which fat cows were now grazing. Mrs. David's cows.

I nodded.

Gilbert turned to face me. "What's it like?" he asked. "I mean, what does it mean to study film these days?" Obviously he had somehow gotten the impression that Uncle would like him better for paying attention to me. I remember thinking that there are *some* strategic disadvantages to being a stranger, no matter how loving.

62

"When I'm not at home, I live in a room in somebody else's apartment in Greenwich Village," I said. "I have a TV and a VCR. No cable. I spend a lot of time alone with the VCR."

Gilbert grinned, so I went on. "We have many cockroaches. Not as many as they used to have before the widespread introduction of Combat. But a good many. I've seen *Triumph of the Will* five times. I've seen *Body Double* three times. Alfred Hitchcock was a genius. I don't much like Peter Greenaway."

Dr. Gilbert was smiling. He had a terrific smile.

"My favorite film is *It's a Wonderful Life*," he said.

"I like the movie," I said. "But it's not. A wonderful life, I mean."

"You want to make movies?"

I shrugged. "I want to make something. Actually, I wouldn't mind going to work for an advertising agency."

The doctor nodded enthusiastically. "James Dickey did that," he said. "Peter Mayle."

I was uncomfortable. "So did a lot of nameless drudges," I said.

Now Gilbert looked quizzical. "Is that what you aim to be?" he asked. "A nameless drudge?"

I shrugged. "A useful nameless drudge. With a wife I love and children. It's been done."

Jonas was clearly impatient with all this. "Nelson has low self-esteem," he explained. "I think it must be the auto mechanic's gene. You know, his father makes a living fixing cars."

"Thanks," I said. "Tell everyone."

Gilbert looked blank.

"But Nelson is also highly empathetic," said Jonas. "So much so that I suspect he has second sight. I think he should be a doctor."

"You want to send me to school for another four years?" I asked.

"Oh, come on now," said Uncle. "You know I'd be delighted to pay the tuition at any medical school that would have you."

I pretended not to have heard the last part. It was nasty. And it wasn't true. If I hadn't had a scholarship, I sincerely doubt that we could have afforded NYU.

Uncle cleared his throat. "While I'm certain that Dr. Gilbert would like to discuss your career endlessly, I also think that if I am going to show him any of the grounds, I should begin to do so before we lose the light."

"Go, walk," I said, trying to keep the petulance out of my voice.

Dr. Gilbert seemed concerned that I might feel left out. Apparently, he still thought that allowing me to be overlooked might someday be held against him by Uncle. Talk about slow learners. "You're welcome to join us," he said.

"I've seen the grounds."

"I guess that settles it," said Jonas, getting up and reaching for his cane.

"The situation is gorgeous," said Gilbert, also getting up. "It's practically incomprehensible that you can have all this and still be less than an hour from Manhattan. It looks like God's country."

"Actually," said Jonas. "We're about fifty minutes from Lincoln Center. Standard Oil of New Jersey had a great deal more to do with it than God."

Gilbert smiled. "The Lord works in mysterious ways."

"Right," said Jonas. "Although it seems they've busted his trust as well." Uncle maneuvered around the glass table. The two men headed off down the path, which led from the back of the house across a corner of the hayfield. They were moving slowly, and I could hear the gravel of Uncle's voice. He was being informative. "They call it the cottage, but it's not. It's really a sort of bastard ranch house."

Gilbert nodded.

"I think it must have started life as some sort of storage barn. Then they fixed it up as a guest house, so we have a pantry and a living room. The bedrooms are small. There's only one bath."

"No Jacuzzi?" asked Gilbert.

"No," said Jonas, and chuckled. "But we do have the park, fifty or sixty miles of dirt road."

"This must be the biggest piece of open space in the county."

"There is the Ward Pound Ridge Reservation," said Jonas. "Not nearly so beautiful. Much of that land was farmed before it was set aside. You can see the stone fences; the trees are second growth. A lot of this property was held in estates, so we have these giant beeches and sweeping fields. Unlike the people in charge of the reservation, the Rockefellers are not afraid to take an active role. The trails were very artfully laid out. They've also worked to preserve the past. So we have some elms, and many horse chestnut trees. Some of the land has been deeded to the state, but it's still meant to look like a rich man's park."

By now Jonas and Gilbert were halfway across the field and heading toward one of the paths that weave through the woods. Jonas was working the cane vigorously with his left hand. He put his right arm around the stranger. The gesture wasn't particularly affectionate, but it stopped me, bothered me. I couldn't remember the last time Uncle had put his arm around my shoulders.

But then I wasn't a medical doctor. Nor had I ever written a literary biography.

I went back around the corner of the house and into the kitchen. Elspeth had appeared. She had some apples she wanted me to put through the Foley food mill, and I was happy to oblige. I always liked working in the kitchen with Aunt. Uncle didn't approve. Sometimes, drunk and angry, he'd call me "the sous-chef."

After I was done with the apples, I set the table, with an extra place. I opened one of the bottles of wine. It was Chianti Classico. I opened the second bottle.

"They need to breathe," I said to Aunt, when she looked a question, but actually I had darker motives. I thought that if both bottles were opened, I would be more likely to get as much as I wanted, and the guest would be considerably less apt to bring the excess home.

I was just putting out the glasses when Nar was dropped off by the Melon. I could hear the car before it got halfway up the drive. Crenshaw drove a Mercedes diesel. The engine had a distinctive idle. It sounded like the Ford had sounded the time the water pump went out. "Perfect American car," Nar had said after her first outing. "It's made in Germany, he can't afford it, and it's supposed to save money." She came through the kitchen in a rush.

"There's company," I said, but Nar still wanted to change into something comfortable. She and the Melon had been in town, I think to the South Street Seaport. She was in a skirt and blouse. When she came out of her bedroom fifteen minutes later, she was in a pair of blue jeans, dramatically torn at one knee. Over this she wore a T-shirt with the message "Life's a bitch, then you die."

The shirt had been the last gift from Duncan Weston, a Princeton freshman she had dated and then betrayed. Duncan had Federal Expressed the shirt with a note: "I'm not sure about life, but you certainly qualify."

I think he had expected a response; he didn't get one. Sister kept the shirt. She had also kept Cameron's Mark Cross pen-and-pencil set, the one that had been given him by the school board "in recognition of an outstanding commitment to the needs of our children."

Now she settled at the kitchen table and watched as Elspeth and I finished up the preparations for the evening meal.

"You could have invited your young man to dinner," said Aunt.

"I like Allen," said Nar. "But there's only so much confidence a girl can bear."

Aunt was just taking the London broil out of the oven when the kind stranger and Uncle returned from their walk. Nar and Elspeth were introduced, and we all settled at our places.

Jonas sat at the head of the table, Elspeth at the foot. I sat on one side, and Nar on the other. Gilbert's place was set toward Elspeth's end of the table and beside mine. We hadn't bothered to put in the holiday leaf, so the seats on my side were squashed together. Gilbert was left-handed. I wield the fork with my right hand, and so I thought our shoulders would probably rub throughout dinner. They did not. This is one of the talents of those born to privilege: They can fill a room, or they can take up no space at all. Gilbert's elbows took up no space at all. His admiration for Uncle filled the room.

Jonas gave a lengthy grace: "Let us assume that the human soul is immortal, able to endure every sort of good and every sort of evil," he began. Then there was a bit about the kindness of strangers. He closed by calling on the Almighty to help calm the tempers of "my sometimes too passionate wards." Obviously, he was afraid we were going to break out into civil war, as was common, and disgrace him in front of his new, literary admirer. The dinner was served. Gilbert poured the wine. Uncle unbent and took a half a glass. I noticed that our guest didn't take any himself.

"I'm driving," he explained, "and it's not my car." Then he started up with the questions.

"I've stayed at Il Pellicano, of course," he said, "but I don't have any feeling for Porto Ercole itself. What's it like?"

"It's quite an ordinary fishing village," said Jonas. "Or that's what it used to be. You could see the sardine boats at night."

" 'Their torchlights circled like those of an enemy encampment,' " said Gilbert. This I recognized as a quotation from one of Uncle's earliest and least distinguished novels.

"I believe they still fish," said Jonas, not acknowledging the quotation. "The largest single source of cash is now the tourist industry."

"English? Germans?"

"No. There are English, of course, and Germans and Americans. But there's also a big contingent of Italians. The village is quite close to Rome. The old castle, La Rocca, is now set up as some sort of multiple residence. Go over the dry moat and there's an electric gate. And a wall of locked mailboxes. I've been told that many of the people who stay there are from Rome."

"But it wasn't that way during the war?"

"No, no," said Uncle. "Conditions in the castle then were extremely primitive. If the place had been fixed up, the Germans would have used it. As it was, they stayed down near the water."

Dr. Gilbert turned to Nar. I could see him reading her undershirt.

"Have you ever been to the Mediterranean?" he asked.

"No," said Nar.

"But you do like the sea?"

"I go to Jones Beach whenever I get a chance."

"Swim?"

"Yes," said my sister, coyly, taking a sip from her glass of wine. "I also like to lie there on the hot sand and do nothing."

"And what an ornament you must be," I said.

"Oh, shut up," said Nar.

"If you children are going to squabble," said Jonas, "please go out into the kitchen."

After that, I subsided. Nar and I had eaten in the kitchen when we were young, and so the reference hit a nerve. Uncle had a rare talent for making me feel infantile when I got out of line. Besides, I didn't really want to have a shouting fight in front of this stranger. Nar piped down as well, although she was careful to top up her wine glass whenever a bottle came within reach.

Most of the talking was done by our loving stranger. Uncle was right. This was clearly a man of parts. Nine out of ten of these parts were hot air. It's become popular in the last decade to say "Money talks, bullshit walks." While I have no firsthand experience of money walking, it's abundantly clear, even from my limited experience, that in our time, in our country, bullshit does most of the talking.

Dr. Gilbert wanted to know if Uncle had ever heard of a Professor Hugh Donaldson.

"Certainly. Didn't he write a book about the poet Emmanuel Glessing? Very well thought of."

"That's right," said Gilbert.

"What was it called?"

"*The Seven.* That was his argument, that Glessing was guilty of the seven deadly sins. I forget what they are."

Jonas smiled. "The mnemonic is 'PC Lages,' " he said. "Pride, covetousness, lust, anger, gluttony, envy, and sloth. Didn't that book win the Pulitzer?"

"That's right."

"I never read it. Never much cared for Glessing's verse, although Elspeth used to love it. And Elspeth's sister, Lily, named her shop after him: The Emmanuel Glessing Book Store and Tea Shop. It's in San Francisco." Uncle took a sip of wine. "But there had been a number of biographies. What was it that so distinguished the Donaldson book?"

"Research," said Gilbert. "Glessing's life was one of the best documented of his time. He kept notebooks, a memoir in three volumes. And unlike many poets, he was revered during his lifetime. But he was also a terrible old deceiver. Up until Donaldson, nobody thought to question his word. So all those earlier books were riddled with inaccuracies."

"What was that biography I read and loved so much?" asked Elspeth. "It had a green cover. The copy I read was part of some series of classics."

"You mean *Emmanuel Glessing: Warrior, Statesman and Poet*?"

"That's right," said Elspeth. "I read it when I was fourteen, and I remember that I wanted more than anything to grow up to marry a man like Emmanuel Glessing."

"It's an inspiring piece of fiction," said Gilbert. "But Glessing was nothing like the man in that book. You know, he killed his first wife. Louisa wasn't swept away by some tender illness. She was swept away by head injuries. Glessing threw her out of his carriage."

"I won't believe it," said Elspeth. "What about the time he gave his last baguette to Emily? They were crossing the Pyrenees together on foot."

"Well, Donaldson thinks he may have done that," said Gilbert. "There's nobody who can refute the story, because Emily died of starvation before they reached France." Gilbert took a sip of water. "Glessing, on the other hand, was quite fit when he crossed the border. Emily's body was never found."

"Well, I'm glad I didn't read your friend's horrid book," said Elspeth.

Gilbert smiled.

"How could they have gotten it so wrong?" I asked.

"There's no FDA for books," said Gilbert. "There are certain facts that are easy to check, and some subjects are defended by interested parties. You couldn't write a scurrilous and inaccurate book about IBM, for instance. Or about L. Ron Hubbard. At least you couldn't publish such a book without being taken to court. But as much fiction passes for nonfiction now as ever did."

"Really," said Jonas. "Don't the critics watch out for inaccuracies?"

"I suppose," said Gilbert. "But it's not their job. And they don't have time to do original research. So they pretty much have to take the author at his word. If it sounds true, then it must be. Some of them have very keen ears, but an ear isn't always enough."

"So what's the difference between fiction and nonfiction?" I asked.

"Well," said Gilbert, laughing, "there are those three letters: n, o, n. And also, nonfiction is usually about something."

"Hear, hear," said Nar.

Gilbert shrugged. "It's also not as well written."

Jonas cleared his throat. "You're not going to deny that there have been novels about something. Or that there have been distinguished works of nonfiction. *In Cold Blood. The Enormous Room.*"

Gilbert nodded. "*In Cold Blood* was highly factual," he said.

"You're not suggesting that Cummings lied?"

"Actually," said Gilbert, "I've never read the book. But I do know of it. Didn't most of the other prisoners die?"

"I suppose," said Jonas. "But Estlin was not a fraud."

"No," said Gilbert. "He was a poet."

Jonas reared back in his chair. I thought he was going to continue the argument, but then he looked off to one side, as if remembering something pleasant. He returned to his dinner.

Gilbert cut himself another piece of meat. Chewed, swallowed, and wiped his lips. "I suppose Donaldson's success weakens my argument," he said, "but I've always felt that the really interesting biographies bypass these inflated literary celebrities. The worthwhile books are about quiet characters with real substance, writers who might otherwise have been overlooked.

"By the way," he said, giving THE SMILE to Elspeth, "this is delicious. How exactly was it prepared?"

"Broiled," said Elspeth.

Gilbert shook his head. "It's an exceptional piece of meat then," he said.

Elspeth colored again. "Not particularly," she said.

70

"Then you've done something to it," said Gilbert, almost triumphantly.

Elspeth nodded.

"Marvelous," he said. "Really, this is superb."

Elspeth blushed. "Thank you," she said.

"In any case," said Gilbert, turning back to Uncle, "I used to hang around with Donaldson when I was an undergraduate. Biology was my major, but I always had a minor in literature. He'd just broken up with his first wife."

"He must have been something of a campus celebrity," said Jonas.

"No," said Gilbert, "not at all. He'd been working on that book for fifteen years then. It started out as his doctorate. Nobody thought he was ever going to finish it. We used to play basketball with the same group and go out sometimes afterward for a beer. We were both Red Sox fans."

Jonas was very carefully cutting a piece of meat.

"He thought you should have gotten what Hemingway called 'the big thing,' " said Gilbert.

Jonas cocked his head. "Hummm?"

Gilbert: "The Nobel thing."

The silence after this one lasted seven beats. Nobody spoke, nobody even chewed. The guy was a master. I had a long pull on my glass of wine. "God," I thought, "if bearing false witness still matters to you, you'd better strike this one dead."

But there was no crack of thunder. The lights didn't even blink. Consolidated Edison is our electric company, so the lights often do blink. Sometimes, for no apparent reason, they'll go right out. Stay out for hours.

"I thought you should get it for the entire body of your work," said Gilbert. "Donaldson thought you should win for the Agricola books."

Jonas was wagging his head sternly, but obviously he'd been moved. "This is very kind of you to mention," he said, "but it's also a little outrageous."

"No, honestly," said Gilbert. "Just suppose that you'd been

from Asia, or even Eastern Europe . . ." He took another bite of meat.

Nar broke in. "I read today in the *Times*," she said brightly, "where they're exhuming the remains of President Zachary Taylor."

Now Jonas was scowling. "I don't think it's profitable for an artist to speculate on his place, if any, in the literary firmament," he said.

"It was a good paper," said Nar. "The science section had a picture of an asteroid crashing into the Earth. Did you know, I have a much better chance of being killed by an asteroid—one in six thousand—than of being killed by botulism—one in two million. Or even dying in an airplane crash—one in twenty thousand."

Gilbert smiled up at Jonas and took a sip of his water. "You won't deny that the judges are greatly influenced by world politics?"

"No, of course not," said Jonas.

"Although it's still an honor," said Gilbert.

"Yes," said Jonas. "It's certainly an honor."

"And if there's any justice, it's well within reach," said Gilbert.

Jonas nodded gravely.

Nar was beginning to giggle. The doctor shot her a chastening glance, but she couldn't contain herself.

"I think if Daddy's going to win a Nobel prize," she said, it should be for peace."

"Oh," said Gilbert, changing tack but not lightening up in the least. "I didn't know you were involved in politics."

"He's not," said Elspeth, and she snapped her eyes at Nar.

"Well," said Nar, trying hard to control her mirth, "he is the sort of Desmond Tutu of this dinner table."

I laughed. Nar laughed. Elspeth smiled. I saw her smiling. Jonas actually looked bewildered for a moment, in the same way a street fighter must when the opposing hoodlum gets a blade in under the arm. He was hurt and surprised by the attack. It was astonishing to me how susceptible the old flatterer was turning out to be. Matthew, I thought, 26:52: "For all they that take the sword shall perish with the sword."

Gilbert paused for a moment but then went right on, like a

politician with hecklers. "Honestly now," he said. "If you'd been a Knopf or even a Random House author, you would certainly have won the National Book Award for *Agricola, Agricolae*."

Again Jonas didn't answer. He seemed to be terribly interested in his food.

"There's a nobility to being published for years by a firm that specializes in farm equipment, but Brindle's distribution system was frightfully inadequate. I can't imagine there was any publicity department at all. And that's leaving aside the whole question of advertising."

Jonas smiled. "As Trollope says in his autobiography, 'Many a book—many a good book—"is born to blush unseen, and waste its sweetness on the desert air."' "

"But that can be changed," said Gilbert. "Marketing is much more sophisticated than it was in Trollope's time. A good publicist can make an enormous difference."

"I wouldn't want a good publicist," said Jonas, with a touch of hauteur. "A book goes into the living room, sometimes the bedroom, of the person who buys it. I wouldn't want strangers to take me into their homes. Not if I didn't feel that I could comfortably return the invitation."

"That may be so," said Gilbert. "Unfortunately, there are probably a great many people you would like who have never heard of your books."

"Maybe."

"Classic will change all that," said Nar.

"They do have an adequate sales force," said Gilbert. "Brindle did not. I remember when *Puella* had been reviewed quite favorably in the *Globe*. I went right out to get it, and they didn't even have it at the Coop."

"The way I understand it," said Jonas, "the bookstores order the works of authors who have sold well for them in the past. It's just possible that nobody in Cambridge, Mass., wanted to buy *Puella, Puellae*."

"I lived in Cambridge, Mass., in 1975," said Gilbert. "I was taking a survey course in American literature, and we were studying the Agricola books. I wanted to buy *Puella, Puellae* very much. Besides, I don't think your work is abstruse in any way. I see you as being right in the tradition of the popular American novel. Donaldson used to say that Sherwood Anderson was your closest parallel."

Jonas shrugged. "I'm flattered, of course," he said, "but I wouldn't agree."

"Neither did I," said Gilbert. He moved about uneasily in his chair, and his arm did rub my shoulder. "This is silly," he said, and paused.

"Go on," said Jonas.

"Well," said Gilbert, "I make you out as a sort of a cross between Charlotte Brontë and Ernest Hemingway, with a touch of Emerson."

"Quite a ménage," said Nar. "Probably illegal in most states."

Elspeth glared at her daughter. "*Basta.*"

Sister reached for the Chianti.

Gilbert seemed not to have heard the exchange. "You won't deny that you were influenced by these writers?" he said.

Jonas wouldn't deny it.

"I rest my case," he said. But he didn't rest his case. There was quite a lot more about Uncle's place in the literary pantheon, and although Jonas certainly didn't encourage this particular line of inquiry, his hearing never seemed to quite go out either.

It was Nar who brought up the Classic contract. "I guess they think Daddy has been undervalued."

"I confess to having heard something about such a contract," said Gilbert, "and I must say I'm surprised at this demonstration of acuity on their part."

Elspeth got up to clear. "They don't want him to write fiction," she said. "They want a memoir."

Then Gilbert gave the biggest smile of the evening. "Correct me if I'm wrong," he said, looking at Jonas. "But hasn't everything you've written come out of some deep personal experience?"

Jonas nodded. "Yes," he said. "I suppose that's true."

"Well then," said Gilbert.

Elspeth was still standing by the table, holding two dinner

plates. I got up to help. "They did send a man out here with instructions," she said.

Gilbert chuckled. "Take their money," he said. "Please take their money. Ignore their advice. You're a class act. They can't afford to turn down Jonas Collingwood. At this point in your career, you could hand in a laundry list and they'd print it. On vellum."

This time it was Nar who insisted we get up from the table, and Uncle who would happily have lingered over Elspeth's espresso. There was a lot of toing and froing at the kitchen door. Gilbert had never eaten such a fine meal. "Mr. Bronfman has been very kind. I've been able to rent a wonderful cottage, but it can be sort of gloomy, sitting on the wide-board floor, eating shrimp with lobster sauce out of a cardboard box."

"Oh, you mustn't," said Elspeth. "Come here instead."

"All I need is an invitation."

"Well," said Elspeth, blushing slightly, as our guest backed politely out of the door. "You certainly have that."

Jonas went off with a novel and Nar took the telephone up to the jack in her bedroom. Elspeth and I cleaned the dinner dishes. "You and Jonas have to scour this oven someday soon," she said.

It was a tradition in our household that the men cleaned the oven. It was felt that the poisons used to cut grease might be too much for a woman.

When the kitchen was clean, I went to my room. I took off my shoes, propped myself up in bed on a pillow, and began to read from John Cremony's *Life Among the Apaches*.

"It may be entered up as an invariable rule," Cremony had written for publication in 1868, "that the visits of Apaches to American camps are always for sinister purposes."

I'd just started chapter eight when Nar appeared at the door to my bedroom. She was holding a half bottle of the Chianti Classico in one hand and two empty jelly jars in the other.

Sister came in, settled beside me on my cot. My bed is against a wall, so we could both sit on it and have something to lean against. I gave Nar the pillow. She poured us each a drink.

"So what did you think?" I asked.

Nar tossed her head. "Shit stinks," she said.

"He's handsome enough."

Nar rolled her eyes. "He's already in love," she said.

"With Uncle?"

She shook her head. "He's in love with a doctor."

"How would you know that?" I asked.

"A girl can tell."

I shrugged, held out my glass for more wine. "I met him before," I said. "He came into the office of the *Commons*. Wanted to place an ad. The guy can't write his way out of a paper bag."

"Why do you have to see everything in terms of writing?"

"I suppose it has to do with Jonas. That's what he does. He's the model."

"The model for what?"

"For an adult male."

Nar raised her eyebrows. "He's not even your real father."

"If he's not, who is?" I said.

Nar shrugged.

"He's more father than a lot of real fathers might have been."

"I guess," said Nar. "But I don't want to be a writer. So why do you?"

"This is going to sound corny and melodramatic."

Nar shrugged. "That's my brother," she said.

I didn't say anything.

She took a sip of wine. "Go on. Spit it out."

"When I die," I said, and took a pull on my jelly jar, "there's going to be this old man who looks a lot like Jonas sitting up on one of those high, rickety chairs they use to judge tennis matches. He'll want me to explain myself. The choice of words is going to be crucial."

"You don't want to be a writer. You want to be a lawyer."

I moved around a little on the bed. It was awkward trying to sit without my pillow. But Nar looked so comfortable that I didn't have the heart to ask for it back. "For one thing, law is boring," I said. "Besides, I somehow doubt that the great scorer is going to go by the same rules that they apply in the courtrooms of this state. Certainly the laws of evidence will be a lot less arbitrary."

Nar nodded. "Maybe," she said. She got up, looked at herself in the mirror that hangs over my dresser, plumped her hair, and returned to the pillow. "I don't like having somebody snooping around Uncle's life any better than you do. But I bet he can write."

"Why do you say that?"

"Professor Donaldson."

"You give him too much credit. Gilbert doesn't have that vivid an imagination."

Nar took another sip of wine and smiled. "Obviously the guy exists. Uncle had heard of the book. But all that Nobel stuff."

"You think he made that up?"

Nar smiled. "Boys are so helpless."

I didn't respond. Neither of us moved. We lay beside each other on the bed. She was comfortable. I was not comfortable. But both of us were quite still.

We used to do that sometimes, Sister and I, just lie beside each other in bed. I looked at her profile. She isn't a beauty. Not in repose. She has a perfectly good face, but that's not what makes her such a man-killer. What makes her deadly is what she does with that face, the way she can light it up. She used to let it go out when we were alone together. I could never tell for certain if this was an insult or a compliment. I don't think she knew either.

"I'm going to have a glass of water," she said finally, and stood. "You'd better have a glass of water too. Neither of us is going to be exactly chipper in the morning."

"I worry more about Uncle," I said. "The poison we had will piss out."

My alarm went off at 6:30 A.M. I smelled coffee. This was odd. I was always the first one up, the one who made the coffee. I was also the one who bought the beans at the supermarket and had them ground. I went into the kitchen. The Melitta was half full, its contents piping hot. Then I heard the sound of typing. Uncle was typing. Furiously. *Poison*, I thought, pouring myself a mug of coffee. *Maybe. Maybe not.*

8

I was in the second grade at Pocantico when I got into my first serious fight. This was with Bill Grafton. Bill said I hadn't winged him in dodge ball. He thought that because he was an upperclassman, a fifth grader, he could intimidate me into pretending that I hadn't hit him, and so stay in the game. He was mistaken. And I called in other witnesses, made him look foolish.

So he said I was blind and that my mother wore combat boots. Nobody laughed.

He said my mother was like a B-52: large cockpit. Nobody laughed.

He said: "The day they handed out brains, you thought they

said trains and asked for a small set." And this time he got a couple of titters.

"Take *your* brain," I said, "blow it up a million times, shove it up a flea's asshole, and it'll still rattle around like a BB in a boxcar." This got real laughs.

So Bill said I was an asshole.

"Asshole," I said, "you should know. If the Defense Department ordered a container ship full of assholes and you washed ashore, nobody would be disappointed. The contract would be fulfilled." More laughter.

So he called me a bastard. Just like that. One word: bastard. He was still out of the game, and I still had majority support. But I did notice that a couple of kids snickered. It was as if Bill had said something original, something truly clever. Which wasn't at all like him.

That evening, after dinner, I approached Uncle. He'd been drinking, and you never knew, when Uncle had been drinking, if he wanted your company or if your company was the last thing he wanted. I guess he wasn't too fond of his novel, because he put it right down and heard my story.

"He was out," I said.

Uncle went into the root cellar and came back with his *Funk & Wagnalls Standard College Dictionary*. "Bastard," he read aloud. "Noun 1. An illegitimate child." Then he shook his head sadly. "I don't like Bill Grafton either. But he's got you dead to rights." He lit a cigarette, went back to his novel.

I couldn't sleep well that night, but I didn't formulate any particular plan either. The next day, during play period, I left the second-grade area, found myself wandering over to the baseball diamond. There were bats lying near the foul line. I picked one up. It was an old-fashioned wooden bat, but painted, black with silver lettering. Bill Grafton was at the plate. Then the memory goes out.

It comes back with Bill lying on the ground, crying, begging me to leave him alone. Which I did.

I still have no recollection of the fight. And people who saw it will remind you that Bill had a bat too. Tried to use it. And he was a good foot taller than I.

One of the conditions of nobody's pressing charges was that I be sent to a therapist. I went to an office in an apartment building in White Plains and was given a battery of tests. I had to fit pegs into holes, look at inkblots, that sort of thing. The trouble with the mind sciences is that they don't seem to care much about motivation. It's true that I used to lose my head when I lost my temper. And I didn't mean to lose my head. But it's also true that after the fight, I always felt much better. Much, much better. Remorse would come later, but there was a little bit of glee in there between the violence and the return of the superego. And glee is quite the little motivator.

This would never have occurred to Elspeth. Jonas had his suspicions. "Damn it," he used to say, "responsibility is the very first article of my faith."

He came in with me once, talked with the psychiatrist. The doctor was asking if there was anything Uncle could remember that I might have forgotten, anything that could give them a clue.

"He did have colic."

"Well, the indications at this point are that colic has no predictive force on later life."

Jonas nodded. "The first time I laid eyes on Nelson," he said, "he was just a tiny baby. I guess he was sick. His face was red. His little fists were waving around. I'd never seen anybody so angry."

Anyway, they couldn't explain what the matter was. The tests did confirm Pocantico's theory that I had severe dyslexia. This turned out to go a long way toward explaining the trouble I'd had with reading. But nobody really supposed that my bad eyes justified my violent temperament.

One of the staff psychologists suggested that we look up my biological parents, check for genetic clues. This was not done.

Shortly after the incident, I was personally approached by a woman in social services who seemed to want to follow this trail. But she was so painfully condescending that I couldn't bear the idea of being helped by her. Besides, I didn't really want to track down some mother who'd forgotten all about me. I also knew for certain that any such attempt would have broken Elspeth's heart.

Neither Sister nor I could recall another mother, or having lived under the thrall of a man other than Jonas Collingwood. And really, objectively speaking, Jonas and Elspeth were as connected with us as any biological parents could have been. Elspeth has been the dearest mother imaginable. When you consider the fact that I was an SPCA baby—that's what Uncle called us—and that I got into more than my share of trouble, even Jonas could be intensely loving. He hated to see me cry.

9

All that lonely summer, I was driven to work by Laura Grafton. Laura was my staff. She was also one of the Enablers, so she and I had known each other since we were babies, although we came from vastly different backgrounds. The television was by no means the only way in which the Grafton and Collingwood households differed. In fact the Grafton television was just about the only thing we shared. That, and being from roughly the same species and geographic region.

There's an antique sofa in the Grafton living room—crushed red velvet with wooden combing. Laura and I played house on the floor behind this, while the grown-ups sat on it and in the flanking armchairs, watching the blue eye of the news.

Nar wouldn't stay in the living room. She'd go off somewhere with the boys. The Enablers had three male children, and they followed Sister around like a pack of obedient and somewhat melancholy hound dogs.

I was five, Laura seven, when we got in trouble. I'd been given a toy stethoscope for my birthday. I don't remember whose idea it was, but we went out in the backyard of the Grafton house and played doctor. Bill Grafton caught us at it. I don't know what the Graftons did to Laura, but I got locked in my room for a day. Then I got spanked. And spoken to. Something about betraying hospitality.

Now Laura was a young woman, about 5 feet 4, with a woman's figure and Farrah Fawcett's hair. In her maturity she had developed a deep bosom, a slight tendency to get fat around the hips when sad, and an apparently terminal attachment to a very handsome, very tough young lawyer. His name was Albert Positano. Albert did something harsh and lucrative in White Plains. I think he was twenty-eight or thirty. He drove a black BMW and had studied the martial arts. Why do pretty girls always have old boyfriends? Mean old boyfriends.

Laura had dropped out of Penn State and come back to Westchester so that she could be near Albert.

Our friendship had stopped abruptly after the incident with the stethoscope. Now we got along just fine. I liked Laura. And she was kind to me, although we never, ever touched.

I was given the job of office manager because I would work Saturdays sometimes, and Laura could not. Albert wouldn't allow it. I also got the card. That was the badge of office, a corporate American Express Card. It had a monthly ceiling of something like $500. But you could use it. The bill went directly to Albany. Most of the receivables were sent to headquarters anyway. I paid the small ones out of petty cash. But still, I enjoyed the credit card: my first perk.

The man in Albany responsible for us was a retired cop named Walter Paige. He'd heard about my troubles. "You have balls," he once told me. "That's good."

If you know something about fighting and you're wondering

why I wasn't ever hurt myself, the answer is a simple, if a shameful, one. People thought I was lucky, but it wasn't that. It was just that when I did lose my temper, I lost my sense of honor right along with it. I wouldn't engage in that warm-up, that slow dance that usually begins even the most deadly combat. I'd kick the other guy in the shin, then hit him with a chair. I always won.

Elspeth was horrified by this quality. "I know this sounds dreadful," she said, "but I don't mind about the other people. I just can't bear the idea of you going to jail because somebody cuts in front of you on the bank line, or whistles at a girl, and then you kill him."

10

Laura and I stayed late on Wednesdays to put our section of the next week's *Commons* to bed. We worked on a picnic table, the sort with metal tubing for the legs. The tabletop and seats were of linoleum, mottled gray and white. The surface had been pitted at the factory so as to give the impression of very old marble. The piece, such as it was, appeared in our back room shortly after the state closed the Signal Hill Reformatory. Laura thought I was jumping to conclusions. "It may be from a private home, for all you know." I didn't argue, although several different sets of initials were carved on the attached benches. Nobody has that large a family anymore.

Above the table hung an enormous fixture that buzzed at us from its harness of stainless-steel chains. There were four long bulbs, at least two of which could be counted on. I used to cherish the light they gave off: buttercup yellow, mild as candles. It may have been the antique bulbs. It may have been the dust and the bodies of the dead flies, which lay on the fixture's translucent plastic guard. The glow was calming; it softened the edges on Laura's otherwise slightly threatening little face.

At about 4:30 P.M. one of us would go to the doughnut shop for coffee. Then we'd lock the front door and flip the orange sign in the window so that it read "Closed" to the outside world. I liked coffee at that time of day. But mostly I liked Laura. I took great pleasure in moving about freely with her, smelling her dark hair, joking about the ads. She used to wear pants on Wednesdays, stone-washed jeans, with a wide leather belt. She didn't want to spill hot wax on a good skirt. She looked great in pants. Doing the layout was commonly the climax of the week.

But on this particular Wednesday I was not having fun. I told Laura I had a sinus headache. I think she believed me. I look about the same with a sinus headache as I do with a broken heart.

Our favorite new ad was in the Help Wanted section:

JOBS IN KUWAIT—TAX FREE. Construction Workers $75K. Engineering $200K. Oil Field Workers $100K. Call now: 1-900-(A)RAB GOLD.

"It's the classic con," I told Laura. "People think they're going to take advantage of some rich towel head. They've heard about the war. They couldn't have not heard about it, but still they consider themselves clever for knowing something. They're distracted by their own feelings of greed and guilt. That's when the man who has placed this advertisement can clean them out."

Laura wanted to know what a "K" was.

"It's like what J. P. Morgan is supposed to have said about yachts."

"And what's that?" she asked, frowning.

"He said if you have to ask how much one is, then you shouldn't get one."

"You know, you really are an elitist," Laura said, and she said it with genuine bitterness.

"I was just trying to make a joke," I said. "A 'K' is a thousand dollars."

"Oh," said Laura. "Well, I personally don't care what they do in Kuwait as long it doesn't involve yellow ribbons."

Laura had very nearly lost her job that winter when the ribbons failed to appear at the top and bottom of the full-page ad she had sold and put together for the local Neighborly Pharmacy. The Neighborly had phoned headquarters in Albany. I don't know what Walter Paige said to her exactly, because she had the receiver to her ear, but I saw her go red and then a sort of blue. He was director of human services, and I guess he must have had special training.

The guy was a fabulous bully. Even when he liked you, he was a bully. He used to come in, sit on my desk, show me his firearm. He had a nickel-plated automatic.

Once, after he'd had something to drink at lunch, he came into the office afterward, gave me the gun. Then he walked about three feet from the desk, spread his arms. "Go ahead, shoot me."

"I don't want to shoot you."

"Yeah, maybe not. But you couldn't shoot me even if you wanted to. You know that?"

"Yeah," I said. " 'The best lack all conviction, while the worst are full of passionate intensity.' "

"Who said that? A cop?" Paige wanted to know.

"No."

"You sure?" he said.

"Yeah," I said, "I'm sure."

It seemed odd to me that this guy cared so much about guns. He didn't really need one. He was the sort that would beat you to death with his key chain if he had to. He'd beat you to death with your key chain.

It was because of the not-yet-forgotten contretemps about the ribbons that we had to go into Pleasantville on the way home. Laura needed "supplies." The Neighborly was right across the street in New Sussex. Laura insisted we go elsewhere.

We didn't reach Pocantico until it was almost 6:00 P.M. Somebody had placed a gigantic convex mirror on a stand in the woods across from our driveway. The thing must have been two feet across. Laura and I both remarked on it. I had no idea what it was.

Laura said she'd seen one before. "Across from an estate somewhere in Vermont. I think it has to do with safety."

When we got to the house, she came in to pick up a couple of mechanicals. The door to the pantry was open, and she heard the ruckus going on in the root cellar. "Your aunt?" she asked, as she backed out of the house, holding the folder of ads against the breast of her white nylon shell. "Sewing?"

"What a philistine you turned out to be," I whispered. "That's art going on in there. That's Jonas. Writing." I smiled. Laura didn't smile back. She turned on her heel, went to the car.

I felt guilty then for having teased too hard. She's always suspected me of being a snob. Besides, I understood her confusion. When Uncle was hot, he sounded a lot more like a treadle sewing machine or a rivet gun than a novelist. When Uncle wrote, he was always hot. White hot.

I didn't want the rivet gun to know I was home. Amy had sent me a Dear John letter. Actually, it wasn't a Dear John letter. It was just a chatty note about this other guy: how handsome he was, how honorable. His name was John Delman. Then she wanted to know if I'd replace her broken hair dryer.

If Uncle found out how upset I was, he'd be in a fever to give me the benefit of his wisdom. The benefit of his wisdom was precisely what I did not want.

I've never had any talent for stealth. When I was six years old, I used to try to sneak up on Elspeth in the kitchen. She always knew I was coming. Even when she was operating the Mixmaster, she'd know. She'd wheel away from the counter, kneel down, and fold me in her arms. "You're the dearest little Indian still living in the Hudson Valley," she'd say, "but you are also the noisiest one."

I guess time hadn't lightened my tread any, because when I turned from closing the door on Laura, Jonas had already come through the pantry and was stationed at the entrance to the kitchen. He was scratching his beard and beaming, actually beaming. I opened the refrigerator door, took out the iced tea.

"Want some?" I asked.

"No," he said. "Do you know where that check is?"

"What check?" I took one of the jelly jars down from its place in the cupboard.

"The one from Classic."

"The last place I saw it was in the scissors drawer." I poured myself a jelly jar of tea. I took a sip. It was heavily sugared.

Uncle opened the drawer in question. He removed a book of matches from the Plaza Hotel, a half-empty package of novelty birthday candles—the sort that relight themselves when blown out—a communication from the IRS, and finally the size-ten envelope from Classic. He put the envelope in the pocket of his chinos. He left everything else out on the counter.

I returned the jar of tea to the refrigerator.

"Are you coming down with something?" he asked.

"No."

"You look like hell."

"Thanks, but I'm fine. Just tired."

"You put in a long day," he said.

"Not as long as yours."

I got another big smile. His teeth were yellow. I happened to know that many of them were false and had been stained to match the few surviving originals. He told me that. Still, he had a great smile. He was like Sister: Uncle could light up his face.

"No, actually not that long a day," he said. "Gil came over for lunch. We went for a drive."

"Gil?" I asked. "The doctor from Harvard? You're calling him Gil?"

"Yes, why not?"

"What does he call you, Colls?"

Jonas shrugged. He was still smiling. "I wanted Gil to see the

Rockefellers' Potemkin village. I showed him the Chagall windows in the Union Church. And we put up that mirror."

"What *is* that?"

"Well, it means I can always see who's coming. So when the turnaround is blocked, I won't have to come out blind."

"It's a good idea, I guess, but won't the Rockefellers object?"

"No, Gil called Greenrock first. And the thing works like a charm," said Jonas, chuckling. "I'm going to have to find some other way to die."

"Good," I said. "Or rather, I hope you don't."

Jonas smiled. "You like Gilbert?"

"Yes," I said. "Although I don't exactly trust him."

Uncle's face darkened. "Why not?"

"I guess he's too, I don't know, blue-blooded."

"You're not going to hold that against him?"

"No. Of course not," I said, and tried to produce a smile of my own. I most certainly *was* going to hold it against him; I also knew that this was an argument not worth having. The ploy worked. Uncle grinned, patted me on the back. I borrowed his Funk & Wagnalls and escaped to my bedroom. "Dear Amy," I wrote.

> When I close my eyes I can still see you walking barefoot through your father's vegetable garden. You're wearing cutoffs and that sweatshirt David Hitchens gave you: Property of the University of Pennsylvania. You walk like you should rule the earth: shoulders back, head up. The sun is caught in your hair.
>
> Remember when that stockbroker stopped us in Grand Central? He asked if you'd been on television. I know it's unusual for somebody to approach you, to speak up, but his reaction wasn't extraordinary. You give the distinct impression of having come to us from another world: someplace where the headache medicine works and the toilet water is as blue as the Caribbean. [I remember stopping to think that this observation might

go a long way toward explaining my passion for advertising.]

You suggest I "see other girls." I do "see other girls." Every day. I'm in love with you.

No, we can't be friends!

Best,
Nelson Ballard

P.S. I'll look for the hair dryer.

I signed the note boldly with a red felt-tip pen, initialed the P.S. Then I remembered that when Abraham Lincoln was furious he'd write a letter, put it in the stove, wait a day, then write the one he sent.

Our only stove was in the root cellar. And it was July. So I used a wastepaper basket.

Jonas came down the hall that evening and looked into my room.

"Reading about your sachem?" he asked.

I nodded.

He stalked off.

Uncle never had understood my interest in the Apache. He thought it childish. Nar was the one to point out how similar the old writer was to the Wolf of the Warpath.

"For starters," she said, "they both have the cheekbones. And they're both taciturn."

It went well beyond the shape of the face. They were small, womanish men. Both were eccentrics. Both were fighting a losing battle against progress. And they were both killers.

I'd been reading for half an hour when she came in. Sister was wearing the suede skirt and the controversial camisole. She had some papers in her hand. "I found this on the kitchen counter," she said. "Did you see it?"

It was the IRS letter Jonas had taken out of the scissors drawer.

"No. I mean, I saw it. I didn't read it." She handed it to me. It was addressed to a Mrs. Lily Ballard:

Dear Taxpayer:

Thank your for your inquiry dated January 7, 1991.

We are sorry, but the information you provided does not establish reasonable cause or show due diligence for adjusting the penalty. This is your notice that your request for penalty adjustment is denied.

A review of your account history shows that similar penalties have been charged in the past. We find no indication that you have taken steps to correct this situation.

Carelessness or forgetfulness are the same as willful neglect and do not meet the criteria for practicing ordinary business care and prudence.

The total in penalties and unpaid taxes is $63,756.23.

I stopped reading. Looked up at Nar. "Shit," I said. "How's Lily ever going to get that kind of money?"

Nar smiled. "Jonas has gone to war."

"What do you mean by that?"

Nar leaned over the bed, patted me on the shoulder. I could smell her perfume. "Brother," she said, "I can only guess." She smiled and left.

I would like to report that it was my concern for Lily that kept me up that night. I thought about Lily and worried about Uncle, but Amy Snodgrass Rose was the one who kept me up.

It was as if a large and important organ had been removed from my body without benefit of anesthesia.

I know something about pain. I fell off a borrowed two-wheeler and snapped my right arm when I was five. Uncle had been trying to teach me the art of balance. Elspeth called an ambulance. Jonas sat there beside me on the lawn until the volunteers arrived. He promised to buy me my own bicycle if I would just stop crying. It's still mysterious to me why he would have thought that the thing I wanted right then was my very own personal engine of torture. But I saw the horror in his face. And I stopped crying.

The pain I felt now was as intense and as localized as had been the shock from that early fall. It was in my chest and belly, though, not in the arm. The arm bone mended until it was as good as new. Actually, a little stronger than it might otherwise have been, according to Dr. Bernstein, the family pediatrician. I wasn't at all sure that the same would be true of a broken heart.

If you'd ever seen Amy, known her, you might be better able to understand my grief. Nar's beauty is something she does to you. Amy's beauty is something that was done to her. By somebody else. Maybe God. And it's a favor she passes on. Even when she doesn't mean to, she passes it on.

Aunt Lily has the same kind of looks. Put her in a pair of Uncle's chinos and a man's shirt, have her dig in the garden, get dirt on her nose, and she still looks as if she'd been posed for a fashion shot. Men who don't know her well always assume that Lily is a snob. She has a snob's bearing. The force of her presence is so great that it often excites fear and then a sort of preemptive condemnation.

Amy has similar difficulties. At high school parties she was often the last one asked to dance. It was dangerous enough to give a homely girl a chance to belittle you, but nobody wanted to be rejected by the young woman they met in their dreams. And everybody at Briarcliff High School dreamt of Amy Rose.

She has a narrow waist and pale white skin, but she's healthy, and a little dense about the spectacular impression she makes on members of the opposite sex. She's bright, cheerful, and it's terribly easy to make her laugh. She uses Ivory soap.

Elspeth also buys Ivory, so I can't wash my own hands for dinner without summoning that pretty face.

I make Amy sound like somebody who's in love with her own body. She's not. She's very serious about other things, like her grades, which are excellent, and those little seals that are slaughtered for their skins. People *do* stop her in the street, ask if they haven't seen her on TV. She's always surprised.

I know that modesty is supposed to be admirable, but Amy's brand drove me wild. Men were constantly inviting her off for the weekend. Inevitably, she was flattered. "Oh, Nelson," she'd coo at me on the phone. "Billy Squires wants me to come up to New Haven for the football game, and then to spend Saturday night. Do you think I should go?"

"Where will you sleep?"

"Billy says he'll sleep on the floor. I can have his bed."

Not having a car put me in a terrific bind. My alternatives weren't convincingly attractive: "Well, if you could just get your parents to drive you to the mall Saturday, I'd take the bus."

She'd do it, though. She'd turn down the invitation for the Harvard-Yale game, meet me at the White Plains Galleria. I'd buy her an egg roll, and she'd eat the shrimp out of it, dipped in hot mustard. We'd talk about David Hitchens. For some reason David didn't bother me all that much. They rarely saw each other. And her love for him seemed too romantic, too admiring, to ever blossom into carnality. John Delman hurt. He was now; they were together.

Like modesty, an imagination is supposed to be an asset. On that particular night I would have given almost anything to be able to shut mine off. I kept seeing Amy: Amy baking Delman his corn muffins in the Dutch oven; Amy waking Delman up to see the sunrise; Amy wrapped in John Delman's arms.

Jonas would say I was crazy. He'd tell you that Amy and I were never that close. I'd probably only kissed her a dozen times.

We went on a picnic once, in the Falcon, to Bear Mountain State Park. We walked away from the people, ate our lunch, and then read to each other from *The Crock of Gold*. She put her head in my lap. I sat there, running my fingers through her hair until she fell asleep. It got late. It even got a little cold. But I just sat there, hardly breathing, proud as the boy with his thumb in the dike.

The Falcon wouldn't start. But I'd brought cables, and we got a jump, as well as a cup of hot, sugared coffee, from the Puerto Rican family parked in the next slot.

After that, it seemed to me that I had a couple of options. I could marry Amy, or sanctify Bear Mountain State Park as the climax of my life. I'm not an optimist, but even to me, eighteen seemed too damn young for a high-water mark.

Almost two years had passed since then. I'd purchased egg rolls, sent flowers, written letters, postcards. I was out there, paddling furiously, frantic with yearning. And losing ground.

11

When I brushed my teeth the next morning, the face looking back at me was as haggard as that of any old sinner. Sleep may not be the main nourisher in life's feast, but it certainly is the first and most necessary cosmetic.

In the kitchen, I could hear Jonas off in his bunker, typing. I fixed myself a mug of coffee, then mixed skim milk and Equal into a cup of Fiber One.

I'm not quiet. I already told you that. So I expected the commotion to draw Uncle away from his labors. But I finished my coffee without his making an appearance. When I looked out of the window, Laura's Subaru was in the drive.

"I'm going," I said. "Back at the regular time." No answer. The typewriter was clacking away. I went out, took the Kleenex box off the passenger seat, climbed into Laura's little station wagon, and closed the door. I didn't even glance at the driver until we hit the traffic light where Route 117 crosses Route 9A. There was a deep red mark under her right eye.

"You look like I feel," I said.

No answer.

I thought I'd better ask. I couldn't pretend not to have noticed. "What happened to your cheek?"

"A broom," she said. "I was sweeping up a broken glass, tripped, and the handle poked me in the face."

"Sorry," I said.

"Not your fault," she said.

"Have you seen a doctor? I can cover for you."

"It's only a bruise. I don't need to pay cash money to have some elitist condescend to me: 'Well, Miss Grafton, cluck cluck, you *are* lucky the handle didn't hit you an inch higher.' "

I nodded. But I also knew this wasn't about money. Rather it was about the questions any good doctor would ask: "Do you live alone? Do you find that you have a lot of these accidents?"

She was wearing a denim skirt and another white nylon shell. Laura must own a dozen white nylon shells. She was little, but not quite as little as her clothes. I suspect she thought that if she bought smaller clothes, she'd shrink into them. It's not possible for a young and sexual woman to be thin enough anymore. The prettier they are, the more convinced they are of some personal obesity.

We were stopped at a traffic light in Yorktown behind a light truck that still had "Nuke Iraq" in black electrician's tape on its tailgate.

I pointed this out to Laura. She wanted to know if I'd seen the message they had outside the stone church in Briarcliff.

"No."

"Said, 'War hath no fury like that of the noncombatant.' "

I chuckled. We drove the rest of the way to New Sussex in silence. Laura opened the office. I walked to Dunkin' Donuts and fetched us each two cups of coffee.

"I have this letter I want to try to write."

"You'd like me to take the phones?"

"That'd be great, if you would."

"Sure, of course. It'll keep my mind off my wound," she said. And then, "Does this have to do with that Amy person?"

I didn't answer. My silence was answer enough. Laura may be dumb about some men, but she's not dumb about me.

She smiled. "I knew you didn't have a sinus headache."

I shrugged.

"I thought she was in Washington State or someplace. On a dig?"

"She is. She wrote me a letter."

"I told you she wouldn't understand about those cards with the picture of that awful Indian on them."

"It's not the cards she doesn't like," I said. "It's not even me she doesn't like. It's somebody else she likes better."

"You want to know what I think?"

"I know just what you think."

"I think *you* should dump *her*."

"Maybe I will," I said with almost perfect insincerity. "But I have to have her first. You can't dump somebody who doesn't care."

So I got out the old blue IBM Selectric and set myself up with a chair, right there at the end of the counter.

Dear Amy,

I'm sorry you don't like the postcards. I didn't mean to give a somber tone to our relationship. When you look at Geronimo's face, you might try to remember that he was still young when his wife, his mother, and his children were all treacherously murdered.

In 1905, he sent this letter to President Theodore Roosevelt. The old Apache was living then—had been living for almost twenty-five years—as a prisoner of war on a reservation at Fort Sill, Oklahoma:

"There is no climate or soil which, to my mind, is equal to that of Arizona. We could have plenty of good cultivating land, plenty of grass, plenty of timber and plenty of minerals in that land which the Almighty created for the Apaches. It is my land, my home, my fathers' land, to which I now ask to be allowed to return. I want to spend my last days there, and be buried among those mountains. If this could be I might die in peace, feeling that my people, placed in their native homes, would increase in numbers, rather than diminish as at present, and that our name would not become extinct."

All he ever wanted to was to live in Arizona.

All I ever wanted was Amy Snodgrass Rose.

I understand how attractive an individual like John Delman must be. I can't help but admire a man who finds a rattlesnake in his sleeping bag, catches it with a forked stick, and returns it to the wild. A sort of Saint Francis of the reptile world. Goodness, however, is not always linked with the complete absence of sexual appetite, and I sincerely doubt that Delman hasn't "noticed" you. If he has eyes, he's noticed you.

He has a car. I do not have a car. He has a doctorate in archaeology. I'm an undergraduate at NYU.

I love you.

I love you.

You owe me nothing.

Nelson Ballard

I love you.

P.S. If I can find the hair dryer, I will certainly buy it for you and ship it Parcel Post. If I can't find the Emerson 407, would another model do?

I was just starting what I hoped would be the final draft when Laura broke in.

"Pick up on line 35," she said. I figured it was an ad and reached for a form.

Laura wagged her Farrah Fawcett at me. "No," she said, cupping the mouthpiece of her phone with one hand. "It's not business, Nelson. It's personal, for you."

Amy, I thought. But this was a man's voice, smooth enough to be a woman, but a man's voice nevertheless.

"Look," said the voice, which was fast becoming familiar, "I have to go to New Sussex. I need to pick up some planks for book-shelves. I thought we might have lunch. I mean, if you do that."

I didn't say anything.

"It'll be my treat."

"That would be great," I said. I didn't think it would be great, of course, but I also knew Uncle would be furious if I refused.

"I figured we'd just get together," he said. "Chew the rag."

I held my tongue. "Chew the rag" was not the sort of phrase that would come naturally to Dr. John Gilbert. Clearly I was being condescended to. I let the silence lie for seven full beats.

"I'm not an expert," I said, finally. "I mean, I've read the books, but there are other people who have studied them."

"Oh, I know that," Gilbert said. He sounded a little surprised, as if I were being gauche. "Look," he said, "if you don't have time, just say so."

I didn't say anything.

"I *am* going to be in New Sussex," he said.

"All right," I said. "That's fine. I just didn't want you to have ex-pectations."

Gilbert laughed. "Don't worry about me," he said. "When's good?"

"A lot of people place ads during lunch breaks. I like to wait un-til 1 P.M.," I said. Actually the office was busy right up until 2 P.M., and I liked to wait until then to eat, but I didn't have the crust to say so.

"That would be fine. Is there any kind of food you prefer?"

"In New Sussex?"

"That's right."

"There are two kinds of restaurant in New Sussex," I said. "The kind that serves you in your car, and the kind that has chairs."

Gilbert didn't laugh. There was another pause. "I've only been in that area once or twice," he said. "I ate at a sort of hamburger place. Only nicer: The Mark Twain? The Samuel Clemens?"

"Huckleburger Finn?"

"That's right."

"It's a little pricey."

"The restaurant I'm speaking of specializes in hamburgers."

"That's right. Pricey hamburgers."

"I think I can swing it. Just don't have the lobster salad," Gilbert said, chuckled, and hung up.

He picked me up at 12:45. Laura didn't come out to say hello. Her bruise had gone from red to yellow. Gilbert wasn't driving the Chevy Blazer he had been borrowing from the Seagrams' handyman. Instead he had a beige Isuzu Trooper II. I could see glue on the back window where the price sticker might have been.

I was just getting in when Laura's boyfriend pulled up in his black BMW. He waved to me, but he stared at Gilbert. Kept staring at him as he got out of his car, and even took one last look backward as he went into the office.

"He looks like a hit man," said Gilbert.

"He is a martial arts enthusiast."

"Yeah?"

"Spent many long years studying the ancient and mysterious arts of the Orient."

"What did he learn?"

"How to be a motherfucker."

Gilbert didn't laugh.

"So why was he staring at me?"

"His girlfriend's inside, and he's very possessive."

"Jesus," said Gilbert, turning on the ignition. "Remind me to leave his girlfriend alone."

As we backed out, I looked into the rear seat and noticed that there was a rawhide dog toy on the floor.

When we got to Huckleburger Finn there were already five people waiting. There was an old woman at the front of the line with an aluminum walker. Her head was elaborately wrapped in a red

102

and brown silk scarf. I couldn't see any hair. It might have been there, but I couldn't see it. She was with a younger female whom I supposed to be her daughter: too well dressed for staff, too solicitous for friendship. The old lady was holding her walker with one hand while she waved the other hand around angrily. Every so often she'd stop expostulating for long enough to get in a good cough. It was one of those deep smokers' coughs I knew so well from having lived in the same house with Jonas. But this one was drier than Uncle's and seemed actually to inflict pain.

There was a slender young woman behind the little podium that separated the entrance hall from the dining room. She had long, straight, blonde hair and was dressed as a riverboat cardsharp: black pants, a black vest, and a white shirt with a black bow tie. She was tall and had the sort of blank expression almost universal among hostesses in midprice, wait-to-be-seated restaurants.

"The name is Vanderhooven," the old lady said. "We had a reservation."

"I'm terribly sorry for the misunderstanding," said the hostess, "but we don't take reservations at lunch." Then she picked up four menus, went to the group that had come in behind us, and ushered them to a table.

The back of the old lady's neck went pink, and she turned to her daughter. "Ask for the owner," she hissed.

"He's not here," said the daughter. "It must be his day off."

"How would you know that?" said the old woman. "You haven't asked. That's always been your problem, Amanda, you haven't any spine." Then she went into a long series of dry coughs.

I looked at Gilbert and rolled my eyes. He wouldn't smile. We stood there, practically touching, not knowing each other, not saying anything to change that. Every so often, I'd glance at his profile. Thoreau wrote that every man's face is his own masterpiece. It's a fine thought, but you can be a shit and have a handsome face.

Whenever Gilbert caught me looking at him, I'd give him a big smile, stretch every muscle, light up the eyes. After ten minutes of this, I was exhausted. I've always found insincerity to be extremely hard work.

Ultimately, Gilbert and I agreed to be seated in the smoking section. The old woman who knew the owner was placed with her back to us in the next booth. Sitting down, I got a good look at the Vanderhooven face. She was lighting up a long, brown, filtered cigarette. "What in heaven's name are you afraid of?" she asked as her daughter blew out the match. "Is death the thing that's got your generation so cowed?"

Our waiter arrived with the bread and water. The soup was cream of broccoli. The specials were a porterhouse, for two, and tuna, which could only be ordered medium rare.

Asked about drinks, Gilbert looked encouragingly in my direction. "Well, Max," he said, "what do you think?"

But Maxwell Perkins thought he'd start with a Diet Coke.

Gilbert also wanted a Diet Coke, "but without citrus."

"I believe we can order," he said, and then to me, "Are you ready?"

I said I'd like the Huckleburger Finn with farm-fresh bacon and the Alpine cheese. Medium. Gilbert wanted "the sirloin tips. With their hearts still beating."

"Your uncle knows," Gilbert said, when the waiter had backed away. "I didn't want you to think I'm trying to slip anything by anyone."

I nodded.

"I've told you how much I admire your uncle's writing," he said. "He's one of the only men alive today whose style is truly lapidary."

The waiter arrived with the Cokes.

"What does lapidary mean?"

"You know what lapidary means."

"No, I don't."

"It means brief, direct, and yet full of emotion: something you might carve onto a tombstone."

I smiled. Gilbert wanted to know why I was smiling.

"That reminds me of a joke," I said. "The waiter's headstone. Have you heard it?"

Gilbert hadn't.

"Here lies Joe Boston, waiter. God finally caught his eye."

I laughed. Gilbert scratched the bridge of his nose. "Your uncle's finally getting the attention he deserves," he said.

"I guess there's more interest now that it's felt he's been writing nonfiction," I said.

"What do you think?" Gilbert asked.

"He lived in Italy. He was wounded."

Gilbert seemed not to be listening. "In Europe," he said, "this would be quite a complicated situation. We'd probably have to go riding, shoot quail, or at least play tennis. I wouldn't dare broach so sensitive a subject until we'd spent several hours together."

I sipped at my Diet Coke. I don't ride or play tennis. The only living thing I had ever fired my rifle at was a large, black snake that Nar found wrapped around the toilet bowl one August night. I missed. I mean, I missed the snake.

"But we're not in Rome, or Paris," said Gilbert. "We're in New Sussex. Both you and I are American."

I put my paper napkin in my lap. I fiddled with my fork. Gilbert didn't put his napkin in his lap. I was surprised and wondered for a second if I had gotten it wrong.

The doctor sipped thoughtfully at his Diet Coke. "I'm going to be direct," he said, finally. "Is that all right?"

I squeezed the lime into my drink.

"Okay," he said, as if in response to an acquiescence not yet voiced. "Don't answer any questions you don't want to."

I fished an ice cube out of my glass and began to chew on it.

"Now, as I understand it," said Gilbert, "both you and your sister were adopted."

I crunched my ice.

"Same family?"

"That's right. Or at least from the same mother. As far as I know. Although I've never met her."

"But you do remember living someplace else? I mean before Pocantico?"

"No, I don't. I'm supposed to have lived in Montvale, New Jersey, with my Aunt Lily and her husband, Hamilton."

"Hamilton was a lawyer?"

"That's right."

"You don't know what sort of law he practiced?"

"I know he did taxes for Uncle, and he handled some divorces."

Gilbert took the big pen of out his blazer pocket and began scribbling on his napkin. "You don't mind if I take notes?" he asked.

I said I didn't mind. "You might talk with Lily," I said. "She's in San Francisco."

"But the Ballards aren't your real parents either."

"That's right, although they adopted us. One at a time."

"Do you remember why the Ballards couldn't have children?"

"Her tubes were scarred. He went to the University of Virginia. Played football. And the field. He got this infection, gave it to her. Her tubes were badly scarred. That's justice for you: The axe falls, but it cuts off somebody else's head."

"How did you learn that?"

"Uncle told me."

"Rough stuff to tell a kid."

"Why would you say that?"

Gilbert took a piece of bread, buttered it, chewed, swallowed, and dabbed his lips with the napkin from one of the places that wasn't being used. "Isn't that precisely the sort of detail parents keep from their children?"

"I don't know what parents do. But that's not what Uncle does. Conversationally, we've always been treated as peers."

"He's forthright with you, your uncle?"

"He's always saying that he and I operate on a basis of absolute candor."

"Do you think he means that?"

"I know a lot more about him than most of my friends know about their real fathers. But then he's more interested in telling a good story than he is in protecting himself."

"You've never caught Jonas in a lie?"

"Uncle lies all the time. He doesn't even know when he's doing it. But he won't tell the common household lie. He doesn't lie to make himself out to be respectable. Or to protect us from unpleasant but undeniable facts. He also won't lie to make himself a hero. Just as a for instance, he's never talked about the war."

"Why do you suppose that is?"

"He'd consider it boasting. Also, I don't know if you've noticed this, but most of the people who talk about combat were not in it."

Gilbert didn't say anything.

"It's practically a rule," I said. "There were a lot of men around when I was growing up who'd been in the army during Vietnam. The ones who wanted to talk about the fire fights, wanted to show you the ears they'd taken, well, it always turned out that they had spent the war in Japan, or South Carolina. The guys who were in combat, you'd bring it up, they'd get solemn."

"But Jonas has agreed now to write about Italy?"

"Yes, and I think he'll do it."

"Why now?"

"He has his reasons."

Gilbert seemed not to want to follow up on this one, and I was relieved.

"When does he lie?"

"He lies to give resonance. He lies to make life more dramatic but never, I think, to make it simpleminded. That good-guy-versus-bad-guy stuff you see on TV or read in books, it makes him furious."

"He aims to be evenhanded?"

"It's not that. He just wants his writing to have something to do with life."

The waiter arrived with a salad for Gilbert. The sirloin tips came with a salad. The Huckleburger Finn did not. The waiter went away and came back with a pepper grinder the size of a nightstick. He needed to know if Gilbert wanted fresh ground pepper on his salad. Gilbert did not want fresh ground pepper on his salad. He didn't want his salad at all.

The waiter was nonplussed. "But it comes with the meal," he said. "I don't care," said Gilbert. "I still don't want it."

The waiter nodded, took the salad away. About fifteen seconds later he came back, gave me the sirloin tips, gave the Huckleburger to Gilbert. He asked if we wanted anything else.

"Ketchup," I said.

"Tap water," said Gilbert

The waiter went away. We traded plates.

I took a bite of the hamburger. Gilbert began poking at his sirloin tips with the serrated steak knife they'd given him.

"What do you know about your biological mother?"

"Almost nothing."

"Your father?"

"He's supposed to be an auto mechanic. But I don't think I inherited his talents. I tried to tune the Ford once. Spent two afternoons on it. Finally had to have it towed to the service station. Cost sixty-three dollars to get it running again."

Gilbert looked bored. "I don't know that anybody thinks auto mechanicing is an inherited talent," he said.

I shrugged.

"Does the adoption ever come up, I mean in the course of dinner-table conversation?"

"When Nar was younger, she used to torture Elspeth with it. 'My real mother would get me the new Barbie doll,' that sort of thing."

Gilbert nodded. "I can imagine."

"You don't like my sister?"

"No," said Gilbert, obviously surprised by my sudden hostility. "What heterosexual man could ever really dislike your sister?"

I subsided. "Anyway," I said, "we're a family. As much as any other group of people is a family."

Gilbert smiled. "That's right," he said, took a piece of sirloin, chewed, and swallowed. "So," he said, "who's the literary executor?"

"I don't know," I said. "I guess Uncle is."

"But if Uncle died?"

I shrugged. "He's not going to die," I said.

Gilbert took another piece of meat.

The ketchup arrived. I put some on the side of my plate.

"You know, I never got along with my father," Gilbert said. "He was disappointed in me."

"How could your father have been disappointed in you?"

"He wanted me to be a surgeon. He was a surgeon. Perhaps you've heard of him: Dr. Walpole C. Gilbert. Some of his techniques were revolutionary."

I hadn't heard of Dr. Gilbert's father.

"His father was also a surgeon."

"Why aren't you a surgeon, then?"

"Don't have the hands. I always did well at school, but there are some things that can't be taught. When you get right down to it, there's nothing more important to a surgeon than his hands and his eyes."

"Same with a mechanic," I said.

Gilbert shrugged and smiled, a little sadly.

We ate in silence for a time. Then he reopened the questioning.

"How long have you lived in that house?"

"I've been told I had my first birthday in New Jersey. Since then I've been in Pocantico. So that would make it something like eighteen years. I turned twenty in May, so I guess it's nineteen years. Jonas and Elspeth had been there for a while when I showed up."

"Why has Jonas stayed for so long in that house?"

"We can afford it. You know, he was brought there by the Rockefeller family. He and Nelson had corresponded. I think that originally the governor had wanted Jonas as speech writer. Later, when Nelson died in 1979, the publicity was so unfortunate that the surviving Rockefellers thought it might be worth their while to keep a decent writer on hand."

"How cheap is the place?"

"I guess Uncle pays what it costs them to maintain it, but since they own it free and clear, we don't have to pay much. Or at least it's not much when you compare it with apartments out there in the world."

"Did Jonas ever write anything for the Rockefellers?"

"I don't think so. I'm not sure he was even asked. Some of the family members like his novels. That's enough."

Gilbert took a drink and looked at the notes he'd written on his napkin. "So who named you?" he asked.

"Lily."

"I thought you were named after Lord Nelson?"

"That's right."

"Your Uncle must have had something to do with that."

"I guess."

"He has no children of his own."

"If he had any real children, he'd be pushing them in front of me. I think Jonas is old-fashioned enough to be sorry that he has no legitimate issue."

"You and Nar are real."

I smiled weakly. "We try," I said.

"No, no," said Gilbert. "You are his children. You're terribly important to him. He says so all the time. I think you definitely qualify as children."

"Legally we're not."

"The law is an ass. You can be a common-law wife. Clearly you can also be a common-law child. If I were asked, I'd certainly identify you as his son. You even look like him."

"Thanks."

"Nelson never had any legitimate children either."

"Yeah, I heard. First he was devoted to his stepchild, Josiah Nisbet. Then his real, his biological children were born out of wedlock. Jonas has a copy of the first letter Nelson wrote with his left hand. You probably remember?"

Gilbert nodded.

"Nisbet had saved his stepfather's life at Tenerife by binding up the shattered right arm. I can quote the letter: 'I have become a burthen to my friends and useless to my country: but by my last letter you will perceive my anxiety for the promotion of my son-in-law Josiah Nisbet.' "

"That's right," said Gilbert, smiling with pleasure: 'I go hence, and am no more seen.' Oh, how that man could write."

"He could also exaggerate. That letter was written before he had even become the hero of the Nile. His real fame was all ahead of him."

"I suppose," said Gilbert. "But we must expect a little hysteria in our heroes."

"No question. Expect it. And forgive it."

I ate some more of my bacon cheeseburger. Gilbert sawed at his sirloin tips.

He chewed on a piece of meat, wagged his head. Then he got up and went to another table. Took a napkin from it and spit his meat out into it. "So why would Lily want to name her son after Lord Nelson? I know that Jonas is a great admirer. Is Lily also?"

"The families were very close. Since Lily moved away it's changed, but originally she and her sister were closer than anybody else. So she was exposed to Jonas a lot. He's got quite a charge."

"You're sure Jonas didn't name you?"

"If he had named me, I would have been Horatio. Which would have been terrific on the playground: 'Horatio's it, caught a fit, doesn't know how to get out of it!'"

"But he did name your sister?"

"They figured that was only fair. Lily had named me, and they got me, so Jonas and Elspeth named the child Lily was supposed to keep."

"Did Jonas like the lawyer?"

"They had to get along. The sisters being so close and all. But no, he didn't like him. He thought he was a jerk."

"Was he? In your estimation?"

"I felt sorry for him. There was always the sickness in the background. And he was boastful in the way that some men get when they don't really know what they're doing. He had this great plan and that great plan."

"Schemes?"

"He was going to publish the classics on the back of cereal boxes. He was going to sell miniature monkeys at Yankee Stadium. He was always going to make a fortune. He never did make a fortune." I stopped talking, ate a french fried potato.

"But he did all right?"

"He made a much better living than Jonas. I mean, up until this book, Jonas hasn't earned a lot of money. But Jonas believes in something. Hamilton didn't. And when you don't believe in anything and you're going to die, that makes it worse."

Gilbert smiled and took another piece of steak. "You never tried to find your real parents?"

"I was approached once, by this awful woman. She said she

wanted to help me with my wounds. I never followed up on it. Besides, if I had, I would have broken Elspeth's heart. You understand that?"

"Yes, of course," said Jonas, scribbling furiously on his napkin. "So how much do you actually know about your guardian? I mean about his life before you were born?"

"Nothing, really," I said. "He doesn't talk about his childhood. Almost a matter of principle. You've read the books, you know all that stuff about each man being his own invention. It's in every novel."

"Yes, but I'd like to hear it again. From you."

"Okay," I said, and cleared my throat. "Remember, though, it's his philosophy, not necessarily my own. And that this is a paraphrase."

"I'll remember."

"The great moral issue is often presented as the dialogue between those who believe in an ordered universe and those who do not: Is God dead?" I stopped, looked up. "This is Uncle talking, you understand?"

"I understand."

"It's his point that piety is not the question. He says the only distinction of any importance is between those who believe in free will and those who do not."

"He qualifies it."

"That's right. He says that obviously we are hemmed in or hemmed out by our genetic codes, controlled to some extent by the rapacity of our appetites, by an imperfect understanding of the past." I took a sip of water. "He also believes in coincidence, blind fate."

"That's right," said Gilbert. "He has a pagan's appreciation of the fates."

I nodded. "So it may be that the area in which we act freely is small. Terribly limited. But this one point of impact between the man and his world is all that matters. The rest is furniture."

Gilbert smiled. "So you really don't know much? I mean about his past."

"Nothing and everything. I've read the books. Also, I know that his family lived in Baltimore."

"You've never been to Italy?"

"That's right."

"But your Uncle lived there for years?"

"I thought you'd read the books."

Gilbert had read the books.

I don't know if the doctor considered the lunch a success. I most certainly did not. When we got up to leave, I heard a loud cooing sound coming from behind us. It was the old woman with the walker. She was cooing at Gilbert. He went around the booth and kissed her tenderly on one leathery cheek.

"Are you feeling better?" he asked.

"Yes," she said. "Much better. Thanks to you." And she coughed into the back of her hand. "I don't believe they would have seen me at all, if you hadn't intervened."

"Oh, of course they would have seen you," said Gilbert.

"I don't know," said the old lady, wagging her head. "I just don't know." Then she looked a question at me.

"A friend," said Gilbert.

As we walked by the booth, the old woman's hand snaked out and grabbed me by the forearm. I stopped, and she motioned for me to put my ear down near her mouth. "You're extremely fortunate in your choice of friends," she said.

I straightened and looked for Gilbert. He'd already left the room.

I smiled and nodded down at the old woman. "Thanks for the tip," I said.

When I got to the parking lot, my new "friend" was standing by the Isuzu, holding the keys in his hand.

"What's the story?" I asked.

"Story?"

"The old lady."

"Oh, she's the mother of a friend. We went to Andover together. He's a journalist. Covers culture. Ever read the *International Herald Tribune*?"

"No," I said, and then corrected myself. "Or almost never."

"He also writes about film," Gilbert said. "But mostly books." He opened his door and started to get into the car.

"What about her?" I asked, as I climbed into the four-by-four. "Why is she in your debt?"

"Got her into Sloan-Kettering."

"I understand the doctors are great there," I said. "What will they do for her?"

Gilbert had started the engine. The sound of ignition must have drowned out my question.

"Come again?" he asked.

"What will they do for her?"

"Oh, her," he said, putting the car into reverse. "Nothing."

"Nothing?"

"She's got lung cancer," he said, looking back over his shoulder as he pulled out of the parking slot. "The death sentence."

12

The New Sussex office of the *Westchester Commons* occupies a unit in one of those single-story boxes—orange girders under glass—thrown up on vacant lots and rented to business.

The *Commons* shares the building with two other ventures: a haircutting salon and a travel agency. The Charismatic U represents the last, best hope of a retired police lieutenant who is as bald as the nest egg he squandered on electric clippers and purple sinks. The Road Less Traveled is the perversely titled darling of George and Belinda Frost. The great feature of this establishment's front window is a seven-foot-tall stuffed bird in what Laura calls "this'll-get-their-attention yellow." Big Bird is supposed to be a good guy, a flightless creature without genitals designed to lull preschoolers into an easy familiarity with the alphabet. Still, I can't imagine that he inspires much confidence in the wary traveler. He's scrunched there, gigantic amidst the miniatures of cruise ships and airplanes, positioned to bring down a 747 with the twitch of one vestigial wing.

George Frost must have gotten drunk, bought the outsize toy for some neglected child, and then decided to write it off as a business expense. The bird has not been dusted since and is losing one of his plastic eyes. This may help explain why the Frosts don't get a lot of customers. They do get more customers than the former peace officer. His name is Harold Levin, and if he ever had charisma, he laid it down with his gun and badge. Unarmed, unauthorized, in jeans and a Western shirt, he's a lot less threatening than Big Bird and just about as active. He sits all day in one of his antique barber chairs and reads biographies of Napoleon. Every Tuesday his wife, Sheila, brings in Josephine, her Bichon Frise, to have its hair done.

Harold is a friendly sort; his establishment has the endearing wistfulness of a lost cause. He used to come over every week or so to give us his opinions. He'd stand around while we worked, talking at us in the same way a man might water a shrub with his garden hose. He really didn't expect any response.

Harold wasn't a racist, an anti-Semite, or even a woman hater. He was, however, profoundly depressed, convinced of the absolute corruption of his world. One of his theories was that the medical establishment was hiding a cure for cancer.

"They're not going to let that out," he said. "It's better than TB, better than heart disease ever was. Look at what it costs to die of cancer. It's a gold mine."

"But doctors don't get that money," I said. "That's just what it costs for the machines, the treatment."

"God bless you for believing that," he said, "but you can't tell me that they don't get some part of it, some percentage. And you also can't tell me that if they did find a cure for cancer and it was pumpkin seeds, the AMA wouldn't shit a cow."

I might actually have gotten to like Harold if it weren't for the suspicion that he spied on us for the people in Albany. I knew he phoned Walter Paige regularly, one ex-cop to another. When Laura was called on the carpet for the missing yellow ribbons, the boss had a long list of other particulars that he could only have gotten from the barber next door.

Parking for 102 Apple Blossom Court is behind Dunkin' Donuts, but there's also a small apron of asphalt in front, with two redwood boxes for geraniums. This is where Gilbert dropped me off. He didn't kill the engine, so it wasn't until he'd pulled away that I could hear the slightly muffled ring of our office phone. The sign with the dreadful orange letters had been flipped to read "Closed." The door was locked. Shutting up during business hours is *verboten*. A cardinal sin. By the time I found my keys and got inside, the caller had given up. Laura hadn't even thought to turn on the machine. "Stupid bitch," I said, to nobody in particular. I didn't mean it. Nor did it make me feel any better.

It might have been Amy. It could also have been Albany, checking up on us. Walter does that. Our office, after all, is run by an unreliable, a young person: me.

There were two pink message slips on the counter. The first one said: "Jonas." The second one said: "Had to leave." No explanation, no apology, not even her initials. Talk about lapidary.

I flipped the "Closed" sign. Then I dialed home. I could taste the bacon in my mouth.

Uncle picked up on the second ring. "Unsettling news from the Bank of New York," he said.

"Yeah?"

"The check bounced."

"Which check?"

"The one from Classic."

"That doesn't mean anything."

"It most certainly does mean anything," said Jonas with some asperity. I could hear a match go off. "I thought I had $75,000. I don't have $75,000."

"It's standard business procedure," I said. "They assume that if the check goes to the right person, it will be deposited or cashed within a month or so. After that they stop payment. It's a way of keeping the books tidy."

Jonas didn't say anything.

"Call Classic. I bet they'll send you a new one."

I could hear Uncle drawing in smoke, pausing, and then exhaling. "I don't have their number."

"They must be listed."

Still nothing from Jonas. It sounded like he was having something to drink. "It's embarrassing," he said.

I was at work, and so I was all business. "Sure it's embarrassing. It's also $75,000."

Nothing from Jonas.

"Look, do you want me to do it?"

"Do what?"

"Make the phone call."

"Would you?" he said. And if I hadn't known him so well, I might have thought he was genuinely surprised by the offer.

"All right, but you have to pick me up here today. My ride left."

"Fine. I had the car out yesterday. It should start. I'll see you at five."

I dug the Manhattan directory out of the back room, looked up the publishing house. I don't trust my memory, so I kept reciting the number as I walked back to my desk. I dialed immediately. The phone rang nine times. The woman who finally did pick up sounded so bored that I thought she might actually be sick, bitten by some urban version of the tsetse fly. "Classic Books," she said, and she drew each syllable out for so long that it could have worked as satire.

"I'd like to speak with Paul Whitfield."

"Which department?"

"He's an editor."

No response. There followed three loud clicks, and the line went dead. I returned to the back room, this time with a pen and paper, wrote down Classic's number, walked to my desk, and called again. I got the same bored woman. She made no mention of having spoken to me before. This time she did manage the transfer. I could hear another phone ringing, but now the sounds were more distant, muted, as if the lines had been laid under water.

On the seventh ring, I got another voice, also female, but not the least bit bored. "Paul Whitfield's line," it snipped. This one sounded as if it had been drinking the other one's coffee.

"Could I speak to Mr. Whitfield?"

"And *who* may I say is calling?"

"Nelson," I piped. My voice always gets high when I'm anxious. "Nelson Ballard."

"Please hold," said the voice. And then, rather as if it were my fault, "Mr. Whitfield is momentarily out of the office."

"Can I ask him to call me back?"

"Certainly."

I left my name and the office number. I also gave out our home listing. "For after five," I said.

"Um-hum," she said.

I put the piece of paper with Classic's number into my back pocket.

Then I went to work. I had to produce copy to go with the big layout Laura had sold to a local hotel: "Fat and Lonely? Just Fat? Just Lonely? Spend a weekend in slimming luxury. Visit our Wellness Room and use the Lifecycle, Stairmaster, and NordicTrack. Swim laps in our indoor pool. Network at the juice bar with like-minded executives." I'd have to get it by the hotel manager. I doubted he'd approve. Still, I thought it was worth a try. Who was it said that when you write, you must always write flat out? Never hold anything back.

Jonas didn't show up until 5:30 P.M. "Robert McNamara wouldn't turn over," he explained, when I'd settled beside him on the bench seat.

I nodded. "That battery isn't going to heal itself."

Jonas shifted up into second gear. "So are they sending a check?"

"No. I called, though. They promised Whitfield would call back."

"Who promised?" he said, looking at me as he went down into third and changed lanes. There was a loud honking from behind.

A black two-seater, with the top down, pulled abreast of us, and a man with a ponytail and mirrored sunglasses shouted something. The only word I could make out was "grandpa." Jonas turned slowly in the direction of his accuser and gave his biggest, warmest smile. "Handsome car," he said, in a loud voice. Then he began to let the Ford drift ever so slowly into the lane occupied by Ponytail's highly polished little Chevrolet Camaro.

Ponytail wanted Uncle to "watch what the fuck you're doing, asshole!" I could hear that. I suppose Uncle could hear it too, but he didn't acknowledge it. He looked ahead and kept drifting. Ponytail was in the left lane. We were in the right. There was a blue Ford van in front of us, and a silver BMW in front of Ponytail. He was trapped.

We'd traveled about fifty yards in this manner before the Camaro had to bang over the curb and go up on the shoulder. There was an ugly scraping noise as the little car's undercarriage hit the cement curbing. The BMW sped up, and Ponytail, still hollering, managed to bang back onto the road ahead of us and pull through a light that had just gone yellow. The Ford's brakes wheezed, and Uncle coasted to a full stop. Law abiders, we.

"Shouldn't you signal when you change lanes?" I asked.

"Your point," said Jonas, and nodded. Not very interested. We took the slow route to Pocantico, through three towns. Uncle always used to avoid parkways whenever possible. "They're boring," he said. "Featureless."

I explained to him once that the highways were not just faster, but also statistically safer. "Most accidents take place within twenty-five miles of the home."

"I don't take local streets because I'm afraid of being killed on the highways," he said. "I take them because when I drive on the highways for any distance, I feel like I've already died and am being punished."

Many of the trees that lined the back roads were still cinched about the waist with yellow ribbons. The bows had drooped, and the material had been blackened by the weather.

I nodded at a big sugar maple whose gigantic sash was particularly disheveled. "The patriots are making Mother Nature look like an old whore," I said.

Jonas took the box of Marlboros off the dashboard, shook out a cigarette, and used the car lighter to get it going. "War has always been in bad taste," he said, inhaled, and then let the smoke out through his nose. "I hope it always will be."

When we got home, I went straight to the refrigerator. Took out the tea. My mouth was dry.

Jonas sat down at the kitchen table. "When do you suppose they'll get back to you?"

"I don't know."

"They promised?"

"That's right."

"Why don't you call them again?"

"Whitfield wasn't in his office this afternoon. What makes you think he'd be there after five? He's a gentleman editor, not an arbitrageur."

"Just try."

"This isn't like you."

Jonas sighed noisily. "I have my reasons," he said. "Please try."

So I took the piece of paper with the number out of my back pocket. This time the phone at the publishing house rang fourteen times. The person who finally did pick up spoke with a thick accent. An industrial-strength vacuum cleaner was raging in the background. I put my hand on my Adam's apple in order to lower my voice. Nar says it's all in the tone of voice. "Whitfield," I barked, "Paul Whitfield."

I heard a couple of clicks. Then I got the snippy one: "Paul Whitfield's line."

"My name is Nelson Ballard. I called earlier today, to speak to Mr. Whitfield," I said, clutching at my throat.

Jonas had taken a seat at the kitchen table. He was sipping thoughtfully at my glass of iced tea.

"I'm terribly sorry," said the woman. "Mr. Whitfield is not in his office at the moment."

"Should I call tomorrow?"

"Mr. Whitfield works at his home in Connecticut on Fridays. May I suggest that you phone him here on Monday?"

"Oh." I said. I was looking at Jonas. "That's too bad." I didn't mean to sound melodramatic, but I guess some of Uncle's disappointment got into my voice.

"Is this going to be all right?" she asked.

"Well . . ."

"May I ask what this in reference to?"

"It's about my guardian, the writer Jonas Collingwood." There was a clicking sound in the background, and a man's voice came on the line.

"Jonas," said the voice, inquiringly. "Is that you?"

13

The writer made the coffee again the next morning and was at work when I got into the kitchen. But he came and sat with me while I drank mine and ate my mug of Fiber One. He seemed uneasy, kept pulling his ear. This used to mean he had something to say, but he hadn't gotten to it when Laura's Subaru appeared in the drive.

I had been afraid she wasn't going to show up. Correction: I had been certain. So sure that I had put the battery on trickle charge the night before. But there she was, bright and early. The Subaru had been washed. Laura wasn't looking all that bad either. She'd used pancake makeup and had managed somehow to conceal the mark on her cheek.

That morning at the office was completely ordinary. Which said a lot about how little Laura and I really trusted each other. Albert, the lawyer/boyfriend, drove in from White Plains and got there at noon to take his belle to lunch.

I was at the table in the back room working on a layout. Laura wanted to powder her nose. Powder her wound, more likely. So Positano sat opposite me. Neither of us said anything. Positano is a small, dark guy. Saturnine.

I had tried to talk with him once, and that had been in the early spring. I asked him about his martial arts training.

"What do you care?"

"I thought I might take a course."

"Sure, great," he said. "Hit somebody, go right to jail. Do not pass go. Do not collect two hundred dollars. You forget, I'm not just a martial artist. I'm also a lawyer."

So this time I held my peace and was relieved when somebody rang the service bell. It was Bill Grafton. Despite Thoreau, Bill's turned into a good-looking guy. He's got black hair, blue eyes, and a chin that indicates the character he so completely lacks. He was wearing black jeans and a black polo shirt. Bill's mother irons his jeans. He'd just washed his hair, and it was still a little bit wet. His skin is light, so he looked like he'd been snipped right out of a Ralph Lauren ad: one of those vapid young Englishmen we see lounging around, just about to be called to the Somme.

He wanted to know where Laura was. I said she was in the bathroom.

Bill: "Figures."

"She'll be out in a minute."

"I'll wait."

Positano came out of the back room, joined us. Bill was enrolled at the University of Pennsylvania. That's where Positano did his undergraduate work. So there was a certain amount of toing and froing about dorms, the cafeteria, Paul Fussell.

I was moving around, not paying a lot of attention to the conversation. I thought I heard Bill use the word "bastard." He might have been talking about me. He might also have been talking about any one of a number of prominent figures in European history.

Laura appeared. Bill hit her up for $60, and everybody left.

Jonas called at 12:30. "The battery charger is plugged in. Is there something I should know? Are you going out tonight?"

"That was for this morning. I thought Laura might have car trouble."

"Listen, are you okay?"

"Yeah, fine."

"Look," said Jonas. "I saw that letter. The one you wrote to Ms. Rose. I found it in your wastepaper basket. I was in your room. Looking for the dictionary." He paused to light a cigarette. "The letter was on the top. I assumed that you meant for me to find it."

I didn't say anything.

"It's practically a father's obligation to look through his son's garbage," he said, and chuckled awkwardly. "That's what the hand-outs on drugs say."

"Yeah," I said, "I've read them. Very subtle: 'How big are your son's pupils? Is he tired in the afternoons? Are all his friends in jail?' "

"I want to be able to talk to you," he said. "I don't want to be the father for you that my father was for me."

"Oh."

"And I may not know much about love, but I do know something about prose."

"Yeah."

"It is devoutly to be hoped that you didn't send a letter anything like the amateurish one I read."

"No."

"It wasn't very well written. Or considered."

"That's why I threw it away," I said. But my feelings were hurt.

"All I want to do is help."

"Okay," I said, and I noticed that my voice was rising. Someone might walk in. "If you really want to help me, leave me alone."

Jonas didn't say anything.

"Look, would you hang on a minute?"

He still didn't say anything, so I said, "I'll be right back." I got up, went to the front door, and locked it. I figured anyone with a pressing need to place a classified ad could knock on the window pane. I didn't want to be walked in on when I was quarreling with Jonas.

"Okay," I said, when I got back.

"It seems to me," said Jonas, "that you have been more than a little foolish about this girl. I understand, of course, why you'd be intoxicated. She's quite a good-looking woman. On the other hand, I've never seen a shred of evidence that Ms. Snodgrass Rose feels at all for you the way you do for her."

"Now you're making me feel much better."

"Unrequited love is not only foolish," said Jonas, "it's also a cliché."

"Maybe, but I can love her even if she doesn't love me."

"That's what I'm so concerned about," said Jonas.

There was a knock at the door. "Could you hang on a second?" I asked.

"Okay."

I got up. It was the mailman.

"I thought for a minute that you were closed," he said.

"No," I said. "Wednesdays we close at 4:30 P.M. But otherwise not until 5 P.M."

He nodded. "You were closed yesterday," he said.

"Yesterday was the exception." He nodded again, but I could see he didn't believe me. I gave him a plastic bin full of outgoing mail, took another bin with the incoming, and went back inside. I shuffled through the envelopes. Nothing from Amy. I picked up the phone.

"I just don't think you're in a position to give advice about love," I said, a little lamely.

"Relationships between men and women are mysterious and unpredictable, of course," said Jonas, "but I don't think Elspeth and I have anything to be ashamed of. We don't hit each other with chairs. We haven't been a bad example for you."

"You haven't been any example at all."

"What do you mean by that?"

"You hardly touch. I've never seen you kiss. You say there's nothing between me and Amy, but I've kissed Amy more than you've kissed Elspeth."

"I'm no longer twenty years old."

"You're not 106 either."

"Thank you," said Jonas, stiffly.

"You respond to other women. Lily, for instance. You respond to Lily."

The line seemed to have gone dead.

"Well?" I said.

Still no sound. Then I could hear Jonas clearing his throat. "If I were you," he said, "I would be extremely cautious when assessing intimate unions. Nobody who is not actually in the bedroom ever knows what goes on in the bedroom. You are grievously mistaken about the relationship shared by Elspeth and myself. Grievously mistaken."

"I'm sorry."

"Okay," said Jonas, but he didn't sound like it was okay.

Laura came back from lunch at 4 P.M. She was wearing a diamond ring. I didn't comment.

She had the posture and attitude of somebody who was ticked off. And it seemed it was me she was angry at. There was nothing I could put my finger on, but I got the distinct impression that if I'd put my feet in a pool of water and then touched that girl, I would have gotten a solid, deadly charge. Two hundred and twenty volts at least.

She lightened up a little at closing time. Not enough for me to feel that it would be prudent to bring up the ring.

When we got in the car, Laura turned to me and smiled. "I like this," she said. "Driving you."

"Thanks."

"No," she said. "You're good company. We go back a long way."

"That's certainly true. I mean about us going back."

Laura nodded. "But you know I won't always be able to do this."

"I know."

"Good," she said, and she sounded relieved. As if she'd gotten something off her chest.

When I reached home at 5:30 P.M., the house was empty. Nar had torn a page from last week's issue of the *Commons*. This was on the kitchen table, with a jelly jar to hold it down. A couple of ads had been circled in blue ink:

> Get a jump on your new life. This 7-year-old will not only win the hack but will jump 3'6" with ease and style. This beauty is a MUST SEE. Bedford Village.

Nar had also circled:

> Palomino gelding. 15.2 hands. 10 years old. Excellent trail horse. $1,650 or B.O.

The *Times* was on the kitchen table, so I poured myself a jelly jar full of iced tea and sat down to read. The drink tasted odd.

Elspeth came in at 6 P.M. She'd been for a walk. "I saw two bluebirds," she said. "This is late in the year for them to be around."

"That's nice."

"A couple. Male and female."

"Good," I said. "Where's Jonas?"

"He and Gilbert went to the fights in White Plains. I felt sure he was going to invite you."

"No. He didn't mention it."

"He certainly is becoming forgetful in his old age."

I wasn't convinced that forgetfulness had anything to do with it. "What's in the tea?" I asked. But Elspeth was on another tack. "He's been talking with Lily. He always loses his bearings when he talks to Sister," she said, and there was bitterness in her voice, real bitterness. "You'd think she was a movie star."

"Well, she acts a little like one."

I'd left the tea jar out on the kitchen counter. Elspeth returned it to the refrigerator. "I thought it would be better after Lily moved to San Francisco," she said. "Salt water and distance wash away love. Out of sight, out of mind. But it's not better. If anything it's worse."

"Absence makes the heart grow fonder."

"It's not his heart I'm worried about, it's his wits. She's got some sort of money trouble. I'm afraid he's going to send her every nickel. He didn't even deposit that check from Classic until he heard about Lily."

"What about Lily?"

"Some kind of debt. Damned if I know the details. Or care."

"He is silly about her. What's in the tea?"

"Blackstrap molasses. It has potassium. Guards against muscle cramps. We all eat too much refined sugar."

I nodded. "Thanks."

Elspeth smiled wanly. "I hope you aren't counting on me to keep you company this evening," she said.

I said I wasn't.

"Good then, because I'm going up to the library tonight. I promised to help Jody Rensible with some sorting."

"Where's Nar?"

"Out with that nice young man."

"You mean the Melon."

"I mean Mr. Crenshaw."

I nodded. "The Melon."

"Why must you insist on attaching a derogatory nickname to everybody you know?"

"That's what Nar calls him," I said, wounded.

"Well," said Elspeth, who had gathered up the supplies for her evening at school. "There's no need for you to be so assiduous in your imitation of a younger sister." Then she swept out the door. She was back in a moment. Concerned but unrepentant. "There's macaroni and cheese in the red casserole in the back of the refrigerator," she said, standing at the threshold. "The string beans are right beside it. Take the plastic cover off the beans. Fifteen minutes at 400 degrees." Then she was gone.

Agricola, Agricolae begins with a wife preparing Cornish game hen, scalloped potatoes, and creamed spinach for a husband she loathes. The narrator muses: "The impulse to victual the mate survives the loss of all tenderness. This is what makes the serving of the last breakfast on death row such a poignant event for the rest of us to read about. For the convicted murderer it's a detail of little significance: bacon and eggs on a nervous stomach. He may find himself in sudden sympathy with the pig, but the taste of the food is unimportant.

"For you, dear reader, for me, it's not one meal but a thirty-year marriage: buttered toast, whipped eggs; the long march to the gallows. On death row the food has lost its taste. For us it tastes of death."

I picked up Nar's disfigured copy of the *Westchester Commons* and went with it to the bathroom. It's the juxtaposition that makes it such an interesting read. We'll have ads for belly dancers, roofers, plumbers, and spiritual counseling all in a couple of inches. And we charge them by the word, so everybody means to be concise.

"Help Wanted" had a new item:

> We will teach you to earn BUCKS YOU CAN SEE selling protection from TINY TICKS YOU CANNOT SEE. If you've been bitten that's a +. Dial TIC-LYME.

When the phone rang, I thought it might be Amy, so I leapt up and raced to the kitchen with my pants down around my ankles. I picked up on the third ring. It was Lily. "Nelson," she said, "how is my baby boy?"

"Fine," I said, pulling up my pants and trying to keep the disappointment out of my voice.

"Look, is Jonas there?"

"No, I'm afraid he's in White Plains. At the fights," I said, fastening my belt.

"And you're not with him?"

"I had work to do," I lied.

"Can you take a message?"

"Sure, of course. Here, let me get a paper and pencil."

"No, it's not that sort of message," said Lily. Then she made a little purring sound. She always makes a little purring sound when she begins to talk. "Tell him not to worry. I haven't deposited the check. I've spoken with my accountant. Personal bankruptcy is not the horror we imagine." She paused.

I didn't say anything.

"You know about all this, don't you?"

"I know something about it."

"When I moved out of New Jersey, I owed the IRS. Actually Hamilton owed the IRS. It wasn't very much money. Or at least it wasn't prohibitive. But they kept sending the bill to Elm Avenue in Montvale. And, not surprisingly, I kept not paying it."

"Didn't the new people forward the mail?"

"No, they're still sore about that septic situation. I mean, really. They had the house inspected."

"So now the IRS has found you?"

"And in the meantime they worked up a lot of interest, and penalties. Quite a bit of money. Jonas has been a dear about it, of course."

"Yeah," I said.

"You knew about this?" asked Lily.

"Sure," I said, but it sounded hollow.

"Then it looked like his help wouldn't be necessary. I got this hotshot lawyer. Or should I say," she trilled, "this hotshot lawyer got me. He said I had a great case. I'd win in a walk."

"So?"

"I lost. In a canter. Now I have $20,000 in legal fees."

"Your hotshot lawyer sounds like a crook."

"That's what lawyers do. You pay them to say you're going to win. It makes you feel better to have somebody spewing confidence at you. Even if it does cost a couple hundred dollars an hour. But if you don't win, you still have to pay them."

"How much do you owe? I mean, if you don't mind my asking?"

"Matter of public record. We don't have to pay all the lawyer's bills immediately. But right now, I need something like $70,000."

"Wow," I said.

"Sixty-five thousand something, or seventy-five thousand something. I'm not certain which. And Jonas wants to be my white knight."

"Wow," I said again, and it sounded different this time. A little less exclamatory.

"I would certainly pay him back in time. I mean, if he even has that much."

I had trouble with this one, but I didn't lie. "Yeah," I said. "He has it."

"Does Elspeth know about this?"

"I think so."

"She doesn't mind?"

"No, I don't think she minds," I said, and thought, "Oh what a tangled web we weave, when first we practice to deceive."

"She's always been a saint, my sister."

"That's right," I said. "She has always been a saint."

"You'll tell Jonas I called? And that I'm going to deposit his check."

"I'll tell him."

"I shouldn't try again later? I'm going out now, but I could call tomorrow night. Around midnight your time."

"No," I said. "We're all asleep by then. You needn't try and call again."

"I can consider it done?" she said.

"Consider it done," I said.

"Good," said Lily. "I had told Jonas that I would probably be able to raise the money myself. I was going to use the bookstore as collateral, get people to invest in the business."

"Oh, I didn't know that."

"There just isn't sufficient interest. Although I could still go bankrupt. There's no reason to rule that out."

"I don't think Jonas would want you to lose the store," I said.
"Well," said Lily, lightly, "that's up to him."

Federal Express delivered a fresh check from Classic on Saturday morning. The van had just pulled out, and Jonas was still standing in the drive holding the big, colorful envelope, when Gilbert arrived. The biographer had gotten up at the crack of dawn, gone into Manhattan, bought a Krups coffee grinder, six navel oranges, and as many chocolate croissants. He'd also bought a pound of mocha beans and two pounds of Vienna roast. "You use two parts Vienna to one part mocha," he told me. "It's like a cruise ship martini, with the gin being the Vienna." Then he ground the beans. When the water boiled, I operated the Melitta.

Afterward, Elspeth said that she hadn't broken a fast so well since she left Italy.

Afterward, Jonas and Gilbert drove off in Gilbert's Isuzu Trooper II to Ossining. Jonas wanted Gilbert to see Sing Sing. "The Ossining Correction Facility is what it's called now," he explained, "but it's still the big house, it's still up the river, the place where the Rosenbergs died."

I stayed home. The battery had been in the trickle charger for more than twenty-four hours. I put it into the Ford and drove to ShopRite for Elspeth. We were out of tea bags.

Nar didn't appear until time for lunch. Jonas and Gilbert had picked up sandwiches at one of the gourmet delicatessens in Pleasantville. There are five delicatessens in or near the center of the village. Three are within bagel-tossing distance of each other on Wheeler Avenue. Two of these sell frozen yogurt. There is also a frozen-yogurt store.

During lunch, Black Forest ham with Bibb lettuce and honey mustard on toasted oatmeal bread, Nar and Elspeth made a plan to take Gilbert to Sunnyside. That's the home of Washington Irving. It's about ten minutes from here. Set up now as a museum.

Gilbert obviously presumed that Jonas would accompany them. Jonas said he would not. If Gilbert was disappointed, he didn't let on. Elspeth let on.

"Come now," she said. "We've lived here twenty years. He's the father of American literature. You've never even seen his house."

"And I never shall," said Jonas.

"Why's that?" I asked.

"I suppose this will sound heretical," said Jonas. "Dead writers who are remembered at all are always held in such high esteem. But I don't admire the work. If Washington Irving were alive today, he'd almost certainly be writing for television. You forget that he's the man who coined the phrase 'almighty dollar.' It was only the built-in morality of his epoch that kept Irving from being ridiculous. Born in our time, he'd be a great public oaf. They'd call him the Legend of Sleepy Hollow, the networks would interview him poolside whenever anybody overslept. And think of the tie-ins. He's been dead for a hundred years and he's still a hot commercial item. Imagine if he were alive today."

"Not a bad idea," I said. "The Rip Van Winkle Mattress Outlet: Conk out for twenty years. Don't wake up until the dog is dead."

Nar laughed. "Mr. Winkle here actually slept right through the American Revolution. He doesn't feel like he missed a thing. So what are the rest of us staying up for?"

"Enough," said Elspeth. "Enough. Jonas needn't come."

"I think I'll skip it too," I said.

"Jesus," said Nar. "I hope this doesn't mean that pretension is a contagious disease."

"No. I've already been to Sunnyside."

Gilbert wanted to know when.

"I had a girlfriend who worked there. Or a girl I was interested in."

Nar nodded. "Amy," she said.

Gilbert wanted to know how often I'd gone.

"I don't know, a couple of times a week."

"Did you learn anything?" he asked.

"They used to have a break, and I'd bring her tea and cigarettes. We'd go out behind a far building, and I'd watch her smoke and drink her tea."

"I mean about history."

"Well, I learned that Amy looked good in a hoop skirt."

"If you don't come," said Elspeth, "who will drive the Ford?"

"I will," said Nar.

"You will not," said Jonas.

Gilbert said they could all go in the Isuzu. He smiled at Jonas, almost coyly. "I'm sure you're right about Irving," he said. "But I'm still curious."

Nar took the front passenger seat. Elspeth got into the back. She looked young, almost childish, sitting up there waving at us as the high, square car headed down the drive.

I returned to the kitchen and found Jonas at the table, beaming. I was beginning to wish he'd get writer's block again.

"Now," he said, rubbing his hands together, "how much does a battery cost?"

"I don't know. About a hundred dollars."

"Okay," said Jonas. "Let's do it. I think we'd better spend this money before Nar settles on a $20,000 horse."

"Speaking of which," I said, "did I tell you that Lily phoned?"

Jonas raised a hand. "I don't want to hear right now," he said. "You'll tell me later. Now about that battery."

So I dug out the Westchester directory. When I found the heading "Auto," Jonas wondered if that meant dealers as well as auto supplies.

I said it did.

Then he wondered if they had a listing for Ichabod Motors.

I found it.

Then he wondered if I would mind terribly if we called them first.

"They won't sell batteries. Or if they do, they'll sell them at a terrific markup. If we're going to buy a battery from them, we might as well buy it from Joe and have him install it."

"Call them anyway," he said.

"Now," he said, moving close to me after I'd dialed, "ask if they sell the Miata."

"Why?"

"Just ask."

I got a girl with gum in her mouth. I asked if they sold the Miata. She put me on hold. They had country-and-western music for the people they put on hold. Kenny Rogers was singing "The Coward of the County." We'd just reached the point where the coward's girlfriend was brutally raped when the salesman broke in.

"This is Ralph," said a sugary voice. "Ralph Ingersoll. And what is your name?"

"Nelson Ballard," I said.

"Well, Nelson," said Ralph, "how can I help you today?"

"Do you sell Miatas?"

"Yes, we do."

"How much do they cost?"

"It depends what you want on them. Leather-wrap steering. Alloy wheels. AC. They can go up to $20,000."

I put my hand over the speaker and turned to Uncle. "They can cost $20,000," I whispered reverentially.

Uncle's eyes glistened. "Ask them how little they can cost," he whispered.

I took my hand off the speaker.

"How little can they cost?" I asked.

"Well, Mr. Ballards, it's quite a coincidence your asking that. We just this week got a 1990 model on the lot."

Jonas was signaling. I put my hand over the speaker again. "Ask them about color," he whispered.

I took my hand off the speaker.

"What color is it?" I asked.

"White with a black top. Very smart."

"Isn't a white car hard to keep clean?"

"I suppose so, but it looks great. And a car like this, you don't want to carry garbage in. Outside of red, white is our most popular color."

"What do you want for the white car?"

"Thirteen thousand. It's got the alloy wheels. Wrapped steering. Full AC."

"Why would anyone want to sell?"

"Go figure. Some people, money isn't a consideration. They have to have a new car every year. Rich people aren't the same as you and me."

"Sure they are," I said. "They just have more money."

Ingersoll didn't laugh. One thing about living in Westchester, you don't have to worry about attributing your quotes. Nobody's that interested in words anyway. Most communication is carried on in a not-so-subtle sign language involving make of car, type of clothing, neighborhood, and job.

"So there's nothing wrong with it?" I said.

"These people, they wouldn't own a car if it had anything wrong with it. Nelson, I know it's still a lot of money we're talking about, but you've got to see this one to believe it."

I didn't say anything.

"Can I ask you a question Mr. Ballads?"

"Sure."

"Have you ever driven one of these cars?"

"No."

"Then you have to come down for a test drive. Can we make an appointment? How about this afternoon?"

"I'd rather wait," I said. "I'm still just considering. How many miles on the odometer?"

"I'd need to check that. Ten, fifteen thousand. No more than fifteen thousand."

Uncle was signaling again. I turned to him. "Ask them," he whispered, "do they have anything in red?"

Saturday-afternoon traffic is light around here, so it took about fifteen minutes to get to Sears in White Plains. We had an hour to kill while they installed the new Die Hard. I told Uncle I had to go to the bathroom. I did have to go to the bathroom. It wasn't a lie.

I left him in hardware and rushed upstairs to small appliances. They didn't carry the Emerson, so I bought the most expensive hair dryer in stock. The Lady Godiva was whorehouse pink and came complete with rollers, a helmet, and a device for drying nail polish. I tried to use a check, but that process was going to take hours, so I gave them the American Express Card I'd gotten for expenses incurred by the *Commons*. I would pay that part of the bill myself. I had the dryer sent to Amy. The whole thing, with shipping, came to $138.29. I figured she'd have to break up with Delman or throw it away. (And Jonas says I don't live in the real world.)

I found Uncle near the escalator where it comes out in the basement. He was holding some literature and watching a man in a three-piece suit who was scattering iron filings and dog hair onto a thick carpet and then vacuuming them up. The suit was brand new. It looked like it had just been taken off the rack. The shirt was also brand new. The man inside was not brand new. Nor had he bathed recently. His hair was greased, and some of the iron filings had gotten stuck to his pompadour.

Uncle thanked him for the demonstration and said that he would seriously consider purchasing the Royal Buckingham. The man with the pompadour looked sad. "If you want the machine, you'd better buy it now. The sale ends tomorrow."

"I know," said Jonas. "But still, I have to think about it." Then we went up the escalator and out to the lot where we'd left the car. Jonas showed his receipt to a bald man in a white jacket that was supposed to remind us of surgical procedures. The faux doctor was standing at a sort of podium. He spoke into a microphone, and in a couple of minutes the Ford came screeching up out of the sub-basement. A striking youth in green electrician's pants and a matching work shirt got out. He had thick blond hair, slicked back, and that bouncy walk that used to be associated with professional boxing.

Jonas presented the receipt. The blond smiled. "This your car?"

"Yes."

"You want my advice?" he asked.

"No," said Jonas, "I don't." But the young man didn't hear, or if he did hear, he didn't care.

"Fill her with peat and plant tulips," he said.

"Why, thank you," said Jonas, his voice heavy with sarcasm. "Any particular color?"

"Well," said the young man, who seemed to be completely unaware of his customer's rising choler, "that's the advantage white gives you. It goes with anything." And he handed Uncle the keys.

Jonas reached out, took the mechanic by the arm of his green shirt. I was afraid for a minute that we'd have a fight, but Uncle was smiling. "Surprised to find a person of your diplomatic skills working at Sears," he said. "I'd expect Washington, the State Department."

The young man smiled and shrugged. The anger still hadn't touched him. "No languages," he said, and walked off.

We drove home in frosty silence. By now I really did have to take a leak.

When we got to the house, we could hear voices on the back terrace. One of them was Gilbert's.

I started for the bathroom. Uncle wanted to know where I was going.

"To the john."

"You just went," he said.

When I got to the one bathroom in the house, the door was closed. Water was running.

"Nar?"

"Yes?"

"What are you doing?"

"What do you think I'm doing?"

I went back down the hall, out the kitchen door, and ran into the woods.

By the time I joined the family grouping on the terrace, Nar was also there, looking pretty and refreshed. Uncle was beginning a lecture, one in the series Sister and I had titled "Pocantico Hills: Fact & Fable."

"Building Kykuit, and working on all the trails, there were a lot of laborers around," Jonas said. "Mostly they were well behaved, but there was one problem. The Rockefellers would put out food for the wild animals, and the workmen would eat it or take it home for their families."

Gilbert smiled. "I can see how that might have been frustrating."

"They solved it," said Jonas. "They'd pay the local kids to collect acorns, and then they'd put out the acorns for the wild animals. Most workmen won't eat acorns."

When Elspeth saw me, she said somebody had called.

"Who?"

"I don't remember."

"Man or woman?"

"I don't know."

"Did they leave a number?"

"No. They said they'd call again."

"I'm afraid our household could not exist if it weren't for the Rockefeller family," said Jonas.

"Does that bother you?" asked Gilbert.

"Certainly not. Joyce accepted Rockefeller money, why shouldn't I? The family has a real sense of social responsibility. In 1929, the old man issued a statement saying that he and his son were buying stock, confidently buying stock, in the expectation that it would hold its value."

"He must have lost his shirt," said Gilbert.

"He did," said Jonas. "He had other shirts. And right then, he wasn't trying to turn a profit. Right then he was trying to save the economy."

Gilbert nodded, not entirely convinced. "Was he here a lot?" he asked.

"Yes," said Jonas. "Mr. Senior was the lord of this creation. There are still people around who remember the son, John D. Rockefeller, Jr. He used to ride the trails in a little buggy. There was always a man in the back with a rifle across his knees."

Gilbert smiled. "Isn't he the one they called Mr. Junior?"

"That's right. Harry Emerson Fosdick wrote a biography in which he said that every man is faced with some problem, some handicap, and that John D. Rockefeller, Jr.'s handicap was to have been born with an enormous fortune."

"Some handicap," said Gilbert.

"Well," said Jonas, "he might have given it up if he could. He took his responsibilities very seriously. And if money counts for anything in this world, he did an enormous amount of good. But it was work. Hard work. I think it may well have taken some of the joy from his life."

"Nobody can select the family he is born into," said Gilbert.

"That's right," said Nar, "but if you were allowed to pick, I bet there'd be a jam-up, with all the babies crawling into position to be the next Rockefeller."

Jonas turned on her. "That's precisely the sort of foolish and superficial observation I'd expect from you," he said.

"What do you mean by that?" asked Nar.

"If you, for instance, had been born a Rockefeller," said Jonas, "and comported yourself as you have done for the last three years, you'd already be a national scandal."

"Wow," said Nar, looking at me and waving her right hand about, as if it had just been dipped into fire. "What's the matter with him?"

I shrugged. "The usual," I said.

"While children cannot pick their parents," Gilbert said, smiling at Jonas, "parents also cannot select their offspring."

"You picked us," said Nar.

"That's right," said Jonas. "The fire-sale babies."

We had pork chops, brussels sprouts, and baked potatoes for dinner. The whole happy family. Biographer and all.

Nar and I both expected Gilbert to show up with Sunday breakfast. When he hadn't arrived by 9 A.M., Elspeth went ahead and scrambled eggs. I walked down to the end of the drive and got the paper. Then I made the toast. We spread out the Sunday *Times* and ate in silence. We were deep into the second pot of New York coffee when Jonas came out of the root cellar.

"So," said Nar, without even looking up from the travel section, "where's Boswell?"

Uncle put his empty coffee mug in the sink. "He couldn't come today," he said. "I think he'd offered to fill in for a pediatrician he knows in Yorktown. He still practices medicine."

"Likely story," said Nar. "Bet you anything he's in New Rochelle. Bringing lox and bagels to E. L. Doctorow."

Jonas scowled menacingly but said nothing. He took a fresh package of Marlboros from the carton, which was on top of the refrigerator. Then, moving slowly, with exaggerated dignity, he headed toward the root cellar. He was not wearing shoes, and it was in the pantry that he caught his big toe on the leg of a brass coachman. There was a little bleat of pain, and Uncle hopped the rest of the way into his office. Nar giggled.

"Really," said Elspeth, from her post at the sink, "you shouldn't." She returned to the frying pan and began angrily to scrub.

Nar tilted back languorously in her chair and cocked her head so that she could see Aunt. "You're wrong about me," she said. "I'm only trying to establish perspective."

"I don't recall your ever having been so nasty," I said.

"Jonas has never really needed my help before this."

"Sshhhh," said Elspeth. "He may still be able to hear us."

"Let him overhear us," said Nar. "That would be good. Daddy, can you hear me?" We all paused, listened, to see if Uncle was going to say anything. We didn't hear him. Or rather we didn't hear his voice. What we heard was the typewriter.

By the time he reappeared at 10:30 A.M., I was dressed and ready for the 11 A.M. service at the Union Church of Pocantico Hills. Nar was in the bathroom with the tap open. The water is always running when Nar's in the bathroom. It runs when she washes her hands. It also runs when she thickens her eyebrows. Elspeth lectures her: "Well water and electricity are not infinitely renewable resources. Why don't you listen to music instead?"

Nar never attempts to refute these arguments. She's fully in sympathy with Aunt's position. Still, the moment she gets into the bathroom, she opens the tap. Apparently, she can't help herself. I think it's a little like George Bush used to be with his cigarette boat: burning fossil fuel by the five-gallon jerry can. The impulse to rape the natural world can be led into civilized channels, but—at least in some people—it cannot be stopped.

Unlike the old battery, the new one made vigorous clicking sounds when Jonas switched on the ignition. But the car still wouldn't start.

So Jonas called the Mobil station. And by the time Nar got out of the bathroom, the mechanic was in the drive.

I don't trust myself to describe Joe Orsini. He's not really a handsome man. He's lost most of his hair, and he's a good ten pounds above what Metropolitan Life Assurance would recommend.

But if Joe lived in California, if he taught history to undergraduates instead of fixing cars, they'd say he had an aura. I don't know if he gets it from being outside a lot, at the pumps, or because he understands his work and does it well. Maybe he's just never done anything he thought reprehensible.

He has the quality that second-rate politicians and movie people are always striving for and rarely achieve. He has presence. He knows himself, and what he knows is not bad.

When Jonas and I came outside, the Chevy Impala was pulled up next to the Ford. Both hoods were up, both engines firing.

"Dottore," said Joe. He and Uncle embraced. "Come sta?"

"Bene, mio figlio. E lei?"

"Molto bene."

I often wondered how Uncle got away with calling Joe his son. They were only about ten years apart. The mechanic didn't seem to mind.

This demonstration of affection—which took place every time the car broke down—always used to disgust Nar.

"It's enough to make me think the old man's gay."

Sister isn't homophobic. She's not exactly open-minded either. I think it's a practical matter. She knows that heterosexuality is her bread and butter. So when she sees men loving each other, it's the loss of influence she resents. She reacts like the carriage manufacturer who stepped off his shop floor one bright morning in 1908 to see the first Model T.

Jonas and Joe never saw each other, except for business. They didn't fish together in the Croton River, which they might have done. And Joe never even asked Jonas to address the local Rotary, although he, Joe, was an officer, and the Rotarians often invited local writers to speak.

Yet I believe the affection was deeply felt. On both sides. Certainly the friendship was theatrical in the way European relationships are apt to be. But it was also genuine. Rock solid.

Once the car was going, Joe left. Nar got into the back seat; Jonas and I got into the front. Elspeth will not go to church. "I'm sure I believe in a lot of nonsense, but I like my hokum the same way I like my dinner, fresh and cooked up from scratch."

Jonas didn't argue but continued to go to church himself, and when we were at home and otherwise unaccounted for, Nar and I would accompany him.

By the time we got to the church that morning, the bells were sounding the hour. We had to wait in the foyer while the choir paraded up the aisle. Then we went in, found our seats.

Nar thought the man on the left aisle, three rows back from the front, was a Rockefeller. "Look at the square head," she whispered. "He's either a mutant or a Rockefeller." Jonas shushed her. "You don't have to pray," he said, "but you mustn't gawk either."

The sermon on this particular morning was given by a visiting minister. The Reverend Arnold Arnold informed us that he had just renewed his subscription to a weekly news magazine. As a consequence of this act, he was going to get, as lagniappe, a digital pen stand.

"And that got me to thinking," he said. "Because I realized that we, as Christians, must also renew our subscriptions to the teachings of Christ."

The sermon went on for half an hour, but it wasn't until we got into the Falcon, which started, that the postmortem began.

Nar broke the silence. "I'm sure he was a Rockefeller," she said. "Probably he was Stephen."

Jonas seemed not to have heard her. "Not since the crucifixion," he said, "have men of the cloth had any grasp of the limits of metaphor."

Elspeth wanted us to spend the afternoon cleaning the oven, but Jonas thought it too fine a day. He had an outdoor project. Several large granite blocks in the stone retaining wall that embraces our house and drive had been loosened by the winter freeze.

I went out to the shed, got the wheelbarrow and shovel, loaded up a bucket and a bag of cement.

The bearings on the old wheelbarrow are shot, and the squeal of metal on metal is so high pitched as to be almost entirely subliminal. Sensing the sound before hearing it, I invariably take the disturbance for a portent of disaster. When I figure out, as I do each year, that it's metal on metal I'm hearing and not a premonition of death and damnation, I'm always enormously relieved.

I mixed the water and powder while Jonas scrubbed at the empty sockets in the wall with a wire brush. Then I spread the cement, and together we fitted the stones back into the places where they seemed properly to belong. This is a ceremony that we perform each summer. Each winter the stones pop out again. (Something is there that doesn't love a retaining wall. Or at least one that's been imperfectly repaired.) "There's a skill, a serenity possessed by the original masons," said Jonas, "which you and I can only guess at." Parts of the wall that had never required our doctoring went for years, for decades without so much as a hairline crack in the mortar. The sections that we worked on always needed to be fixed again.

Laura showed up on Monday at the regular time. The scar was gone, the diamond was not. We didn't speak. Or not until we got on 9A north.

I started it. "Ever hear the one about the newlyweds?"

Laura didn't say anything. Didn't even look my way.

"Stop me if it sounds familiar."

She nodded.

"The wedding was beautiful. Now they're in an open carriage with two horses, one white and one chestnut. They're heading off for the honeymoon. A storm is blowing up, so the groom is driving the horses hard. Using the whip. 'I don't want my little lamb to get wet,' he says. Well-wishers have put flowers around the horses' necks. The wreath on the white mare comes undone. The animal catches her foot in the heavy twine, trips and falls. The groom jumps down out of the carriage, helps the horse up. 'That's once,' he says, and climbs back onto the seat. The skies darken. A clap of thunder spooks the white, who gets tangled again and stops. The groom jumps down, frees the horse, gets back onto his seat. 'That's twice,' he says.

"Now the rain is coming down in sheets. The ground is muddy. The white horse falls. Again the husband climbs out of his seat. 'That's three,' he says, cuts the mare out of its harness, takes a revolver out of his coat, and shoots her dead. He mounts the carriage, picks up the reins.

"The bride is horrified. 'Lambkins,' she says, 'you shouldn't have done that. I'm not made of soap. The rain won't hurt me.'

"Her husband turns to her. Smiles. 'That's once,' he says."

Laura didn't laugh.

"A joke," I said.

"Hardeee har har," she said.

That was it. We didn't talk again until noon. Then I got the call. Laura took it and passed it on. "Line 27," she said, "personal."

"Nelson. Nelson, is that you?"

I controlled myself. And when I said "yes," I said it stiffly.

"Ohhhh," she said, and drew it out for long enough to give me an erection. "I'm so glad. I've been trying to call you for days now." And then Amy burst into tears.

I didn't get off the phone for an hour and a half. Laura went out for her lunch, ate it, and came back. When other lines lit up, I ignored them. By the time I hung up, I was beaming, really crimson with joy. "Praise God from whom all blessings flow."

I had hoped Laura wouldn't notice, but of course she did.
She came right over to my desk. "Well?" she said, and smiled.
"Well what?"
"Oh, come on now, you can't hide that."
"All right," I said. "That was Amy."
"Now tell me something I don't know."
"She wants to start seeing me again."
"I thought she was in love with that other guy."
"She was."
"Is he married?"
"Nope."
"What, then?"
"She's reconsidered."
"Don't be coy with me."
"Well, he's not the marrying type."
"Oh."
"He likes her. He told her that," I said, shifting around on my metal chair. "He's really a very gentle man. But she didn't take it too well. Now she says she always knew, I mean on some level, and must have fallen so hard for him because she loved me and was trying to avoid the commitment."

Laura put a hand on my shoulder, looked down into my face with real and suddenly undisguised affection. "Amy Snodgrass Rose may really love you now. I'm not denying that. But she never loved you before this moment. If she loves you now, it's on the rebound."

I got up. "I'd like to stay," I said. "Discuss this at length. But I've missed my lunch. I'm going down the street to get a frozen yogurt. You want anything?"

"No thanks. I ate."

It took me about a minute to get happy again. I liked Laura. But I didn't care why Amy Rose had turned to me. What mattered was that she had. If I could have Amy's love and my dignity too, that would be just swell. But if it was going to be a choice between just Amy, or just my dignity, I knew which way to go.

By the time I got back to the office, she'd called again. I was supposed to call her back. "She's waiting," said Laura. "At a pay phone somewhere. Here's the number."

The line was busy. I dialed it again. The line was still busy. I went over to Laura's desk. I asked her if she was sure about the number. She was sure about the number. I dialed it again. This time I got Amy.

"I'm so glad you called back," she said. "Look, I want you to come out here."

"To Washington State?"

"Yes."

"When?"

"Now. I mean, as soon as possible."

"Oh."

"You sound halfhearted," said Amy, her voice falling.

"It's just—I don't know. A surprise."

"You'll love it out here. It's so wild. So primitive."

I could hear trucks roaring and rumbling around in the background. "Sounds like you're in a truck stop."

This drew a laugh, but there wasn't a lot of mirth in it. "That's true," said Amy. "I'm in a parking lot, and there are trucks, but it's nothing like you imagine. There are also these wild mountains in the background. I'm at the diner we come to for breakfast. It's called the Wooden Indian. There's a cigar-store Indian at the end of each aisle. But it's not precious or overdone, like it might be back East. The food is good and cheap. The men all wear cowboy boots and Western ties."

"Frontier life," I said.

"That's right," said Amy. "It's great."

"But aren't you coming back here? Soon?"

"Yes, but I miss you. I miss you now."

I didn't say anything. It cost me, but I held my breath.

"You can meet John Delman. You'll like him."

"I'm sure I will like him. Now. But I've got this job."

"Which job?"

"I'm office manager at the *Westchester Commons*. You know. The shopper."

"Oh, you mean the giveaway?"

"That's right," I said, "the giveaway."

By the time I hung up, Laura was on the other phone. My frozen yogurt had melted. I wondered what it would cost me to fly to Washington State. Once I'd paid for the Lady Godiva, I'd be down to about $200. Everything else was in savings. If I cashed out and spent the money, I might not be able to go to NYU again in the fall. Correction: I would not be able to afford to go back to college.

In the meantime I had proofs to read:

> Getting married. Must sell 4½-foot boa constrictor with 75-gallon terrarium, 2 heating rocks, 2 heating lamps, one bathing bowl, and 40-lb. bag of bedding. Seventeen white mice. Everything for $750.

I showed this to Laura. She smiled. "Poor guy," she said.

"I know," I said. "And what if she married him for the snake?"

It was about half an hour later that Jonas called. "I'm going to be in your neighborhood this afternoon. Why don't I give you a ride?"

"Sure, that would be fine. But you'll call me if the car won't start?"

"If the car won't start," Jonas said, and laughed, "I'll call Joe. You shouldn't worry. We just bought a new battery."

Half an hour later, I looked up from my copy to see Laura standing beside my desk.

"Well?"

"You'll hate me."

"Maybe. But that's a risk I'm willing to take."

Laura turned to face me, grinned. "I don't know, sometimes I think that you and I have a lot in common."

I raised my eyebrows. "You mean we're both suckers," I said.

Laura bobbed her head. Her masses of hair jounced around. "You said it."

I shrugged. She was smiling. She looked good. The prospects of a bad marriage seemed to have worked as a sort of beauty aid. Her face was filling out. She was wearing a tan skirt, gabardine, and a man's blue dress shirt. Probably it was Albert's shirt. She looked quite beautiful, womanly. If I hadn't known her for so long, I might well have been in awe of my old friend. Also the hair. The hair was still just a little ridiculous.

"That's a nice skirt," I said. "Fetching."

Laura blushed. "Thank you."

"I don't need a ride home."

"Good," she said, and that was that. I applied myself to the tasks at hand. Of which there were a great many. The young people who run the New Sussex branch of the *Westchester Commons* hadn't been a model of efficiency. Our office is one of three. We're responsible for a section of the publication, but not the *Westchester Commons* in its entirety. The layouts we were supposed to send to the printing plant had gone out a day late. And now we were already behind with next week's work.

Laura left at 5:10. I worked alone until 5:30. Then I called home. No answer. So I worked until 5:45, packed the orange nylon knapsack I use for a briefcase, locked up, and sat outside on the edge of one of the redwood flower boxes. All of the begonias were dead.

Harold Levin closed his shop and came and stood with me for a few minutes. He wanted to know if I was sleeping with Laura. I told him I wasn't.

"She wants it," he said.

"Maybe, but not from me."

"So who are you with?" he asked.

I shrugged. "Nobody."

"So you've never done it?"

"I've done stuff," I said, "but no, I've never done it."

"Jesus," he said, running his palm over his bald head. "You got the whole world in front of you. You know, I still remember the first time."

"What's it like?"

Harold put a hand on my arm. "Don't let me scare you," he said.

I shook my head. "I'm not scared," I said.

"It changes everything," he said.

"Really."

"First you hear this incredible sound."

"What sound?"

"Like a watermelon breaking open."

"Really?"

Harold nodded. "And afterward," he said, "you're not afraid of heights anymore."

"But I'm not afraid of heights now," I said.

Harold grinned. "Maybe you should stay a virgin, then," he said, and walked off.

I opened the knapsack, took out a proof to read. The day had been hot, and the evening stunk of melted tar and car exhaust.

A stranger in a bright red roadster pulled off the road. He was wearing an outsize black beret, pulled low over his forehead. I took him for one of those foolish old men you see in convertibles sometimes in the spring and early fall. They've cashed in the life insurance. The dishwasher will never be replaced and little Sarah won't go to medical school, but Daddy has a brand-new car. This particular asshole had obviously gotten lost. He was stopping to ask directions. Probably looking for someplace to get his teeth bonded or his hair thickened. Then I recognized the beard.

14

The Miata was so low-slung that I felt bashful standing beside it, peering down at Uncle in his ridiculous hat. It was almost as if he were the boy, I the man. I thought he might have picked up on my uneasiness because he seemed nervous, had trouble opening the door.

"The catch needs oil," he explained, hoisting himself with difficulty up out of the bucket seat. "That's what Suspenders told me," he said, shutting the door, which sprang open again. "Sorry I'm so late," he said, slamming the door, which held this time. "The paperwork took longer than we expected."

"Suspenders?"

"Ingersoll. The salesman. You like the hat?"

"I do," I said. Then, awkwardly, "I didn't recognize you."

"Paul Whitfield sent it. He's in Paris."

I shrugged. "It's very French."

"But you *do* like the car?"

I nodded.

"You don't look like you like the car either."

"Oh, no, I like it a lot. It's just a sort of, well, sort of a surprise."

"It's not me?"

"Yeah," I said, nodding some more. "It might be the new you. Is it the new you?"

Jonas chuckled. "Like the new Nixon, the new Coke?" he asked.

"That's right," I said, "although I'd market you as a Classic. The Classic Coke. The Classic Nixon."

Jonas came and stood beside me, so that we were now both looking down into the toy automobile. I picked up the sweet smells of scotch and tobacco. He fished a Marlboro out of his shirt pocket. I held out my hand.

Jonas looked a question.

"Just one. In honor of your new car," I said, and grinned weakly.

Uncle shook another Marlboro out of the pack. Then he fished a damp, flattened book of matches from the back pocket of his chinos. It took a while, but we got both cigarettes going.

I inhaled deeply, regretted it almost immediately.

"It's not meant to be me," said Jonas.

"What's not meant to be you?"

"The car."

"Who is it meant to be, then?"

"You. It's meant to be you."

I took another drag on the cigarette; then I reached down, put a hand on the windscreen to steady myself. I couldn't tell if it was the cigarette smoke that was making me dizzy, or Uncle's generosity. In either case, I didn't feel at all well. Now I think it might have been a premonition. But then, at that moment, I was simply nauseous. I actually wondered for a minute if I was going to have to throw up. I dropped the burning cigarette onto the road, stamped it out.

"I'm sorry," I said. "I don't know what to say."

"This was the absolute last one on the lot. Ralph Ingersoll, the salesman, told me that in New Jersey people are bribing the dealers just to get on the waiting list."

"I believe that."

"It's been compared to the Mustang," said Jonas, happily. "Not that the cars are similar, but rather that each of them was somehow a perfect expression of its time."

I'd seen the ad. I didn't say so. "This car must have cost a fortune," I said.

"That's exactly what it did cost," said Jonas, "a fortune."

"So why'd you do it?"

Uncle smiled crookedly. *"Carpe diem,"* he said. "I'm grabbing the gusto. It's Miller time."

"You're not supposed to grab the gusto for other people. If you grab the gusto, it's supposed to be for yourself."

Uncle didn't say anything.

"Besides, you can't afford the gusto."

"I most certainly can. I paid them with a certified check. You can't get a certified check for gusto you don't have."

"What about the Emmanuel Glessing Book Store and Tea Shop?"

"Last time I spoke with Lily, she'd found some California sugar daddies just aching to invest. Lily has plenty of admirers," said Jonas. "I'm the only admirer you've got."

"When did you last speak with her?"

"A week ago."

"Shit," I said.

Jonas scowled. "Nelson," he said, "please watch your language."

"Lily called Friday. When you and Gilbert were at the fights. The backers went away."

"All the backers?"

"All the backers."

"Shit."

"I'm sorry. I forgot to tell you. I didn't see the need."

"How bad is it?"

"Without your money she'll have to go into bankruptcy."

"She said that?"

I nodded.

Jonas took a long draw on his cigarette, threw it down. Stamped it out. He walked over to the car and sat awkwardly on the hood. He lost his balance for a second, and the hood dimpled under his weight. He hopped up, as if he'd been given an electric shock, and we both waited uneasily until the front of the car popped back into its original shape.

"Can we return it?" I asked.

"We can try," said Jonas, and I remember being surprised to find that I was disappointed. Apparently, I was already attached to this wicked little contraption.

"You should drive."

"No," said Jonas, wearily. "You drive. It may be your only chance. Besides, I haven't the heart."

So I climbed down into the tight little cockpit. Jonas showed me how to move the seat back. I noticed that the steering wheel wasn't wrapped. I wondered if this model had alloy wheels. I hadn't looked. I wasn't sure what an alloy wheel was.

The door certainly needed lubrication. I had to slam it four times before it held. Jonas got in beside me. He removed the beret and rolled it up. There was a hammer on the floor in front of his seat.

"Where'd that come from?"

"The Melon gave me a ride down to the showroom," Jonas said. "Apparently, he'd borrowed it a while ago, when Nar helped him put up pictures in his apartment."

"It doesn't look like our hammer," I said.

"No," said Jonas, "it doesn't. Here," he said, "let me help you find reverse." I put my hand on the shift. He covered my hand with his own, and we went through the gears. I went through them again before switching on the ignition. I eased into first and pulled out into traffic. The Miata *was* fun to drive, or it seemed as if it might have been fun under ordinary circumstances. But then under ordinary circumstances I wouldn't own a crimson two-seater.

When we got to the dealership, I pulled into the lot and parked beside a Range Rover with a crumpled front fender and "Lion Hunter: $19,999.99!!!" written on its windshield with a bar of soap. Jonas said he wanted to stay outside. "If you don't mind?"

I did mind, of course, but I wasn't going to say so. "How will I recognize the guy who sold you the car?"

"He's the only one with red braces."

There were three salespeople in the showroom, two men and one woman. One of the men had red suspenders. He was sitting at a tin desk with a sign on it that said "Ralph Ingersoll." He looked to be in his late twenties or early thirties, with hair not quite long enough for a ponytail and a prominent forehead.

I went right up to him and stuck out my hand. Ingersoll stood. He was a little taller than I. We shook hands.

"I'm Nelson Ballard. We've spoken on the telephone. About a Miata."

Ingersoll whistled. He pointed to one of the two metal chairs that were ranged in front of his desk. "Have a seat," he said.

I sat.

Ingersoll sat. He picked up a white coffee mug that was on the desk. Looked into it. "Nelson," he said, "I'm afraid I've got some bad news. We just this afternoon sold our last Miata. It'll be a month at least before we get another one. Although, if you're really interested, I'd be glad to call around." He put the mug down, leaned back in his chair, scratched behind one ear. "I believe there are still some units in New Jersey."

Then Ingersoll took a comb out of his back pocket, ran it twice through his hair. "I'd better warn you at the outset that these cars are very hard to locate. In some cases you actually have to pay a little more than list. Would that be a consideration, Mr., uh. . . ?" He fiddled with the mug, and when he was done, I could see that it had "You don't have to be crazy to work here, but it surely helps" written on the side in black letters.

"Ballard," I said. "But no, I don't want to buy a Miata. You sold your last car to my guardian, Jonas Collingwood. That's what I'm here about."

"Oh," said Ingersoll, smiling. "Congratulations, then. You're an extremely fortunate young man."

"I want to bring it back."

"Something the matter?"

"No," I said, smiling and shrugging in a way that I hoped the salesman would find winning. "We changed our minds."

Ingersoll crinkled his forehead.

"We don't like the color."

The salesman opened the center drawer to his desk, withdrew a folder. "Name Collingwood?" he asked.

I nodded.

"Car's red?"

"That's right."

"Red's our most popular color. Bar none."

I smiled, nodded. "There are four of us. This is going to be a family car. Red isn't appropriate."

Ingersoll sighed. "You don't mind me asking you a question?" he said. "To satisfy my personal curiosity?"

I shrugged.

"How old are you?"

"Twenty."

Ingersoll scratched at his nose. "You're a twenty-year-old boy and you don't want a red Mazda Miata?"

I didn't say anything.

"What color would you like, then? Pink?"

"It's not so much the actual color," I said. "We aren't really in a position to afford a sports car."

"In that case," said Ingersoll, "I can set your fears to rest. Your uncle bought that vehicle free and clear. No loan." He pointed to the manager's office, a large cubicle of smoked glass and tin. There didn't seem to be anybody in it. "We've got a certified check in there for $19,875."

"I suppose he has the money," I said, lamely, "but it's already committed. Elsewhere."

Ingersoll held out his hands, palms upward. "He doesn't have the money anymore," he said. "He has a brand-new Mazda Miata. We have the money."

"Well, I was wondering if there was anything we could do about that."

"You mean you want to sell the car back to us?" The phone on the tin desk rang. Suspenders looked at me and shrugged. "Do you mind?"

"Go ahead."

Suspenders picked up the phone, listened.

"I'll stop on the way home," he said. "Get the syringes and some more of those paper things." He sat leaning forward, holding the phone to his left ear with his left hand. With the thumb of his free hand he began vigorously to scratch the porch of his right ear. "I guess the doctor must know," he said, listened, then nodded again. "Not a spring chicken. No." He leaned back in his chair and put the heel of one surprisingly small, black Reebok aerobic shoe up on the desk blotter.

I turned to look back into the showroom and saw Jonas. He was quite some distance away, obviously avoiding us. He stopped and studied the sticker on an enormous green Peugeot station wagon. A salesman approached him. Jonas said something, and the salesman went away. Uncle walked to the back of the car, looked at the sticker price, walked to the front, opened the door, got into the driver's seat. I could see the windshield wipers going. Then the spritzer.

Ingersoll was still on the phone. Now he was shaking his head. "No, it never is," he said. "And no, we still can't afford a nurse."

He took his foot down, leaned forward, picked up a pencil and examined it. He put the pencil on the desk. It rolled to my side. I could see from where I sat that the pencil said "Courtesy of the Half Moon Convention Center: All the Conveniences with a view of the past and windows on the River."

"Look," he said finally, into the phone, "I've got a customer. I should be home by seven-thirty." He hung up and turned to me. "Now where were we?"

"You've been to the Half Moon?" I asked.

"What?"

"You've been to the Half Moon Convention Center?"

"No," he said. "Why do you ask?"

"I just thought you'd been there."

"No. Look," he said, rearing back in his seat, "am I on 'Candid Camera' or something? Most embarrassing home videos? Is this part of some kids' prank?"

"Of course not," I said.

"You sure?"

"Look, Mr. Ingersoll, what I'd like to do," I said, leaning forward in a supplicatory way (I actually had my hands clasped together in an attitude of prayer), "what I'd like to do is just cancel the sale. Act like it never happened. We could pay you a couple of hundred dollars, if you wanted, for your trouble. But essentially you'd rip up the check and we'd take a cab home."

Ingersoll leaned back in his chair, put his hands behind his head. Jonas had moved to the part of the showroom that was behind Ingersoll's desk. He was spooning Cremora into a Styrofoam cup of complimentary coffee. I kept expecting Ingersoll to recognize him, but he did not. Jonas must have had the beret on when he was buying the car. Nobody who knew him bareheaded would recognize him with that hat. Nobody who knew him with the beret would recognize him without it.

Ingersoll sighed. "Of course I'd love to help you," he said. "But there are a number of reasons why we can't do what you ask. The first and most obvious of these is that it would be in violation of the law. Once a car's sold, it's sold. You can sell it again, but you can't unsell it."

"What if we sold it right back to you?"

"You really want to do that?"

"Yeah."

Ingersoll stood up. "Let me speak with the manager. You wait here."

"Okay," I said, and shifted around in my metal chair. Jonas had engaged his own salesman and was trying out the seat adjustments on a Saab convertible. It looked like the one Paul Whitfield owned. Only without the brassiere. I glanced over in Jonas's direction, but he wouldn't let me catch his eye.

Ingersoll's silhouette appeared in the smoked glass of the manager's office. I couldn't tell if there was anyone else in there with him. Whatever was going on took about ten minutes. Ingersoll came out of the manager's office with a folded piece of paper. He put this into my right hand, closed my fingers around it.

"I really had to bust chops," he said, jerking his head toward the apparently empty manager's cubicle.

I nodded. "Thank you," I said.

I opened the piece of paper. Somebody with a fountain pen had written "$12,799."

I looked up at Ingersoll. He had a fountain pen in his shirt pocket. "What's this?"

"That's what we'll pay."

I didn't say anything.

"We can't do it today," continued the salesman, taking his comb out again and running it through his hair, "but if you leave the car overnight, our mechanics can check it out. We'll come up with a certified check at noon tomorrow. For the full amount."

"For which full amount?"

"That amount," he said, pointing at the piece of paper.

"Is this a joke?"

"No," said Ingersoll, and he looked as if he were disappointed in me. "That's generous."

"Generous?"

"Nobody else would give you that kind of money."

"Wait a minute," I said, standing, "You just got done telling me how desirable this car is. And my Uncle just got done paying you $20,000 for it. Isn't that what you said?"

"Nineteen thousand and change," said Ingersoll, and he sounded a little bored.

"So what happened to $7,000?"

"Nothing happened to $7,000. The car you're selling me is no longer new."

"Now you're the one who's kidding."

Ingersoll shrugged. "I don't really want to buy the vehicle back from you at all. I'm making you an offer. A good offer. But this is only because I was a kid once. You're young. And clearly you've incurred some serious debts. Debts that your father wasn't aware of when he decided to buy the car. I don't know who you owe, of course, or how much you owe. It's none of my business. Nor do I feel obligated to notify the police."

"Come on," I said. "Come look at the car. It's got, what, twelve miles on it since you sold it. Come look."

Ingersoll stood. "All right," he said. "If you insist."

He called over to the lady salesperson. "Patty, I'm going out to the lot with this gentleman. I'll be back in five minutes. Then we should close up."

Patty smiled.

Ingersoll and I went outside. The car was right where we'd left it. With the top still down. The beret was on the passenger seat. As was the hammer.

"Still in red," I said, smiling bravely. "Your most popular color. Bar none." I leaned over the cockpit. "And the odometer has 24.3 miles on it."

"Right," said Ingersoll, as if dealing with a very dull student. "But this is not the same car. It's been off the showroom floor. It's changed hands. You say you haven't put much mileage on it. I can't guarantee that. Maybe you've been hotrodding it all afternoon. Disconnected the speedometer." He pointed to the Range Rover. "You want four seats, buy this car. Ever driven a Range Rover?"

"No."

"Fifteen thousand and it's yours. And we'll throw in a new bumper."

I didn't say anything, so Ingersoll turned his attention back to the Miata, began to fiddle with the driver's-side door.

"What's this?" he said, when the catch failed to disengage. The expression on his face was a dramatic demonstration of surprise and then hurt. He was too hammy for film, but he might have been just right for a high school production of *Oklahoma!* or *Death of a Salesman.*

"This door is broken," he said, straightening up and throwing his voice. "Here I am, trying to give a young kid a break because he's in trouble. How do you repay my kindness?"

"Kindness?"

"You try and sell me damaged goods," said Ingersoll.

"Wait a minute," I said. "It just needs a little oil is all. Besides, that's the way you sold it to us. For $20,000."

Ingersoll stopped and turned to face me. "This is Ichabod Motors," he said. "We would never sell a car with a broken door." Then he started back to the building we had just left.

I went around to the passenger side of the car, picked up the hammer. Then I ran up behind him and put an arm on his shoulder. Ingersoll brushed me off. "Get out of here," he said. "Or I will call the police."

I stood there, looking silly, holding the hammer in both hands. The salesman turned and walked stiffly back into the showroom. A minute or two later the lot lights went out. Then the door opened again and Jonas came out. He had some literature in one hand and a Styrofoam cup of coffee in the other.

I got into the passenger seat. I put the hammer on the floor. I was trembling. Jonas got behind the wheel. I gave him his beret. He put it on. He had to slam the door six times to get it to catch. We drove home in silence.

When we got to the top of the drive, we found Nar standing outside, holding the mail in one hand.

"*Quelle chapeau,*" she said, and then, "Whose car?"

"Mine, I guess."

"Wow," said Nar. "Can I try it out?"

"You don't have a license."

"I drive the Melon's Mercedes all the time."

Jonas cleared his throat menacingly. "Love is blind," he said.

Nar looked at me. "What's the matter with him now?" she asked.

"Nothing," I said, bitterly.

"Wow," said Nar. "Somebody writing your biography too?"

I didn't say anything. Jonas didn't say anything. I opened the glove compartment, removed the clear plastic packet with the manual in it. I got out of the car. Jonas got out too. We drifted toward the house. Out of the tail of my eye, I could see Nar get into the driver's seat. I could hear the car door slamming: once, twice, three times.

"Hey, you guys," she said. "This door's broken."

Jonas didn't say anything. I didn't say anything.

"You bought a lemon," said Nar.

Jonas turned on Sister and gave her a long, silent scowl.

Nar made a raspberry sound, stuck out her tongue, settled back in the driver's seat. The windshield wipers started up. The lights popped up and turned on. Uncle and I went through the kitchen door.

Elspeth was at the stove, dropping brussels sprouts into the steamer. "Dinner in fifteen minutes," she said. I nodded. Aunt had a tall water glass of what looked like scotch. It could have been tea, but I don't think so. The half gallon of Old Smuggler was out on the counter. She stopped cooking for a minute, stepped back, and spoke to Jonas. "Lily phoned. I said you'd call her back."

Jonas nodded, unplugged the kitchen telephone, and brought it to the jack in the root cellar. I retired to my room with the manual.

I settled on my bed. Something was wrong. I opened the door to my room. "Is there a fire?" I asked, projecting my voice down the hall.

"Thanks," said Nar. "We know all about it."

"Do you need any help?"

"Nope."

I went back to my bed, back to the manual. Maybe there was a trick to the driver's-side door latch. I couldn't find it. Nothing in troubleshooting either.

I was beginning a study of the convertible top when Aunt called me for dinner. The kitchen was full of smoke. I opened both windows. Then I helped Elspeth set the table. Aunt put the burned chops out on a serving dish with a sprig of parsley and a dollop of mint jelly. The glass that I thought must have held scotch was empty and in the dish drain. Elspeth didn't say anything about a fire in the broiler. I didn't ask.

Jonas was still in the root cellar, still on the phone, muttering passionately. I could see his ragged crew-neck sweater through the pantry. He was all hunched over, the receiver held to one ear and his hand over the other.

Elspeth and I took our places at the table. No sign of Nar, although something loud and atonal had started up on the CD, so I guessed she wasn't too far off. Elspeth put her napkin in her lap. I put my napkin in mine.

Aunt took up her knife and began to hit it smartly against the side of her water glass. The third time she hit the glass it shattered. "Damn," she said.

I fetched a roll of paper towels, gave her a couple of sheets, and we both went down under the table. There seemed to be blood in the water. When we came back up, I could see that Aunt had wrapped a piece of toweling tightly around the two middle fingers of her left hand.

I went to the kitchen cabinet and got another glass, filled this with tap water, and put it at Elspeth's place. We sat down. "That was fun," I said, but Elspeth wouldn't smile. Her face was a mask.

Jonas came out of the root cellar. He looked grave. He took his place at the head of the table and served a burned chop to his wife.

"So?" asked Elspeth.

Jonas paused, looked at Aunt, said nothing. Then he took Nar's plate and put one of the burned chops on it. He served me a chop, gave two to himself, put his napkin in his lap.

"I won't eat," said Elspeth. "Not until you've blessed this meal."

Jonas bowed his head. Aunt and I bowed ours. "For that which we were about to receive," he said, "Lord make us truly thankful."

"Amen," I said.

But Elspeth wasn't placated. "I think one of the guilty ones is called for here," she said.

Jonas bowed his head again: "Almighty God, Father of our Lord Jesus Christ, maker of all things, judge of all men: We acknowledge and bewail our manifold sins and wickedness, which we, from time to time, most grievously have committed, by thought, word, and deed, against thy divine majesty."

He stopped and looked up. Aunt still had her head bowed. He continued: "Provoking most justly thy wrath and indignation against us. We do earnestly repent, and are heartily sorry for these our misdoings; the remembrance of them is grievous unto us; the burden of them is intolerable."

He stopped again. Still no response from Elspeth.

"Have mercy upon us. Have mercy upon us, most merciful Father; for thy Son our Lord Jesus Christ's sake, forgive us all that is past, and grant that we may ever hereafter serve and please thee in newness of life, to the honor and glory of thy name, through Jesus Christ our Lord. Amen."

"Amen," I said.

"Amen," said Elspeth.

Jonas got up, took the glass out of the dish drain, filled it nearly to the top with Old Smuggler, said "Amen" again, and sat back down.

"Where's Nar?" he asked.

"I told her we were out of milk," said Elspeth.

I took my napkin out of my lap. "May I be excused?"

"Yes," said Jonas. I went out to the driveway. The Miata wasn't there. By the time I had walked back to the kitchen door, Uncle was at the threshold, coming out.

"Gone?" he asked.

"Yup."

He turned, without speaking. We both went back into the kitchen again, took our places at the table.

Jonas cut himself a piece of chop, chewed, and swallowed. Then he looked at Elspeth. "Did you know she was going to take the Miata?" he asked.

"Is that what it's called?"

Uncle nodded. "Did you?"

"No," said Elspeth. "I told her we were out of milk. She said she'd get some."

"It's a new car," I said. "With a sensitive clutch. Narcissus doesn't even have a learner's permit."

"The 7-Eleven is less than two miles away," said Elspeth. "I think she can be trusted to drive there and back."

Jonas sawed at his blackened lamb chop. He spoke without looking up. "Nar has many sterling qualities," he said. "But she has never been the least bit trustworthy. Or punctual."

"She'll be back in ten minutes," said Elspeth. "You can hector her in person."

"I didn't check," I said, looking at Uncle. "Was there gas in the tank?"

Jonas nodded. "Ingersoll had them top it up," he said, bitterly. "He was very chummy. Threw in the gas. The floor mats."

"She won't be back in ten minutes," I said.

"She might," said Elspeth.

"She won't," I said. "I know Nar."

"How can you be so certain?" asked Elspeth.

"Something I picked up in the amniotic fluid."

Elspeth stood and passed around the brussels sprouts. I made the mistake of putting an entire sprout into my mouth. It was dreadful. I couldn't tell if it had been scorched or had just soaked up the smoke while the meat was being carbonized.

"So," said Elspeth, stiffly, after the horrid sprouts had made the rounds. "Speaking of sisters, what did *my* lovely sister have to say?"

Jonas still had his mouth full of burned chop; he looked up but had to keep chewing for a couple of minutes before he could get the meat down.

"Well," he said, taking a pull on the scotch, "she *was* counting on the money."

"And now," said Elspeth, "you've spent it."

"I have," said Jonas.

"I had no idea you were planning to buy me the car," I said. "I would have stopped you if I'd known."

"You would have tried to stop me," said Jonas.

I turned to Elspeth. "We went over to the dealership this evening. We meant to give it back."

Aunt had tried to cut herself a piece of burned chop, but she couldn't. The meat was tough and dry; she had two fingers of her

166

left hand wrapped in paper. She asked me to pass her the bread. I did. She helped herself. When I got the basket back, I took three pieces. "If you know the poisoner," I thought, "you eat what the poisoner eats."

"It's a silly little car," said Elspeth. "But I also think, Jonas, that you're extremely foolish about Lily."

"She's in trouble," said Jonas. "She'll lose the shop."

"People in San Francisco will find someplace else to buy their tea," said Elspeth.

Jonas didn't respond.

"Correct me if I'm wrong," she said, "but you never would have agreed to write about the war at all if you hadn't thought my sister needed the money."

Jonas shrugged, raised his eyebrows.

"You had planned to go to Spartan Books with Christabel Gordon. You would have taken less money and written another one of your novels. Christabel wanted you."

"I didn't even know Christabel was still in business," I said.

"There's a lot you don't know," said Jonas, and then he took a drink of scotch. He put another piece of chop into his mouth, chewed manfully for a while, swallowed, and wiped his lips with a linen napkin before speaking. "Hard to say. It's certainly true that Classic's contract came in at about the same time that I learned that Lily was in trouble with the IRS. On the other hand, there is something invigorating about being offered so much money. Besides, Lily is not the only one in the family who may someday have a need for cash."

"I'd like to believe that you were thinking of the rest of us," said Elspeth. "But I sincerely doubt it. You would never have signed such a contract in order to put Nelson through medical school."

Jonas shrugged. "There's no evidence that Nelson wants to go to medical school," he said. "None."

"That's right," I said, helping myself to the bread. "I hate the sight of blood."

Elspeth tried again with fork and knife. This time she was able to cut a little piece of burned gristle off one end of her lamb chop, but having done so, she decided against eating it. She put her silverware down. I noticed she hadn't eaten any sprouts either.

"I suppose this snazzy little car and the IRS debt total more than $75,000," she said.

Jonas nodded.

"You can't give the car back?"

"I don't think so. We tried."

"So Sister's going to have to give up her precious store after all?"

Jonas shook his head. "Not necessarily."

"What are you going to do, then?" asked Elspeth. "Sell your hair and teeth?"

Uncle took a sip of scotch. "I do have some gold fillings."

"Not funny."

"No, seriously, there is a solution."

"What's that?" I asked.

"Finish the war memoir. Classic would owe me $150,000. That way, Nelson can keep his snazzy car. He can go to medical school if he wants to. Lily can bail out her bookstore. Nar can have her horse. Then I'll go back to Christabel. Get out of show business. Write another novel."

"Doesn't Lily need the money immediately?" asked Elspeth.

"No," said Jonas. "We have some time. That's what I was establishing on the phone while you were preparing this extraordinary dinner."

"How much time?"

"Three weeks."

"You're not going to write a book in three weeks?" I asked.

"I most certainly am going to write a book in three weeks," said Jonas, angrily. Then he softened, turned to me, and smiled. "Remember," he said, "it's not writing with a capital W this time. It's supposed to be straight reporting. Your man in London, that sort of thing."

We had frozen raspberries and Carvel Thinny Thin for dessert. Elspeth had two servings. So did I. Jonas was full. As soon as she was finished eating, Aunt retreated to her bedroom. She didn't even clear away her own dessert dish. Jonas followed.

I stayed in the kitchen and cleaned up. The broiling pan took about fifteen minutes. Then I got a screwdriver out of the shed, and using this, I was able to scrape enough of the gunk off the oven floor so that there probably wouldn't be another fire in the immediate future.

While working, I was also listening. The house is old and solidly built, but the sounds coming out of the master bedroom were loud enough to be heard through the plaster-and-lath muffler. I couldn't make out the words, but both parties spoke with passion. It sounded almost as if there were a couple of big dogs in there fighting. I thought maybe I'd been incorrect in my assessment of the relationship. On this particular evening, Aunt and Uncle were acting very much like lovers.

It wasn't until about 9:30 P.M. that I retired to my room. I spent some more time trying to figure out from the manual how the convertible top worked. If the car came back, if the car ever came back, the top would have to be raised. We didn't have a garage, and I wanted to protect the leatherette upholstery from the morning dew. I came out of the bedroom at about 10 P.M. Still no sign of Nar. Jonas was in the root cellar. Typing. I went back to my room, read about the air conditioning. I didn't even know if my new car had air conditioning. At 11, I walked down the drive. It was conceivable that Nar had parked the Miata in the turnaround. She hadn't. I climbed back up the hill. Jonas was at the kitchen door.

"Don't worry," he said.

"Something like fifty thousand people die every year in auto accidents," I said. "A disproportionate number of them are teenagers."

Jonas smiled. "Maybe so, but your sister, Nelson, is not the least bit self-destructive."

Jonas went back to work. I retired to my bedroom.

I dreamt that I drove to La Guardia in a bright red Mazda Miata. The wheels were alloy, the steering wrapped.

I met Amy at the baggage claim. She was wearing stiletto heels, white, without backs. I'd never seen Amy in heels. She was also wearing a nylon warm-up suit, black with an azure lining. Her face was drawn, distant or angry. We did not embrace. She smelled of Ivory soap. I carried the suitcase, duffel, and knapsack out to short-term parking. When we got to the car, I put the bags down and turned to face her.

She had begun to cry.

I reached out to touch a shoulder. She batted my hand away.

"Honey, what's the matter?"

"Your windshield wipers," she said, tears running down her cheeks.

When I woke up, my clock radio read 5:37 A.M. I pulled on my pants, without underpants, and went out into the drive. Barefoot, I limped across the gravel to the car.

Nar had tied the driver's-side door shut with a blue silk scarf. There were 97.03 miles on the odometer. She must have gone to Poughkeepsie for the milk.

The keys were tucked up under the driver's-side visor. I untied the scarf, got into the seat, turned on the ignition.

I came back inside, heard Jonas typing. I walked into the office. He stopped work.

"The windshield wipers are broken."

Jonas picked up the package of Marlboros. He offered me one. I shook my head. He took one himself, lit it, inhaled, and blew smoke out through his nose. Then he looked at me closely. "Anything the matter?"

"Actually, I thought I might go on a trip."

"What sort of trip?"

"To Washington State. To see Amy."

"Isn't she going to be home soon?"

"Yes."

"Will you do me a favor, then?"

"What?"

"Will you wait until she comes back?"

"Why?"

"Chase her," said Jonas, "and you'll lose her."

I sighed.

"Is that a problem?"

"No."

"If I'm going to write this book in a hurry, somebody else is going to have to do all those things I do that aren't writing."

"Anything now?"

Uncle nodded.

"What?"

"Get that damn car door fixed. And the wipers."

I smiled. "All right. But I'd rather not go back to Ichabod Motors if I can help it."

"Afraid of Suspenders?"

"I'm afraid I might hit him."

"Take it to Joe, then."

I made fresh coffee. Brought some to Uncle. Then I went into my bedroom, got the manual. Back to the kitchen, poured myself a mug of coffee, brought it and the book out to the car.

I called Laura at 7:00 A.M. Asked her to pick me up at the Mobil station at around 7:30.

When Joe saw the car, he whistled. I blushed. Cleared my throat. "*E Roto*," I said.

I got out, showed him the door latch. Joe climbed into the passenger seat and opened the glove compartment. There was a piece in the compartment that looked suspiciously like a part of a door latch.

I shrugged. "So, you think you can fix it?"

Joe smiled.

"Try the wipers."

Joe tried the wipers.

"Can you fix that?"

"Pick it up this afternoon. Anytime after 3 P.M."

"Great."

Joe climbed down into the driver's cockpit and took the car into one of the mechanic's bays.

I walked out to the end of the pump island.

The car that came to pick me up wasn't the Subaru. It was a beige VW Rabbit. Bill Grafton was driving. Laura was in the back seat. She rolled down the window. "My car's getting new tires," she said. "Bill said he'd drive us."

I smiled at Bill. "Thanks," I said, and got into the front passenger seat.

"So," said Bill, "I understand you've got that Rose girl on the line."

I didn't say anything.

"Fuck her?"

I shook my head.

"But you tried?"

I shrugged.

"But you want to fuck her?"

I nodded.

"Jesus," said Bill, "you don't seem very enthusiastic."

"Oh," I said, "I am enthusiastic. Very enthusiastic."

"Good," said Bill. "You know you owe me?"

"You mean for the ride?"

"You owe me for the Rose girl."

I didn't say anything.

Bill rubbed his nose with the back of his hand. "You don't get it?"

"No."

"If it weren't for me, you and Laura would still be together," he said.

"Oh, Bill," said Laura from the back seat.

"No, really," said Bill. "If I hadn't caught the two of you out in the garden that time, playing doctor, and turned you in to the parents, you probably would have stayed together."

I peered back at Laura, who was looking acutely uncomfortable.

"That wouldn't have been so bad," I said.

Bill shook his head and whistled. "You're not just an asshole," he said, agreeably, "you're a lying asshole."

I looked back at Laura. She was crimson. I shrugged.

Nobody talked until we pulled up in front of the office. Laura got out first. She was unlocking the door to the *Commons* as I was getting out of the car. Bill was looking at me.

"No hard feelings," he said. "I mean, you won the prize. Although the race doesn't always go to the swiftest," he said, "or to the guy with the biggest dick."

"Thanks," I said, closing the car door. "But I'm not sure of anything yet."

Bill shook his head, signaled for me to stick mine back in the car window. I did so. "Fuck her brains out," he said.

"Thanks," I said, and straightened.

"Thatta boy," said Bill, slamming the car into gear and pulling away.

By the time I got into the office, Laura was at her desk. She didn't look like she wanted to talk.

Amy's call came in at 1 P.M.

"John says you can sleep in his tent. He'll pick you up at the airport. We can fly back together."

I didn't say anything.

"Nelson, are you there?"

"Yeah," I said. "I'm here. And here's the thing. We have a family emergency. I can't come."

"What?"

"Uncle has to write a book."

"Isn't that what your uncle does, write books?"

"It is what he does. But he has to write this one in a hurry. And I've agreed to help."

"Help him write the book?"

"No, I've agreed just to be around, get things for him, back him up."

"Oh," said Amy, "a sort of maid of all works," and her voice fell.

"Well, to be honest with you, I already felt awkward about coming out there. I do also have this job," I said, weakly.

Amy didn't say anything.

"Are you there?"

"Yes."

"Do you understand?"

"No."

"This isn't what I want. I mean, if I had my way, I'd drop everything and fly out there immediately."

"Then why don't you?"

I took in a deep breath. "For a lot of reasons. First, I have a job. I'd probably lose my job."

"What about Laura, can't she fill in?"

"Laura's getting married."

"Oh."

"There's good news," I said. "Uncle bought me a car. A Miata. So when you do get back, we can see each other. It won't be so hard for us to see each other."

Amy didn't say anything.

"It's red."

"Oh."

"I thought you'd be pleased."

"This may come as a surprise to you," she said. "But I have had boyfriends with cars before."

I swallowed hard. "Not me."

"So?" said Amy. "You came by bus."

Now it was my turn to be speechless.

"I liked that," said Amy, softening. "We had romantic assignations in public places. It was like a spy movie or something. Didn't you enjoy it?"

"No," I said. "I liked seeing you, but it wouldn't have killed me if we could have been alone."

Nothing from Amy.

"Look," I said. "If I was the kind of guy who just rushed off whenever he wanted to, who left his job, left his uncle in the lurch . . . It's like that poem. You know."

Still nothing from Amy.

"I could not love thee, dear, so much, loved I not honor more."

Nothing from the other end of the line. "Amy?"

Still nothing.

"Amy?" I said, my voice rising.

"I'm not deaf," she said. And then, "Tell me not, sweet, I am unkind, that from the nunnery of thy chaste breast and quiet mind, to war and arms I fly."

"That's right," I said. "So you do get it?"

Nothing from Amy.

"Do you get it?"

"No, of course I don't get it. In the first place, that's a war poem, and I'm clearly not as sure as you are that war is a good way for a man to spend his time. In the second place, I'd like you to just close your little eyes for one long moment and consider how often it is that a certain type of girl gets that poem poemed at her." Then she hung up.

I called her right back. Nobody answered.

I waited ten minutes and called again. This time I got a trucker. He was friendly, but he hadn't seen any girls in the parking lot.

He wanted to know where I was calling from.

"New York."

"No girls in New York?" he asked.

"No," I said. "None," and hung up.

We closed up at 5:15 P.M. Laura had picked the Subaru up at Mavis Tire in the early afternoon. She drove me to Joe's Mobil. I asked to be let off at the pumps.

Laura was bewildered. "Don't you want me to wait? Just to make sure the car is working?"

"No," I said. "It's working. I'll be all right."

"You sure?"

"Sure I'm sure."

"Okay," said Laura, who shrugged prettily and drove off.

Joe was in the service station office, looking at bills. He had his glasses on.

When I knocked on the door, he waved me inside.

The phone rang. He picked it up and pointed to a metal chair, which I sat in. The wall behind Joe's desk was of cork, and he had bills stuck to it in alphabetical order, more or less. There was also a photo of Joe's son and his bride on their wedding day. Below this there were some business cards, more snapshots of Joe's family. The last photo was a large one, of three men kneeling in front of a fallen tree. Each man was holding a rifle, and one of them looked a lot like Uncle, only without the beard. Standing near the men, just off to one side, was a boy.

When Joe got off the phone, I pointed to the picture. "Anybody there I know?" I asked.

Joe nodded.

"Why have you all got guns?" I asked.

"Hunting trip," he said.

"Which one are you?" I asked.

Joe came around the desk, put his thumb on the picture of the boy. "I was the bambino," he said.

"What were you hunting?"

Joe shrugged. "It's a long story," he said. "Another time. Your car is ready."

"The door's fixed?"

Joe nodded. "They took a part out," he said.

"Why?"

"To make sure you came back in for service."

"Oh."

"*Banditi,*" Joe said.

"What about the wipers?"

"Fixed."

"Nothing else wrong?"

"*Niente.*" Joe gave me the bill, which I put in my back pocket. Then he gave me the keys, and I went out behind the station, got into the car. I looked down at the gas gauge. The tank was full. Good old Joe. Then I looked at the odometer. My brand-new car had 153.7 miles on it.

When I got up that Saturday morning, Jonas was already at work. I poured myself a mug of coffee and went into his office. He sat back in his chair.

"You've got the day off?"

"Elspeth wants me to ditch the peony bed."

"Okay," said Jonas. "Do that. Take a shower. Then come back here."

When I reappeared, it turned out that Jonas wanted me to phone Whitfield.

"On the weekend?"

"He gave me his home phone," said Jonas. "I've got it here, somewhere," he said, riffling through a pile of papers. "I know he lives in Westport."

I went out into the kitchen, called Connecticut information. The only Paul Whitfield they had listed was in Southport. I wrote down the number, returned to the root cellar.

"Southport?" I asked.

"Southport?" said Jonas, looking up. He'd been leafing through a Berlitz pamphlet: *Inglese per chi viaggi: edizione Nord-Americana.*

"Is that where Whitfield lives?"

"Of course. How foolish of me. Look, would you call him? Ask if they can give me the check immediately after I give them the manuscript. I think they usually take a couple of weeks."

"I hope I don't wake him up."

"I doubt very much that Mr. Whitfield will be sleeping at 10 A.M."

He wasn't. He was in the Jacuzzi. That's what the woman said. I told her who I was and who I was calling for.

"Hang on. He's just stepped out. Here he is. Dripping wet," she said, and laughed in a way that led me to believe they had just finished screwing.

I identified myself. "I'm calling for Jonas Collingwood."

"Yes," said Whitfield. "You do that, don't you?"

"He's writing," I said.

"Good."

"I have a question."

"All right."

"Well, the manuscript. The book you bought."

"The Partisan?"

"Right. It's nearly done."

"Well, well," said Whitfield, and I could hear him take a pull on what I presumed to be his own mug of coffee. "This is surprising news."

"So here's what I need to know. Here's what Uncle wants to know."

"Okay," said Whitfield, "but look. I'm going to put you on the speaker phone. It'll sound a little different, but you'll still be able to hear me. And I'll be hearing you."

"Okay."

"You sure you don't mind?"

"I don't mind."

"Good, then. This way I can dry off."

I heard some clicking sounds, and the line went dead. I hung up. I waited a minute and phoned Connecticut again.

The girl picked up. "Is Mr. Whitfield in?" I asked.

"Aren't we formal?" she said, and laughed gaily. "The old goat is right here," she said, and the editor came on the line.

"Sorry," he said.

"No problem."

Then I heard some more clicking, and Whitfield asked, "Can you hear me?"

"Yes," I said. It was true. I could hear him, but I could also hear a roaring sound, as if the editor were on a rocky coast in Maine and the seas were rising.

"Good," said Whitfield. "I can hear you perfectly."

Then I heard the woman's voice in the background.

"Yes," said Whitfield, speaking away from the phone, which made his voice fade as the surf rose. "It works. Perfectly."

Then he turned back to the phone. "Now, what's the question?"

"Well," I said, and took another sip of coffee. "If Uncle could deliver the book to you, a completed manuscript, in two weeks' time, then how long would it take for him to get a check?"

"It takes us about two weeks to cut a check. That check usually goes to an agent, who takes a bite out of it and then sends another check to the writer."

"We don't have an agent."

"So we've saved a step. It'll take two weeks."

"So even if you got the manuscript today, it would take at least two weeks before Uncle got the check?"

"Ordinarily, yes."

I didn't say anything.

"But," said Whitfield, "if we knew the book was coming, I suppose we could start the process immediately. I'll be in Boston on Monday. We could start it on Tuesday. If we did that, we might produce something by Friday. That is, a week from this coming Friday. Which is a little less than two weeks from today. This will be for half the book?"

"No," I said. "The whole book."

"Well, that's a lot of money, then. How much is it exactly? Will you help me with my math on this?"

I cleared my throat. "One hundred and fifty thousand."

"Ummmmm," said Whitfield. "But if Jonas were to deliver the whole book, we could certainly get you a check for $75,000 on that Friday. Work forward from that point."

"Fine," I said. "I'll tell Uncle."

"So," said Whitfield, "should I proceed?"

"Yes."

"We have a done deal?"

"Yes."

"Could I speak with your uncle?"

I looked over toward Jonas. He was sitting at the kitchen table, shaking his head.

"Do you have to?"

"No. Not really."

"I think he'd rather not."

"Okay, then. Do you mind if I ask a question?"

"No, of course not."

"I'm just a little confused. The last time I spoke with your Uncle, he said he wasn't going to be finished with this book for at least a year."

"Something's changed," I said. "It's like a dam broke."

"I don't want to sound immodest," said the editor. "But I wonder if there was any connection, any possible connection, between my visit and this sudden inspiration."

"No question," I said. "The timing is just too close for it to have been a coincidence."

"Well," said the editor, "this is very good news. Will he bring it in, actually deliver the manuscript to our offices?"

"Would you like him to?"

"I think that under the circumstances it might be appropriate."

"All right, then, we'll do it."

"If your uncle can bring in the manuscript a week from this coming Friday, at about 11 A.M. . . . . Wait, let me get my calendar. Can you hang on for a minute?"

"Sure."

I heard him talking to the girl. I thought I heard him call her Sweet Pea. I also thought I heard the word "Filofax."

A minute or so later, he came back on the air. "Will you be coming in with your uncle?"

"Yes," I said. "I mean, if you'd like."

"Have you ever been to the Carlyle?"

"No."

"So, then, here's the deal. You and Uncle Jonas come into town a week from Friday. Get to our offices, that's on Sixth Avenue. You know where? It's on the stationery. I'll send a letter on Tuesday to confirm."

I nodded into the phone.

"We'll take a cab to the bank. What's your uncle's bank?"

"Bank of New York."

"They have offices in Manhattan?"

"I don't know."

"They must."

"I suppose."

"So, we'll take a ride to the bank. Jonas can deposit the check. Then we'll go to the Carlyle, have lunch. Listen, are you an only child?"

"No."

"Brothers?"

"No."

"A sister, then?"

"Right."

"Live at home?"

"Yes."

"Have her come too."

"And Aunt."

"Of course your aunt." The surf rose, and that was all I heard for a couple of minutes. "Look, Nelson," he said. "I've got to go now. But we'll talk." Then he hung up.

When I explained the situation to Uncle, he seemed pleased. "Now," he said, "I want you to go out to All My Friends Are Old Books Now." That's what Uncle called the Old Friends Book Store. "I've got a list here." He gave me a piece of paper with several titles typed on it. He opened his wallet and produced a twenty, a ten, and three singles.

"Will this do it?"

"Books are cheap," he said, and smiled.

"They may be worthless, but that doesn't make them cheap."

The total came to a good deal more than thirty-three dollars. So I used my American Express Card. Correction: I used the American Express Card that had been issued to me by the Albany office of the *Westchester Commons*. I already had one personal item on the card. I was going to pay for that. I'd pay for this too.

"So," the cashier said, as I signed. "Planning a business trip to Italy, are we?"

I brought the shopping bag full of books to the root cellar. Uncle wasn't there. I put my thumb in the ashtray. No heat.

I went outside. Elspeth was in the front garden, with gloves on, weeding the roses. She straightened when she saw me. She was wearing jeans and one of Jonas's antique business shirts. She arched, rubbed the small of her back with the knuckles of one gloved hand.

"Thank you for ditching the peonies," she said.

"You're welcome. Where's Jonas?"

"Gone," she said. "Went into town with Gilbert. I think there's something at the Museum of Modern Art."

Monday morning I intercepted the Subaru at the bottom of the drive. I didn't want to have to explain to Laura about the new car.

Because of the time difference, I had to wait until noon to start trying the pay phone at the Wooden Indian. Nobody answered. I let it ring twenty times. The second time I tried I got a man, a stranger. I presume he was a trucker. The Wooden Indian is a truck stop.

"Hello," I said.

"Hello, Sal," he said.

"I'm not Sal," I said. "I'm calling for a girl. A woman actually, Amy Rose."

"Well this ain't her."

"I know that."

"And I'm expecting a call from Sally, so you'd best get off the line."

I did.

I waited half an hour and tried again.

I got another deep voice. Another trucker, I guess. I started off by introducing myself. His name was Swifty. I described Amy. Swifty was friendly enough but ultimately not helpful.

"Listen, son, if the girl you're after is as pretty as you say she is, and if she were in that diner, I'd be in there with her. I sure as shit wouldn't be out in the parking lot gabbing long distance with some lovesick college student."

When Laura drove me home that evening, I said I was sorry to keep imposing on her.

"That's all right. I don't expect you to walk."

"I have a car."

"Yeah, I know about your car."

"No, I have a new one."

Laura turned to me. She looked a little bit hurt. "When were you going to tell me?"

"I don't know. Soon."

She looked back at the road and nodded. "Men," she said.

"I'm embarrassed. Uncle bought it for me."

"You should be pleased."

"I know, I know," I said. "It's an embarrassing sort of car."

"What kind of car is it? A hearse?"

"No, it's a sports car."

"So why are you embarrassed?"

"It's red."

"So?"

Laura was looking better and better. The wedding was scheduled for October. I figured that by then she'd be a knockout. They'd fly to Hawaii. Positano would knock her out.

"Look, why don't I drive you tomorrow?"

"You drive me to work?"

"Yeah, why not?"

"I'll give you three guesses. No, I'll give you one guess."

So she drove again on Tuesday. At noon, I realized that I'd left some proofs on my bedside table. I borrowed Laura's car. When I got home, I found Elspeth in the front rose garden. She told me that Jonas had taken the Falcon to the 7-Eleven to buy cigarettes.

"He should have taken the new car."

"That's your car."

I nodded and went inside. I'd just closed the kitchen door when the phone started ringing. I picked up. It was the snippy one. "Paul Whitfield calling for Jonas Collingwood," the voice said. "Is this the correct number?"

I said it was. I was just getting ready to explain that Jonas was out when she clicked off, Whitfield clicked on. "Hi," he said.

"Hi."

"Ah," he said, his voice falling, "Jonas. Jonas Collingwood?"

"No," I said. "It's Nelson. Remember me? We spoke on Saturday."

"I do. I do remember. Actually, Nelson," he said, in confidential tones, "the person I really want to talk with today is your father."

I heard Robert McNamara coming up the gravel drive. "Wait,

here he is. He just drove in," I said, and put the receiver down on the kitchen counter.

I went out to the car. Jonas had parked beside the Subaru. "Whitfield's on the phone," I said. Uncle nodded, got out of the Falcon, picked up a brown paper bag, and went into the kitchen. I followed. "I have to visit the necessary room," said Jonas. "Will you speak with him for a minute? I'll be right out."

So I picked up the phone again.

"Hello."

"Hello, Jonas?"

"No," I said. "This is still Nelson."

"Look," said Whitfield. "I know that you're empowered to handle business for your uncle. But in this case I must speak with him directly. Before we start to process this check. I just have to speak with him for a minute. If you could please put him on the phone."

"Sure," I said.

"Is he there?"

"Yeah."

"Can I speak with him, then?"

"Yes," I said. Jonas was just coming out of the bathroom. "Here he is," I said, and handed over the receiver.

"Hello," said Uncle. "That's right. Jonas Aldous Collingwood. That's right, I wrote the Agricola books."

He nodded.

"And *My Life as a Woman.*"

He listened for a minute.

"Well, it isn't exactly a gift horse," he said. "I did contract to write this book."

I found my folder and headed for the door. Jonas put a hand on my shoulder, pointed to the kitchen table.

I sat.

Uncle nodded into the telephone. "No, not a compromise."

He listened for a while. "I wouldn't dream of making this a rush job."

"Well, that's one of the things that are terribly unfair about writing. Some people spend a whole life on a horrid book. And a very fine one can come quickly. Robert Louis Stevenson is supposed to have received *Dr. Jekyll and Mr. Hyde* in a dream. Mary Shelley wrote *Frankenstein* in a weekend. On a bet."

Jonas paused, listening. "No, I don't see you as an entirely commercial house. I didn't mean to say that. I thought *Frankenstein* an admirable work."

"Yes, of course I want my name on this book."

"Yup."

"Uh-huh."

"Well, actually, you know," he said, winking at me, "I'm quite the clever typist."

He listened for a minute.

"The pleasure is all mine," he said, and hung up.

Then he walked into the root cellar without pausing, without stopping to say a word. I went out to the Subaru and drove back to work.

When I got to the office Laura told me that Walter Paige had phoned.

"Am I supposed to get back to him?"

"He said he'd call you."

"Did Amy call?"

"No."

So I tried the Wooden Indian. This time I got somebody with a soft voice. He asked me how I was.

"Fine, just fine. But I really want to talk to this girl. Woman, I want to talk to this woman."

The Samaritan went into the restaurant to look for Amy. A couple of minutes later, she came on the line. "Hello?" she said.

"Hi, it's Nelson."

"You had this traveling minister pull me away from breakfast. I thought one of my parents must be dead."

"I didn't know he was a minister."

"He's a minister all right."

"I want to pick you up at the airport."

"That's okay. I'll find some other way to get to Briarcliff Manor."

"Please let me pick you up. I have this new car."

"I know, but my eggs are getting cold. Besides, there's somebody else out here now, waiting to use the phone."

"I miss you."

"Well that's not my problem, is it?"

I took in a lot of air, let it out. "I'll tell you what. I won't bother you. I won't call again. On one condition."

"What's that?"

"You let me meet you at the airport."

"Is that really all you want?"

"It's what I want."

"I'm coming in on Friday, August 16. I think the plane arrives at 9 P.M. You sure you can do it?"

"Is it direct from Spokane?"

"I don't know, but it's Delta. Flight 564, 664, something like that."

"Okay, great, I'll see you then. I'll be at the arrival gate."

"Fine. I have to get off now."

"See you at the airport. I love you best," I said. I don't think she heard the last part. By the time I had finished talking, the line was dead.

15

For her daughter's sixteenth birthday, Elspeth had presented Nar with her own personal plastic razor: the Lady Something-or-Other. That evening, before dinner, Sister drew a bath and shaved her legs. The next day, she discovered that she'd lost the razor. Ever since then she's been singing a chorus about how she's also losing her memory.

I don't know if the two events are connected; I do know that all this lather about failing mental powers is nonsense. Sister has never forgotten a man's telephone number. Besides, senility at that age would be precocious. Even for Narcissus.

So why the chorus? My explanation is that a girl so free of convention needs something to be remorseful about. She's not the type to regret her actions. Nor is she old enough to complain convincingly about losing her looks.

Jonas didn't believe in forgetting. "The brain can fail to recall," he used to say, "but that doesn't mean the information is lost. A good memory is a survival skill, and we, as Homo sapiens, have distinguished ourselves as a species intent on survival, survival at all costs. But one of the reasons we cling so ardently to life," he would conclude, sourly, "is that we don't exactly remember it."

I can remember my compound fracture. I can actually draw up the sound of bone snapping. The ambulance driver was on the chubby side, with black hair and a gold earring. They covered me with a blanket, bright orange, a color designed to be spotted from the air. All this I remember. The hurt I've forgotten. I haven't a clue.

Which may be why my recollections of those first two weeks in August are so damn sketchy. I couldn't even lead you back to the Carlyle. It's a hotel in Manhattan someplace.

Nar wore the camisole again and had the twenty-four-dollar lobster salad, which she hardly touched. Elspeth and I split the sixteen-dollar chicken club sandwich. Jonas had an omelette and most of Nar's lobster.

That was on a Friday. We'd already been to Classic's home office, met the staff, and surrendered the manuscript.

Saturday Gilbert came over with a chainsaw he'd borrowed from the Seagrams' estate and helped Jonas cut up the hemlock that had fallen in a recent storm. I would have helped them if I'd been asked. I wasn't asked.

I found Nar in bed. Reading *Vanity Fair*. She's read it at least a dozen times. "It's the best self-help book a girl can find," she said. I sat on the floor, pulled a long face. "It's gotten so that you have to go to Harvard in order to cut up a dead tree," I said.

Sister looked down at me. "And I suppose that if Tom Sawyer didn't let you paint his fence, you'd complain about that too?"

"I'm not used to being excluded."

Nar shrugged. "Take advantage of it," she said. "Let him help with the chores. You're still the beloved son. The one who gets all the new cars."

"I like to saw wood."

"Whatever," said Nar. "But you don't have to be proprietary about it."

"I thought you hated him."

Nar shifted around under the covers.

"Well?"

She looked at me for a long second, as if considering. "Listen, Bro," she said, "just take it easy, all right? Cool your jets. Maybe he'll learn to wash the dishes."

Gilbert showed up on Sunday. With some new kind of coffee bean that made the whole house smell like a chocolate shop. After breakfast, I went up to my room to read. When I came back down for more coffee, Elspeth was alone in the kitchen.

"What about church?" I asked.

"They've already gone," she said. "The plan was that they'd park behind Wheeler Avenue, buy the paper and coffee. Then they were going to sit out someplace and read until it was time to walk over to Saint John's for the eight o'clock service."

Uncle used to rotate his churches. He was an Episcopalian and preferred the original text of *The Book of Common Prayer*, but he detested the idea of having to socialize with the other communicants and so rarely visited the same house of worship twice in a row. He ranged widely, sometimes driving for half an hour in order to attend services at Saint Matthew's near the Bedford Cross. "Money may not guarantee happiness, but it certainly has produced an excellent choir."

A number of the churches in our area have gone out of business and been turned into houses or office buildings. Jonas and I did once show up at 7:45 A.M. on a Sunday at the door of a firm that designed software for the IRS. The watchman was courteous. "It's a common mistake," he said. "They've put out for bids to have the steeple removed."

I had always accompanied Jonas when he went to church. I complained, but I went. Up until now, I had always been asked.

I returned to my room and spent some more time with *Geronimo's Story of His Life*: "We had no churches, no religious organization, no sabbath day, no holidays, and yet we worshipped."

After half an hour or so, I went to Nar's room. She was still in bed. Sister stays under the covers until there's a reason to get up. Sometimes she'll come out for breakfast. Sometimes not until the late afternoon. I stood in the doorway.

"Want to go for a walk?"

"Why aren't you in church?"

"Doctor Books is taking my place."

"You should be thankful."

"How can I be thankful to that guy? You were the one who used to hate him. Remember, 'shit stinks'?"

Nar got out of bed, went to her closet, and started to dress. She kept her back to me, but she also did not close the closet door.

Sister pulled her nightgown over her head. "He is smart."

"You can't make shit smart enough so that it doesn't stink. I didn't know you had a mole on your back."

She pulled on her panties, slipped a white lace bra over her shoulders. "Cameron used to call it my beauty mark."

"How is Cameron?"

"Fine. He's got his own agency."

"Good for him."

"I knew he'd land on his feet. Would you fasten my bra?"

I got up off the bed and worked the hooks.

"Thanks," she said. "So men are good for something." Then she began the struggle she always had with her jeans.

"Why are you so touchy about that guy?" she asked, when she was done wriggling.

"I hate having to compete for Uncle's attention."

"Why do it?"

"I don't know exactly. I sometimes feel now like Gilbert's the real son, the better son. The one who writes."

"Well," said Nar, gasping as she snapped the waist of her pants, "actually, neither of you is really Uncle's son. As far as blood goes."

"Thanks."

Once dressed, Nar still had to have her Grape-Nuts. "To get my blood sugar up." After that she needed to call the Melon. "He's a bore. But I promised." She would come for the walk, though, if I waited. "I know I should get some exercise," she said.

The Grape-Nuts took only about ten minutes. But when she got on the phone with the Melon, she started to laugh. Melon's the sort who finds his jokes in some Speechmaker's Encyclopedia, under "Ice Breakers."

His single favorite witticism: "Money isn't everything, but it sure beats second best." I've heard it at least a dozen times. From his lips.

Sister was tinkling away, as if she had Dave Barry on the line. I couldn't bear it, and I went out the door alone.

I walked up over Buttermilk Hill and around to that little paved section of road where the Christian Brothers used to have their building. They prayed a lot, I suppose, but are best remembered for their apple butter. There is still a bit of orchard left, but outside of this, and one patch of asphalt, there is no other sign that this bright shoulder of land, with its gorgeous view of the Palisades, was ever a home to man.

One of the little-known oddities of the Rockefeller park is that it was not cut from undeveloped forest. There were settlers on these mythic hills for years before the formation of the Standard Oil Trust. When Senior and Mr. Junior bought up the acreage, they often found buildings at the most picturesque locations. There was a man whose primary professional responsibility was the destruction of perfectly good houses.

So while trees were being cut down and dwellings put up all

over the county, there was this one little section of land where houses were being cut down and trees put up. Uncle used to say that one of the great blessings of being very rich, like John D. Rockefeller, or very poor, like Jonas Collingwood, is that either condition seemed to nurture eccentricity.

The plaster and wood from the demolished houses were carted away, the basements filled. Little sections of stonework, the shrubs, ornamental trees, and perennials are all that survive. Walking through the dark woods, one comes upon a bank of giant rhododendron, a clump of daffodils, sometimes even a bed of pachysandra.

One Egyptian moneybags named Ousani had planted masses of mulberry trees in an attempt to bring the silk industry to southern New York. Some of the trees are still there, near a large hay-storage building on Mr. David's farm. The silkworms are gone. So is Ousani.

There were rural homes here, and other titans had country estates. James Stillman, the president of National City Bank, had an enormous stone stable on one side of Route 448, a Cotswold mansion the size of a football field on the other. Some of his smaller houses are still standing, but both of the large buildings are gone.

Sometimes, walking on the hill above our house, I'll see a bluebird. They have a darting, irregular pattern of flight, and the color is quite extraordinary. There didn't used to be any bluebirds left in this part of the country. Starlings and house sparrows took all their natural nesting places. So men, cursed men, have built houses with holes in them just the right size for a bluebird.

The Eastern bluebirds are back, and mixing their liquid *turee, turee, queedle, queedle* with the rasping notes of the starling.

A bluebird sighting always cheers me. It seems to be good luck, at least for the bird. Doesn't any reappearance of a previously diminished species represent an uptick, however slight, in the downward spiral of our ecological market?

Coming back down from the monastery I saw a flock of wild turkeys. There were two adults and five youngsters. I didn't like to think what sort of luck seven turkeys might bring.

When I reached the house it was noon. The place was empty. There was a note:

"Dear Indian, Gilbert took us all to Garrison to look at a jumper for guess who? He insisted we eat lunch there. I made you a tuna sandwich. With lite mayonnaise. Oat bread. It's in the fridge. Love, Aunt."

So we got through the weekend, more or less. I had expected Classic to phone on Monday. They did not. Gilbert came to dinner with a great slab of marinated swordfish and a bottle of Dom Perignon. He raised his glass. "No news is good news," he said.

Uncle took his portion of the celebratory champagne, but he didn't share the doctor's confidence. "Don't count my chickens," he said.

On Tuesday, when Laura drove me home, the black Saab was in the drive. I found Jonas, Elspeth, Whitfield, and an unfamiliar young woman scattered uncomfortably in the living room. There was tea, and a white cardboard box, which held the remains of a tart. The Old Smuggler was out. And ravished.

Everybody was glad to see me. I took this as a very bad sign. Introductions were made. The young woman, a senior editor, was named Susan Watchman. She was quite beautiful, with black hair and pale, milky skin. I might have thought her haughty, but she had a pimple on her chin, and I could imagine her gazing at it sadly in the morning glass. Her scarlet dress was done up the front with brass buttons. They couldn't have been brass, could they? Nothing's made of brass anymore. They must have been aluminum, but they were brass colored. They meant to be brass.

The undergarment situation was unclear. The dress was fastened right up to the throat, so there might not have been a slip, or even a brassiere. I'm a lonely guy, but taking windage for that, it was conceivable that the dress was all that Susan Watchman was wearing. In which case, the failure of those fake buttons would have brought our visitor—in one delicious instant—from a PG-13 to an X. I won't say that I found this prospect entirely unpleasing, but it made me uneasy, or added to the drama of what already seemed to be a highly charged little encounter.

Elspeth and Susan were drinking tea. Whitfield and Jonas each had a big crystal glass of Old Smuggler.

I poured myself a cup of Hukwah, and Elspeth cut me a piece of the gift tart. It had slices of kiwi fruit on top.

Whitfield was talking. "This could still be a splendid book," he said, then took a slug from his glass.

"I like the way the story looks," he said. "There's a great stone pile built over the water, a dry moat, and positions for archers. The hill is honeycombed with passages and chambers. There are dungeons, with rusted leg irons chained to the wall. The Germans tell the people that if the Allies bomb the coast, they should go to La Rocca. Go underground."

Jonas nodded.

"The narrator had a girlfriend."

"Not a girlfriend," said Jonas, settling back in his chair. "He was infatuated. They spent time together. But they only made love once. That's quite late in the book."

Whitfield smiled and continued. "She goes to the beach in her *costume da bagno*. It's summer, she's tanned. She's got masses of long, dark hair. She wades in up to her waist. She's carrying her shoes."

Uncle shrugged, "If she leaves them on the beach, they'll be stolen."

Whitfield was grinning. "I like all that stuff about the poverty. A coastline entirely without sea gulls, you say, because they've all been trapped and put in the stew. God is in the details."

"The English shoes, the ones she carries into the water," said Jonas, stiffly, "are a gift from a man named Eric. He's a German officer."

"Fiori's a realist," said Whitfield. "She doesn't like the partisans. She feels about them the same way an Italian matron of our time might feel about the Red Brigade. She thinks they're troublemakers.

"You go into the countryside. You're gone for several months. You travel with one other young man, a boy, and a woman. You have forged papers. You're supposed to be masons."

"Actually," said Jonas, "there's quite a bit about stonework."

"That's right," said Whitfield. "John Jerome published a book titled *Stone Work*. It wasn't his break-out book. We want this to be yours. But it's all right to have some technical detail. Susan says it gives a novel class. Right?" he said, looking over at his junior.

Susan shrugged. "I think the passages on masonry are beautifully written."

Whitfield nodded. "One of the resistance fighters was a woman."

"Sabina," said Jonas. "She passes for a man."

"Yeah," said Whitfield. "As long as you're going over this—I mean, if you do agree to go over the manuscript, I'd play that down. Get rid of her moustache."

Jonas scratched his ear.

Whitfield took a drink, then continued. "They blow up an ammunition dump just outside of Rome," said Whitfield. "The girl is caught."

"That's not clear," said Jonas. "Nobody saw what happened to her. We decided to split up and go back to Port Ercole by separate routes. It was possible that the Germans would take hostages. By then I'd heard that Fiori was going to have a baby. The German, Eric, has asked her to marry him. She has refused."

There was a long pause. Whitfield looked pained. "Correct me if I'm wrong," he said, shifting his position on the sofa, "but I don't recall the first book, the novel, as being so intensely antiwar."

Jonas cleared his throat. "*The Partisan* is a memoir. It's supposed to be a record of what I remember. I remember war as a thoroughly unpleasant exercise."

Whitfield stood, cut himself a small, neatly triangular piece of tart, returned to his seat, and carefully ate the point off it. Then he balanced the plate on the arm of the sofa.

He looked at Susan. "More tart?"

"No," the girl said, "I'm stuffed." And she patted at her narrow waist.

Whitfield nodded. "Susan read the book," he said.

"And loved it," said Susan.

"And loved it," said Whitfield.

"But, Susan, if we had to cut back on the philosophy, how many pages would we lose?"

Susan thought they'd lose about one hundred pages.

"How many pages is the manuscript altogether?"

Susan said there were 373 pages altogether.

"All right," said Whitfield, "we can make it one of those little books, for the reader who has everything but time."

The editor leaned back in the sofa, spread his arms wide. Elspeth was watching his tart plate intently. The sofa—a Rockefeller loveseat—was the only light-colored piece of upholstered furniture in the room. The plate tipped but didn't spill.

The editor coughed into his fist. "Don't you conclude that as much good was done by Fascists in that time as was done by people helping the Allied cause?"

Jonas inhaled deeply, blew smoke out through his nose.

Elspeth needed to know if anybody wanted more tea. Nobody did.

Whitfield shook his head sadly. "Susan and I just wondered what point you were trying to make. Didn't you, Susan?" he said.

Susan nodded.

Jonas didn't say anything.

"I know the skinheads, the Klan, those people get a lot of attention, but actually there aren't very many of them. And, perhaps more importantly, they don't buy books. I'm not even sure anymore who has *Mein Kampf* on his backlist. But whoever does is not making a fortune."

Nobody said anything for a good two minutes.

"The preface," said Whitfield. "I've never been able to abide those things—prefaces, forewords, afterwords. And this one, it's like something the surgeon general might have thought up: 'Pregnant and lactating women shouldn't read this book.' " He chuckled sourly.

"Then there are the transitions," he said. "There's no story at all here; it's just a series of recollections."

"Our man in London," said Jonas. "That sort of thing."

"Well," said Whitfield, "there we can help you. You make the changes I've asked for, and we'll do the rest, stitch it into a book."

We had a bad beat there. Then Whitfield reached over and touched Susan's stockinged leg, cleared his throat, and smiled. "There's one point on which Susan and I are in total agreement," he said. "We like the ending. Whatever you do, don't change the ending."

16

Fast-forward. Now it's Tuesday, August 13. *The Partisan* has been shortened. Elspeth has marked it up with a red pencil. She routinely copyedited Uncle's manuscripts. "I was moved," she said.

Jonas: "Did you like it?"

Elspeth: "I said I was moved."

Jonas: "I heard what you said. I want to know if you admired the memoir."

Elspeth: "Not much."

I hadn't read this book in any version. Nor had Nar, although she had riffled through the manuscript. "I think it's fine," she said. "Had the tummy tucked is all, and the teeth capped."

Jonas didn't appreciate her flippancy. "Had its balls cut off is all," he said. "Its asshole sewn shut."

I was the one who phoned Whitfield and told him that Uncle would make the changes. We had a lot of dead air on that call. He was enthusiastic about the message but tired of the messenger. I wasn't happy with either one.

I also cranked up the Falcon, drove the pages to Sir Speedy Printing. The duplicate was put out on top of the filing cabinets in Uncle's office, right beside that of the rejected manuscript. The original of the new and improved was delivered to Classic by Federal Express. Whitfield phoned the following evening. I picked up.

"Nelson," he said, "I've one word for this."

"Yeah?"

"Whooooosh," he said.

"Whooooosh?"

"Swish."

"Swish?"

"Basket."

"Oh, good," I said, beginning to get it. "Look, Uncle's here. Why don't you talk with him?"

Jonas got on the phone. Listened for a minute. "Whooooosh?" he asked. "Swish?"

He'd made the deadline. Lily's business was bailed out. The day the papers were signed, she sent Jonas flowers. I guess she phoned a local nursery and gave them a credit card, because a truck came to the house with two pots wrapped in aluminum foil.

Elspeth was furious. "You give my sister what, $70,000?" she said. "And she sends you two dozen hardy mums? Which I'm expected to plant?"

Jonas tried to placate his wife. "It is August, honey. There aren't a lot of plants for sale this time of year."

But Elspeth wasn't buying. "And the truck knocked down your precious safety mirror."

"The mirror can be fixed," said Jonas.

"By whom?" said Elspeth. "And when?"

I said, "I'll fix it."

"What if you can't?" asked Elspeth.

"Then I'll buy a new one." There was money in the bank. Whitfield had said that the final check would arrive within a couple of weeks.

"No hurry, right?"

"No hurry," I told him.

And there wasn't. Although Nar had visited a chestnut quarter horse twice.

Uncle had invested in a bar of gold. He called it "Nar's dowry." This was kept beside the shoe rack on the floor of the hall closet.

The gold rested in the coat closet, accruing value. The new car sat in the drive, hemorrhaging same.

The stationary presence of a crimson roadster made Narcissus wild. "Birds gotta fly, fish gotta swim, cars gotta drive," she said. "You two are treating it like some sort of icon, the world's most low-slung vision of the Virgin Mary."

She'd gotten that wrong. I thought the car gorgeous, but I never thought it sublime. It seemed the very essence of carnality. I understand that there are places in California, and perhaps Florida, where people attend church services in their automobiles. But I've always doubted the validity of this form of worship. The cars of my Northeastern upbringing had three purposes. In order of importance, these were: social station, transportation, fornication. It may be regionalism speaking, crass parochialism, but I still think that you have to put your feet on the ground before you can drop to your knees.

Nar wasn't allowed to drive the Miata. Jonas wouldn't. And I didn't. I can only guess at Uncle's motive, something about the sanctity of gifts. He never gave it a name.

My reason was named Laura Grafton. I wanted to see her as much as I could before she vanished into the matrimonial maw. The date had been postponed again, but the final result seemed even more a certainty.

"I wonder if it'll be a full moon," I said. "You might want to wear a cross, or maybe a necklace of garlic bulbs."

Laura laughed.

"You're not going to defend him?"

"Why should I?"

"He's practically your husband."

"That's right," said Laura, giving me a brilliant smile. "When have you ever seen an intelligent woman defend her husband?"

"Isn't there something about that in the vows?"

"Nope. I'm just supposed to cleave."

"And obey."

Laura looked concerned for a moment, then lightened. "More or less," she said. "As others have."

She'd gone next door to the Charismatic U on a whim, one slow afternoon, and had most of her hair cut off.

"How do I look as a boy?" she asked, coming into the office and doing a joyous little pirouette.

"Girlish," I said. "Built."

I must have suspected that all that carefully dressed hair was concealing something: a goiter, or a birthmark. Because I was surprised how moved I was by this unveiling.

Odd that a woman just about to give up her freedom, her identity, should feel so emancipated. It was almost as if she were preparing herself to be sacrificed on the altar of matrimony. God knows, plenty of lively women have perished there. As have plenty of lively young men.

Fast-forward another three days. Now it's Friday, August 16, 1991. The day that my true love is supposed to arrive at Kennedy. It was just after 5 P.M. We had dropped the new proofs off at the printer. Laura was supposed to meet Positano at the Good Time Caterers in White Plains but had agreed to drive me to Pocantico first.

The Subaru was on Route 9A heading south into Briarcliff when we heard the fire whistle. They sound it here for fires, prison breaks, nuclear alerts; most of the time it means a bad car crash. A police car flew by us on the right, exceeding the speed limit. He nearly clipped the bumper. Those guys do love to break the traffic laws.

A mile later we got passed by a volunteer fireman in a sawed-off pickup truck with a flashing blue light on the dash. Then there was an ambulance. When we got off 9A, onto Route 117 west, the traffic was at a standstill. Laura looked at her watch, closed the windows, turned up the air conditioner.

She tossed her hair in my direction. "I'll be late," she said, "but I won't be sweaty."

It took us twenty minutes to go the quarter mile on 117 to the traffic light at which we would ordinarily make our left. There was a squad car parked on the diagonal, blocking both lanes of Route 448.

A cop was standing out in front of it. The summer sky was still bright, but he was using one of those cone flashlights to wave the traffic away. He looked familiar. I know the local policemen, not by name, necessarily, but by their hair, the way they carry themselves. This was the tall man with the red walrus moustache.

When he looked at me, there was a flash of recognition. I couldn't tell for sure if this was because he knew me or I him. Laura pulled over onto the shoulder. I got out of the car, walked up to the roadblock.

"I live off of Bedford Road," I said. "On the Estate."

He didn't even look at me, too busy waving other cars away.

"Road's closed," he said.

"I want to go home."

"I don't care where you want to go," he said, "this road is closed."

When I got back to the Subaru, I offered to walk in. Laura shook her head.

"I thought you were supposed to meet Albert somewhere at 6 P.M." I said. "I'm going to make you late."

My old friend smiled. "Make me late," she said. "See if I care."

We took Phelps Way to Route 9. Then we headed south into Tarrytown, drove down past the old Dutch Reform Church.

Washington Irving is buried in that graveyard. Walter Chrysler is also nearby. I wonder if Lee Iacocca ever comes out with flowers. Wouldn't that make a great ad? Lee looking glum in his double-breasted suit, fine shoes squelching across grass: "You can bury a man, but you can't bury an idea." I'd have to work on the speech.

We climbed the little rise into North Tarrytown and then made a left up the hill onto 448.

There was another policeman at the hamlet crossroads. This was the bald one who smoked the long, brown cigarettes. I remember him as being a genial sort, but on this particular evening he was thoroughly unpleasant. His dislike for me seemed to be out of all proportion to my somewhat less than felonious intention to get home in time for dinner.

I told him I'd take the trail. The cop wagged his head. "No you don't."

"You mean I can't walk?"

He nodded. "We've got a situation up there."

"What kind of situation?"

"A situation."

"So I can't walk either?"

"I said we've got a situation," he said, as if that made everything perfectly clear.

I went back to the car and had Laura turn around and take me down the road to the first of the dirt trails. Then I got out, put on my knapsack, and came around to the driver's window.

"An assassination?" she asked.

I shrugged. "Look, when you reach White Plains, if it's easy, would you call my house? Tell Elspeth there's nothing to worry about."

"Sure."

Then I heard the cop. I looked up. He had seen me, surmised my intention, and was walking down the shoulder, shouting "Hey, you!" at the top of his lungs.

Laura smiled. "I want a kiss," she said.

"I haven't kissed you since I was five years old."

"Hey, you!" said the cop. He was getting closer, but he wasn't going very fast.

"It's all right now," said Laura. "I'm an old lady. Practically a married woman."

So I leaned in the window. We kissed. It wasn't the sort of kiss commonly associated with old ladies. I almost lost my balance. I wasn't sure, but I thought that Laura took my hand, put it on her breast. I thought so, but I wasn't sure. Then I turned away and ran the first fifty feet or so into the woods. I could hear the Subaru pulling out. The cop shouted once more and then gave up.

Go in on the first trail after making the right at the hamlet, and you pass a building that is still painted in a faint, almost camouflage green. I've been told that many houses were once that color: Pocantico green. This was so that the Rockefellers, in their hilltop mansions, could look down on the surrounding countryside— dotted with the homes of their employees and protégés—and imagine that it was entirely deserted.

I took the long route, past the entrance to Hudson Pines, the farm run by Mrs. David. I was afraid the police might actually try to follow me on the trails, so I went down by Swan Lake. I thought that I'd mingle there with any tourists. Also, I needed the time to figure out what to say to Amy.

I'd wear chinos and a blue button-down shirt. With the sleeves rolled. I'd borrow Uncle's blazer. It was small, but I could carry it over my shoulder. I'd stop at the 7-Eleven, get one of those chocolate roses they had been selling at the counter. Amy didn't much like chocolate. She did like roses. David Hitchens was always sending her roses. A rose is a rose is a rose. Even if it is made of chocolate and covered with aluminum foil. Besides, the flower stores close at 5 P.M. Then I'd park on Wheeler Avenue, get a dozen egg rolls at the Magic Wok. And as many packages of hot mustard.

"I love you," I kept saying, with my hands out, palms upward: "When you are old and gray and full of sleep . . ."

I almost stumbled on the turtle. This was a big one—with a shell at least a foot wide—moving slowly across the trail from the swamp to Swan Lake.

I've been told that a snapping turtle that size will eat ducklings, take off a man's hand. But I've never seen either thing happen, or even known of a person who knew of a person who was actually hurt by a snapping turtle. I think we tell these stories to make ourselves feel better about how much they scare us. The turtles have been around for a long time. They've seen us come, and I suppose they think that someday they'll see us go.

Anyway, I stood out there on the land bridge, waiting for the old one to make its transit. I didn't want to take the chance of leaving it alone. A dog might come along and get hurt. Or kids could show up and hurt the turtle.

They don't hurry when they get that big. I assumed it was a female, that she'd laid her eggs in the swamp and was returning to the lake. The monster finally settled into the water, and I yelled, threw a couple of clods of dirt, convinced the ancient one to submerge.

Then I started on toward the house. Amy came back into focus. I imagined her leaning into me. First I'd kiss her on the top of the head. I could feel her shoulder, the warm shape of her bosom against my chest. Then she'd tilt her face upward.

It took me almost an hour to get to the place where the trail crosses Route 448. There's a stone archway so that horsemen and walkers can pass under the road. When I got to this point, I climbed up to the highway. Looking north, I could just make out three police cars, at least five policemen, and what looked like a knot of volunteer firemen.

I went back under the bridge and stayed in the park for the rest of the walk home. I wish I could tell you that I sensed something, had some kind of premonition. I didn't. There were birds, must have been birds, but I didn't hear them. The verges of the dirt road had recently been mowed; I didn't smell the grass. What I saw was Amy. What I smelled was Ivory soap.

17

Now the memory really does go out. I believe I can bring up Phelps Memorial Hospital in August of 1991, but then it might be some other trauma I'm recollecting. I've been to emergency rooms half a dozen times. It's always the same.

Somebody is shouting: "What I need, doctor, is a fucking pain killer. Fucking pain! Fucking killer!" The shouter flips around on the gurney as they rush him through. "You worried about insurance?" he screams. "I'll pay you now. In cash! Fucking pain! Fucking killer!"

A middle-aged husband stands silently in the corner, clutching a ridiculously large black handbag. There's nothing sadder in this world, nothing any sadder than a man with a bad pocketbook.

Meanwhile the doctors and nurses move around slowly, deliberately, and this may be a blessing. But I do wish they wouldn't talk so openly about the ball game, or about the sushi at that new restaurant in Elmsford.

On this particular evening, I seem to remember that the woman behind the desk wore eyeglasses studded with paste jewelry. There was a big stain on her white lab jacket: chocolate or blood? She wanted numbers: date of birth, insurance identification.

Nar was there, Elspeth, and the kindly stranger. He'd driven. We all pitched in, but it was John Gilbert who gave most of the answers. He even had Uncle's Social Security number memorized, reeled it off while Aunt was still searching through her purse. Then a doctor appeared. This was a big man, with thick glasses. The frames had recently been repaired with adhesive tape.

First he wanted to know what the nurse had thought of Tahoe.

"I liked it."

"Win big?"

"Nope."

"Glad to have you back."

"Glad to be back," she said, and then looked at us. "I suppose."

But this could be from another, a different hospital visit. In any case, we followed the doctor. He brought us to Uncle.

There is one scrap of dialogue I'm sure of. Nar was speaking.

"Shush," she said. "He's sleeping." And that's just how he looked. There was a gash on his forehead. Nothing serious. Jonas was in a hospital gown, but I'd seen my guardian in ridiculous clothes before. The most noticeable change was that he seemed smaller. It was as if he'd been shrunken rather than killed.

Clearly we've missed something important here, so we'll have to rewind. That afternoon, Elspeth had taken the Falcon out to the Grand Union. When she'd done her shopping, loaded the car, Robert McNamara wouldn't start. So she called Jonas. He never would have driven the Miata otherwise, but he came from that generation and class of men with a chivalry circuit. When there was a call for gallantry, all else was forgotten.

Friday had been a fine, sunny day. Some asshole must have

parked in the turnaround. So Uncle had to back out onto Route 448.

That's when he got tagged. The truck was a big one. Doing the speed limit. Carrying earth.

Meanwhile, back at the Grand Union, the French Vanilla was beginning to melt. Elspeth called my office. No answer. She phoned the Graftons. They were all out at the edge of the common, trying to get a peek at the tragedy. She called Gilbert. Got him. What is it they say about bad pennies?

The doctor drove right over to the supermarket. He picked Elspeth up and brought her home. I don't know why, but the police let them through the barricades.

Nar was in the house alone that evening. She had Talking Heads on the CD player and so probably wouldn't have heard the world end either.

Sister didn't even suspect until Gilbert and Aunt came in through the kitchen door, each with a pair of brown grocery sacks, solemn as a couple of Supreme Court judges.

It was another hour and a half before I showed up.

Elspeth came running at me. She took me in her arms. "Oh, Indian," she said. "Your new car." Then she burst into tears.

But I still don't get it. Death doesn't exist in our world, except as a concept. And why would anyone want to go out of his way to grasp a concept like that one?

Nobody is dead until a doctor says so. Which means that in order to believe in death, you have to believe in doctors. I have my doubts.

Besides, the people I've seen who were supposed to be dead, they were dressed for church. The women had wigs on, the men had rouge on their cheeks. Somebody once told me that the bodies are packed with sawdust. Who's to say for sure that these are corpses? Maybe they're just dolls, manufactured right along with the coffin.

Twice, I've actually seen a person die when I was right there. Both were strangers, and neither performance was entirely convincing. I saw a young woman jump off a highway overpass. She was wearing jeans, a pair of those short black boots, and a Western-style shirt, green with pearl snaps. She hit the ground like a sack of potatoes, but she didn't cry out or anything. No orchestra swelled in the background. Afterward, one leg was bent at an odd angle. True, she might have been dead. She might also have been a contortionist.

The other was an old man in a white wash-and-wear shirt, a black cardigan sweater, gray doubleknit slacks. The shirt was buttoned up to the throat. He was out taking a stroll with his wife when he keeled over on the sidewalk. First nothing. A circle formed, an officious stranger moved in and looked for a pulse.

"Give him air!" somebody shouted. Then other people took up the cry. "Give him air!" The wife was also making a racket. "Leave him alone," she said. "He's all right. He's fine. Just playing possum." That's what I thought too.

I've seen a lot of people die in movies, of course, and on TV. You can tell they're dead because the camera comes in for a close-up, shows you the mortal wound. And there's always the music. But mostly they aren't dead. When the real-life actors do perish, they keep coming back on the screen. Put on the TV any weekday morning, and you get "Bonanza," an antique Western, in which just about every young, virile hero is a ghost. Hoss is dead. Pa Cartwright advertised dog food for a while, then he died. Little Joe gave press conferences about his cancer. And there they are on Channel 11 fully armed and in color. Peppier than most of us. Better looking. And with rosier prospects.

Now that somebody I knew was actually supposed to have died, the sense was more one of bewilderment than grief. I knew something had changed, but I wasn't at all certain what. Not that I had a high old time either. I was in full possession of many good reasons to feel like shit. Many ordinary reasons to feel like shit. Reasons quite beyond the question of mortality, or even of broken safety mirrors.

When we got back home, the phone was ringing. Nar picked up. It was Walter Paige wanting to know where the hell I'd been.

"At the hospital."

"Are you all right?"

"Yeah, I'm fine."

"I've been trying to reach your ass for weeks now."

"Oh," I said. And then, "Why?"

"You're fired," he said. The man always did have a way with words. Not to speak of timing.

"Isn't this a little sudden?"

"What sudden? I told you I'd been trying to reach you."

"Yes, but why?"

"You fucked up. Your proofs are late. You close the place during business hours. You use the company American Express Card for personal expenses. You're lucky we aren't prosecuting."

I nodded into the phone but didn't speak.

"Still there?"

"Yeah."

"Got anything to say for yourself?"

"No."

For some reason this also didn't bother me much. I put the receiver on its cradle, and then, since I was there, I picked it up again, punched out the number of Joe's 24-Hour Mobil. I asked Joe if he could have the Falcon towed in from the Grand Union, charge the battery. I didn't mention the accident, but it seemed almost as if he knew. He may be psychic. Probably he has friends in the volunteer fire department.

Gilbert needed to make a call. He disconnected the phone from the kitchen jack, set himself up in the root cellar. He wanted to close the door. "Patient, doctor confidentiality," he explained. Uncle had never closed that door, and the wood was so badly swollen that this turned out to be quite an operation. But ultimately, we managed. The doctor was gone for twenty minutes. He came out looking stern, judicious. Nar plugged the phone back into its kitchen jack, where it began to ring immediately. She snatched it. "The Melon," she said. "He'll want to know if I'm all right." It wasn't the Melon.

"Well, Mr. Popular," she said, handing me the receiver. This time it was Amy Snodgrass Rose. At the airport.

"Forget something?"

"Oh, shit."

"That's all right," she said, with surprising venom. "I've already phoned my father." Then the line went dead.

18

Gilbert bedded down on the sofa in the living room. I didn't invite him. I remember thinking it must have been Elspeth. Nar isn't customarily that stupid.

I wasn't sleepy. I tried reading from the Alexander Adams biography of Geronimo. The old warrior recalls the massacre at Janos: "I found that my aged mother, my young wife, and my three small children were among the slain. There were no lights in camp, so without being noticed I silently turned away and stood by the river. How long I stood there I do not know. . . ."

Geronimo and the other warriors had been in town, drinking, when the Mexicans attacked the women and children. I wondered if there had ever been a death without some culpability, without some feeling of culpability. I also wondered, with all the many foolish chores I had done in my life, why the fuck I hadn't found the time to fix that mirror.

The house was still, and by midnight I'd slipped into that band of consciousness which is not sleep, but is not wakefulness either.

Someone walked into the kitchen. I could just make out the sound of water running. The shoes went through the pantry and into the root cellar.

I expected the typewriter to start up, but it didn't. Instead the steps came back up the hall, stopped outside my door.

There's always something hokey about a scene like this. Not even Shakespeare can carry it off with perfect grace. Isn't there a lot of dry ice and offstage thunder when Hamlet's father appears?

Ghost: "I am thy father's spirit; Doom'd for a certain term to walk the night."

But just because a scene is absurd, that doesn't mean it didn't occur at all.

I'm a sensible sort, and I told myself that I was hallucinating. "You miss him," I thought, "so you've willed him back to life." It's a convenient theory. But then why would I have been so scared? I can understand evoking Santa. Or even Jesus. But why would anyone want to invent a monster? Out of thin air?

I had been lying on my stomach when the footsteps started. I didn't move to face the door; instead I turned away, gave the shoes my back. Slowly, I drew my knees up into my chest. I tried to give the impression of somebody moving in his sleep. When I stopped, I could hear myself breathing, and I could hear somebody else, also breathing. My nose itched. I didn't scratch it. I lay as still as I knew how. It shouldn't be difficult to relax, I thought. Just pretend you're dead.

When I woke up the next morning, it wasn't raining. Saturday, August 17, 1991. The moon was in its first quarter, and it was not raining. It should have been, but it wasn't. I put on jeans and a blue T-shirt that had a raccoon on it and the legend "I read books from the Mount Pleasant Public Library." I walked down to the end of the drive. Route 448 still had dirt on it. A lot of dirt. You could have planted pumpkins. I picked up the newspaper. This was wrapped in blue plastic. In case of rain.

When I got back to the kitchen, I made the coffee. I didn't make the chocolate coffee. I didn't mix mocha and Vienna roast either. I thought the grinder might wake up the widow. So I took out some of the already-been-ground stuff I'd bought at the supermarket early that spring. "We had coffee long before we had a biographer," I thought. "We used to drink it. In quantity and with enthusiasm."

But the palate is a quick learner, and mine now knew better. The supermarket brand was stale. I wasn't letting anyone sleep either, because Aunt appeared almost immediately and poured herself a cup. She took a sip and blanched. "Why?"

I shrugged. She pulled the newspaper out of its blue plastic rainsuit and read for a while with uncharacteristic intensity. I was surprised. Aunt has never been a keen student of current affairs. I spread cream cheese on an English muffin, put it in the toaster oven.

"Well," she said, and I believe her voice trembled, "I suppose he'd be pleased."

"Who?"

"Your uncle."

"Why's that?"

"Page one," she said, and handed me the paper.

There was a photo of Jonas sitting in the back of a rowboat. Christabel Gordon had taken the picture for a dust jacket. The caption: "Author dies in car crash. D26."

The notice itself was a big one, with a box full of excerpts and a reproduction of the drawing that Classic had requisitioned for the *Publishers Weekly* ad.

I knew *Times* staffers wrote obituaries of important people long before they died. I hadn't known Uncle was important. I was also surprised that a national newspaper would have such highly burnished contacts with the local police.

Jonas Aldous Collingwood, the author of eighteen
novels, died yesterday evening after his Japanese sports

car was crushed by a heavy truck on a country road not 200 yards from the house he rented in Pocantico Hills. He was sixty-nine years old.

While Collingwood's writing has long held a small but enthusiastic body of readers, it did not draw national attention until last year, when it was reported in the *International Herald Tribune* that sections of *My Life as a Woman* (Brindle Publications, 1989) exactly matched accounts of combat in the journals of an Italian partisan.

That book, *Mea Culpa, Mea Culpa, Mea Maxima Culpa*, was not published in this country until 1985. Further inquiries revealed that Collingwood had lived outside of Rome during the Second World War. When questioned, the American pronounced the diaries of Dominic Pelligrino to be "highly romantic." He never denied, however, that he and the famous partisan had known each other.

There seems now to be little question that Collingwood was an active member of the anti-Nazi, anti-Fascist resistance. His references to the Italian countryside and to the confused politics of that time and place bear a verisimilitude highly unlikely in a work of fiction. Collingwood spoke Italian and had a pronounced limp, which was said to be the result of wounds inflicted by a German rocket.

Four of Collingwood's later novels were set between 1942 and 1945 in what the author termed "a no-man's land entirely without borders. Three armies, several distinct faiths, and more than a dozen nationalities joined here in murderous play. Families were split, brother against brother, father against son.

"The killing all took place," he wrote, "against the background of an extraordinarily handsome countryside, an earthly paradise in which nobody out of uniform could remember ever having had enough to eat."

Thrust before the literary world, the books, which

had long been held in high esteem, were praised conspicuously. Writing a year ago in this newspaper, *New York Times* critic Davis Anderson Miller Helman Wilson Canning Burroughs noted that "we have accustomed ourselves, in recent years, to writers and painters who force themselves into the public eye. Collingwood was of an older tradition. His personal life was flamboyant and courageous, while his artistic life is both quiet and distinguished."

In a piece published in the *New York Review of Books*, Lancelot O'Toole wrote that "his [Collingwood's] wit is so keen, his observations so acerbic and unpleasant, that it was simply easier for a generation bred on the *Reader's Digest* and TV comedies to believe that his work was fiction. A realistic assessment of the nature of this prose and its relation to the little that is now known of the author's life leads the intelligent reader to suspect, however, that we are presented not with eighteen bitter, unsavory novels, but with a memoir in as many parts. These documents are so magnificent in their fidelity to the life as to be virtually a work of science."

While unwilling to do more than hint in public about his Italian adventures, Mr. Collingwood had nevertheless reached an agreement this year with Classic Books to write a memoir.

Reached yesterday at his Connecticut home, Classic's executive editor, Paul Whitfield, pronounced himself "shocked and grieved" by the news of his author's death. He reported that a completed memoir is "in house" and would be published in the spring. Whitfield noted that there had already been inquiries about the book's suitability as the basis for a television special.

"We at Classic are thrilled to have worked with Collingwood," he said. "One of the greatest satisfactions an editor can have is to help win wide recognition for the true artist."

The memoir, titled *The Partisan*, is not the only work expected on the life of its enigmatic author. Dr. John Gilbert, a physician and noted literary critic, has contracted with Faber & Krupp to produce a biography.

Gilbert, who phoned this newspaper from the Collingwood house yesterday, just hours after witnessing the wreck, described himself as "devastated by the loss."

"I've admired Jonas Collingwood as a writer for years," he said, "but I only recently grew to know him as a man. And I am hard pressed to say which of those two exceptional beings was most precious to me. It's as if my own beloved father had died in that car."

I looked up from the paper. Elspeth had the eggs out; she was heating the skillet.

"He hates his father," I said.

"Who hates his father?"

"Gilbert."

"Oh, that," she said, and she didn't sound very interested. "I was just wondering if you'd like cheese in your eggs."

"Cheese would be fine," I said, and went back to the paper. There was a lot from Gilbert about Jonas having grown up in Baltimore, some comparisons to Hemingway.

"Did you read this?" I asked Elspeth.

Aunt nodded.

"Well, then, you've got to hear it again," I said, and read:

> "I know it is a commonplace for the biographer to magnify his importance in the author's life," Gilbert told the *Times*, "but I think that in this case, I did play a significant role. He had no children, and living in the country, Collingwood was often without the sort of intelligent companionship essential to a man of his complexity."

Elspeth was stirring butter in a frying pan. She seemed to be completely absorbed. I'd never seen her so intent.

"No children," I said. "Not even bad ones? Not even a couple of frightful disappointments?"

It was at this point that the kind stranger came into the kitchen. He looked remarkably well for somebody who had slept on a sofa.

I glanced at Elspeth. Suddenly she looked terribly old, with jowls I'd never seen before, whiskers. But she was smiling crookedly up at Gilbert. "Eggs?" she asked.

"Yes," he said, turning in my direction, "and then I think Nelson and I should go out and fix that mirror."

19

When the Stone & Son Funeral Home unloads a "top flight" coffin—burnished wood with brass fittings—they also try to sell an ugly cement or Fiberglas case to bury it in.

"I, personally, like the additional protection." That's what Jeff said. Jeff is the yuppie in Stone & Son, the junior manager and legitimate heir. "Of course, this is entirely up to the family," Jeff said, solemnly, "but we do feel obligated to present the bereaved with all the options."

"What about resuscitation?" asked Nar. "I think we'd be willing to pay a little extra for resuscitation."

Jeff smiled. Jeff didn't laugh, but he did smile.

Elspeth didn't even smile.

"And what's being protected?" Nar asked.

Jeff shrugged. He had a nice shrug. He had a winning shrug. "Your investment."

Nar nodded. "To keep the box from getting wet and dirty?"

"That's right," said Jeff, clearing his throat, "and the deceased."

I should point out here that we all liked the yuppie. He wasn't pompous, nor did he have the minty breath or forced heartiness commonly associated with his profession. The only thing that distinguished him as a mortician was the size and fleshiness of his palms. Ever notice how large and moist the hands are on those guys? Jeff was a jogger. He ran two miles in the morning and was slender everywhere but the palms.

We met in his office. This had dark paneling and several brass lamps. It was set in the rear of what had once been a banker's mansion on Upper Broadway in Tarrytown.

Jeff had a taste for port wine leather; the prints were of sailing ships and scenes from the hunt. We'd had quite a long conference that morning and had already settled the question of gravediggers. "They cost a little more," Jeff explained.

"But they do a better job?" I asked.

"No, actually the machines make a neater opening. But they are, well, they are traditional."

"That's what we want, then," said Elspeth. "Actual men, with shovels."

Jeff smiled, made a note on his yellow legal pad. He liked to sit on the front of his wooden desk. The informality of his style contrasted pleasantly with the absurd rectitude of his surroundings. "And what about the case?" he asked.

Nar rose from the big leather sofa and put a hand on his arm, smiled up at the young mortician. "We'll think about it," she said, and we, the bereaved, all trailed out of the office, regrouped in the parking lot around our rented car.

The rental was Joe's idea. He had had the Falcon towed and had promised to look the car over carefully, but still felt strongly that we should arrange for more reliable transportation.

"Driving with the lights on," he explained, almost coyly, "will be an extra draw on the battery."

Not that there was going to be a funeral cortege in New York. Still, I didn't think the Taurus too much of an extravagance. Elspeth said Uncle's insurance might cover it, at least until we got a check for the Miata. We had the cash. (In fact we had enough money in the bank to subsist at our customary level for five or six years. Provided, of course, I didn't go to college.) And death, like most objects pursued in Westchester County, involves a lot of stop-and-go driving.

Besides, the local rental agency actually delivered the car. This was a sedan, in midnight blue. We had driven a Ford. Lately. But it was a novelty to have a Ford that started. It was also pleasant to drive a Ford that didn't belong to us.

I opened the door for Elspeth, who slipped inside.

"I vote not," said Nar from the back seat. "If there is a Resurrection, it won't matter how damp he's gotten in the meantime."

Elspeth was searching in her purse. She found a piece of tissue into which she honked noisily.

We backed out of our slot. I spoke: "They say the dead carry with them to the grave in their clutched hands only that which they have given away."

"If that's true," said Nar, "Jonas will have a Miata, cash to buy gas with, and a complete set of the works of William Makepeace Thackeray."

I put the Taurus into drive. "That's what we should pack," I said. "I mean, if we really wanted to do something, we should ask them to bury one of those Itty Bitty Book Light."

"It might make a decent ad," said Nar. "First a black background, with block letters in white: The Quick and the Dead. Give a glimpse of the funeral, pass a week's worth of pages on the calendar, then two dark silhouettes climbing over the wall into the graveyard at night. Next, we hear the sound of a shovel cutting into rocky soil. These scenes could be lifted right out of old movies."

"Heavy breathing," I said, "wood splintering. From the grave, there's a light. The violins get manic. The camera pans in on the corpse, establishes the beginnings of decomposition: swollen gums, one milky eye. Then we see the Itty Bitty Book Light. I'd want Charlton Heston or James Earl Jones to come booming in with the text: 'He's still dead, but his batteries keep on ticking. That's Duracell, the one with the copper top.' "

"Batteries don't tick," said Nar, and I noticed that her face was wet with tears.

The light in front of us went yellow. I pulled to a stop, looked over at Elspeth. She was not crying. She wasn't smiling either.

"You don't mind?" I asked.

"Mind what?" said Elspeth, stiffly. She'd taken a compact out of her purse and was applying blush.

"Us joking? He would have joked."

"He would have joked," she agreed, thrusting the compact back into her purse. "On the other hand, I honestly don't see the point of spending all that money on a cherry-wood box if we are not going to at least try to make it last."

That was it. End of discussion. We bought the deluxe Fiberglas shell. The Royalist cost $498, came in "living gold," and actually had some sort of crest. I thought it absurd, but Elspeth was the widow. And remarkably pious for such an outspoken atheist.

Besides, we had saved a lot on cosmetics by opting for a closed casket. This decision had clearly pained the yuppie. "So then I suppose you'll be wanting to come in before the trip and say good-bye to him," he said.

I thought not.

"Well, then," he said, "when will you have your, I don't know, your final parting?"

Elspeth got up out of the chair she had been sitting in and stood there with her head bowed. We expected her to speak, but she did not do so. Nar also rose, went over to Aunt, put an arm around the older woman's narrow dancer's shoulders. Sister looked up at the mortician, smiled wanly. "Never," she said. And now they were both crying.

And she was right. Uncle's presence did not seem to have been diminished significantly by death. He was always in our minds.

Most situations, either Nar or I would think of what he might have said and say it ourselves. It was as if we'd been given his proxy. And when we did speak, Elspeth would get that same tired, bemused look on her face, the one she's had for as long as anybody can remember.

The typewriter wasn't going anymore. And this was a loss. But then there had been times when he was alive and the typewriter wasn't going.

The whole entourage had survived his passing. Gilbert was around a lot too. Elspeth had never stopped liking the doctor. Nar had gone uncharacteristically tolerant.

"Give him a break," she said. "It's a literary biography. Nobody'll read it."

Gilbert nodded. "I'll be lucky if they look at it in graduate seminars," he said. "Dos Passos didn't even get a daily review in the *Times*."

"I hope it's not going to be like the obituary," I said.

And then he apologized. "I'm terribly sorry about that. I was probably as shocked as you were. You know how important I think you all were to Jonas. I've told you that."

"They misquoted you?"

"Well," he said, "not exactly. But they certainly quoted me out of context." Then I got The Smile. Really, there ought to be a law about facial expressions.

I hadn't met Uncle's mother or father, nor had I known or even speculated about the terms of the will. But apparently, aside from an abiding distaste for Baltimore—the city Lincoln had to skulk through for fear of being murdered by southern sympathizers—they'd left their only son with a small plot of ground—in Baltimore.

And so, when all the details had been worked out, Nar, Elspeth, and I took a train south. As did the body. A different train. Or at least we didn't ride in the same compartment.

Gilbert had a meeting in New York, said he would fly down, meet us there.

The church was a stone fortress, built on a rise and with a halo of cracked and crooked tombstones. The positioning was excellent for defense, the walls thick enough to stop small-arms fire. One was given the distinct impression that the forces of evil would be coming soon, on foot, and equipped with pikes and harquebuses.

The inside was as dark as a coat closet. What light there was had been discolored by a set of gory stained-glass panels.

At first I couldn't tell who was there, or even if anybody else had bothered to show up. We were led by the local mortician (Stone & Son had a reciprocal arrangement) to the front of the church. My pupils dilated, and I began to make out the shapes of other mourners.

I know from reading Uncle's books that in Italy, at least during the war, strangers were employed to swell the throng at funerals. "The practice gives melancholy a monetary value," he wrote. "Which is to give it value at all. Which, today, is uncharacteristic. We today have much less tolerance for sorrow than we have for filth, or even violence."

The deceased, we were told, was "deeply creative." Uncle despised the word "creative." He called it an unword, "meaning a person—quite possibly a person of atypical sexual predilections—who performs clever and entirely useless work, for which he is overpaid."

We were assured that "the dearly departed was beloved by his parents, Moses and Abigail Collingwood. . . ." We were told that Jonas, in his turn, adored and honored his parents, "as only an only son can love the mother and father who gave him life and love."

After the service, we got into a rented limousine and followed the hearse out to the Collingwood family holding. The only Collingwood family holding.

The edges of the grave were neat. Inhumanly neat. There was a backhoe parked nearby, a big, orange insect with its single dirt-stained claw. I can't imagine what else it could be used for.

Six of us carried the box out of the car, and somebody whisked it into its shell. This was a ghastly construction painted gold with flecks, much worse than its pictures. The style was Spanish Galleon. A system of straps and pulleys was employed, and the whole costly and tasteless package was lowered into the ground.

Laura was there, without her loving lawyer. She'd driven down with her detestable brother, Bill. She gave me a kiss. She said nothing. Not a word. Which I thought was just right.

Joe appeared with a woman on his arm. We hugged; he moved to one side, presented his companion.

"Mrs. Orsini?" I asked.

Joe grinned. "No, Nelson, no," he said. "Miss Pacula, a friend of your father's."

I shook the woman's hand. She had a fighter's grip.

Susan Watchman was also present. She was wearing a green, double-breasted raincoat, tightly fastened at the waist.

"Paul had work to do," she said. "He was dreadfully disappointed. He wanted so much to come."

"I know," I said. "I can imagine."

Christabel Gordon probably hadn't wanted to come either, but she did. Christabel was in her seventies but still a stately, quite beautiful woman. She wore a white dress that looked a little like a bathrobe and had enormous blue flowers on it. She kissed me, kissed Nar, kissed Elspeth. Christabel smoked and always smelled of violets and tobacco.

After the greetings, she took me aside. "None of my business," she said, lighting a cigarette.

"Ask away," I said.

"Can you stop that book now?"

"Nope."

"Spent the money?"

"Yup."

She shook her head. "He was such a fool for love, your uncle."

I nodded. "You can't hate him for that?" I said.

"Quite the contrary."

The Melon was present. He had offered to drive us all down. We'd refused. Nobody particularly wanted to know what Dale Carnegie thought of the afterlife.

Rolaids came. As did Princeton. And Cameron, wearing better clothes and looking much more prosperous as a literary agent than he had ever looked as a beloved schoolteacher. He spoke with Nar.

Outside, I thought the priest was splendid. I don't mean to sound uncharitable, but there is something about the smell of a freshly opened grave that gives a priest hope. The threat of damnation does not carry a lot of force anymore; the death threat is still a good one. And standing in the open air beside a deep, rectangular hole, it gets your attention.

Also, there was no ad-libbing after we left the church; the good father stuck right to the text. And the texts for traditional Episcopalians are very fine indeed. Parts of the old *Book of Common Prayer* were written, after all, by a man who was burned at the stake for his troubles.

That sunny day in Baltimore, the words from Cranmer's book seemed wildly appropriate, written with Uncle in mind: "Man that is born of a woman, hath but a short time to live, and is full of misery. He cometh up, and is cut down, like a flower . . ."

Nar was beside me. She was making a grunting sound, almost like an animal. A small, a sexy animal, but an animal nevertheless. It took me a while to understand that she was speaking words, then to remember what they meant in Italian. "*Spero*," she was saying. "*Io spero*." I hope. I hope.

The minister said: "The Lord be with you."

And about a third of the gathering in uncertain chorus responded: "*And with thy spirit.*"

"Lord, have mercy upon us."

"*Christ have mercy upon us.*"

"Lord have mercy upon us."

There was a general clearing of throats, a little milling around, and somebody produced a shovel. I was encouraged by a stranger with fleshy palms to throw soil down onto the gaudy plastic shell. This I then did.

I felt a hand on my arm and turned to see Dr. John Gilbert, in gray flannel slacks and the blue blazer.

"Many hands make light work," he said, and I surrendered the shovel. He pitched in briefly, then stopped and began to examine his hands for blisters.

"You all right?" I asked.

"Yes," he said, "but this does remind me of my favorite Sonny Liston quote."

"What's that?"

"Those who wish they dug ditches never dug ditches."

"Yeah, I remember Liston. They rioted at Sing Sing when he lost," I said, and took back the shovel. It was a relief to have the tool in my hands, but when the clods of dirt hit the golden case, they made a cheap, ugly sound.

20

"Public Works Brownies." That's what Uncle used to call them, "because they are produced exclusively for civic events and are sufficiently durable to be used in the construction of sidewalks or sewer culverts." It's a mix, but Aunt substitutes water for milk and uses half the liquid. Eat one and you're chastened. Eat three and you're dying of thirst. Drink a glass of milk and you're just dying.

I understand that in the bad old days in France they used to make the best liver pâté by taking a goose, nailing its feet to the floor, and stuffing it with rich food. Then they'd cut the animal's throat, remove the engorged liver. Eat a plate of Aunt's brownies, wash it down with milk, and that's how you feel, like a Strasbourg goose. You find yourself expecting—nay, practically hoping—that somebody will come along and slit your throat, harvest your organs.

On this particular evening, Aunt had filled two Pyrex baking dishes. She took one to her meeting and left the other in the fridge.

Nar was out with the Melon, seeing a movie with Julia Roberts in it: *Dying Young? Sleeping with the Enemy?*

When the phone rang, I thought it would be Laura. She'd been calling at least once a day, "just to see how you are."

It wasn't Laura. It was the Melon: "I want to be certain of the day your sister is coming back from Florida."

"I don't exactly know."

"Any idea?"

I shook my head but didn't speak.

"Well, look, I'd hate to put you to any trouble, but could you find out for me? Because I'm going out of town myself, a business trip, and I want to schedule it around her being away."

"Sure," I said. "I'll try and find out. Call tomorrow."

"Okay," said the Melon. "And thanks, buddy."

I told him it was nothing, hung up, went to the refrigerator, and took out the Pyrex baking dish. I cut the dessert into squares, ate one, and put the pan back.

Then I took down one of the Parkman histories, but I couldn't read. I sat there, fuming, with the book in my lap. Talk about sleeping with the enemy.

I knew Sister wouldn't appear until long after Elspeth was home and in bed. I also knew that when I told her what a cunt I thought she was, she'd burst into tears. That would wake Elspeth up.

I'd tell Nar we needed something at the 7-Eleven. I'd get her out in the Taurus, burn her tidy little ass. I stood, went to the refrigerator, had another brownie, and hid the only container of milk back behind the orange juice.

The phone rang again. This time it was Laura. She was crying. "I'm in the bedroom," she said. "I've locked him out."

In the background, I could hear somebody pounding on a door. "Do you want me to come over?"

"No," she said. "He'll calm down."

"You sure?"

"Yeah, I'm sure."

"What's this about?"

"He's uptight about the wedding."

"So he's hitting you?"

"No, actually, he's been hitting the wall mostly these days."

"You could break it off, you know."

"I know. But I really do want to get married."

"Marry somebody else."

"Like who?"

"Marry me."

"You have a girl."

"Do not."

"Everybody says Amy Snodgrass Rose has been pining for you."

"Everybody?"

"My brother called her up for a date, and she wouldn't. Saving herself for you," she said. The banging in the background got more intense and then began to recede.

"Yeah, I wish. But what about you? Should I come over?"

"No. Not really. Just having somebody to talk with makes me feel better. Wait a minute," she said, and put the phone down. Then she came back. "He's stopped now. I'll go out and try to reason with him."

"What set him off?"

"I went out with a girlfriend is all. We went to a bar."

"Why'd you do that?"

"I don't know. There was this cute guy. Look, Nelson, I have to hang up now. But thanks for listening."

"You sure you don't want me to come by? Or to call the police?"

"I'm sure."

"Look, if you ever do want me to come by, you tell me."

"Okay."

"Promise?"

"I promise."

"Even after you're married."

"Even after I'm married," she said, and hung up.

I went back to my post. The book I had chosen was Parkman, *Montcalm and Wolfe*, volume two.

When the battle was over, Quebec taken, Wolfe dead, Montcalm mortally wounded, I went back into the kitchen, helped myself to another killer brownie.

Elspeth came home at 10:30 P.M. with her empty Pyrex pan. We exchanged pleasantries, and she tripped off to bed. I was still in the Chesterfield, dozing, when I heard the crunch of tires on our gravel drive.

"Is that you?"

The footsteps stopped. "No, it's Charles Manson."

Sister was wearing her seduction outfit, the camisole and the suede skirt. Her hair was ruffled, her lipstick smeared. She was squinting into the refrigerator.

I leaned back against the counter. "We need milk. Want to come out to the 7-Eleven and get some?"

"No thanks."

"I'll let you drive."

"That's all right. I'm tired," Nar said, and took out the iced tea, then the orange juice. "There's milk here," she said.

"Oh," I said. "I couldn't find it." Then, affecting extreme casualness, I went on, "So how's the man who got his personality out of a book?"

Nar shrugged.

"You were out with the Melon, right?"

Nar nodded. "Did you call Amy?"

"No."

"You know, you should."

"Why should I?"

"Trust me."

"Why should I trust you?"

"Why shouldn't you trust me?"

"Because you're a liar."

"Give me a for instance."

"For instance you weren't out with the Melon tonight."

Nar leaned forward, put the milk back into the refrigerator. She turned and looked at me. "Where are the brownies?"

"Were you out with Gilbert?"

Nar began to reach around in the refrigerator again. "I thought Elspeth baked brownies."

"You haven't answered my question."

Nar closed the door. Looked at me. "You my father now?"

"Allen called here. He wanted to know when you were getting back from Florida."

"Yeah?"

"Well, it was a little embarrassing for me."

Now Nar looked mildly interested but still not the least bit repentant. "What did you tell him?"

"I told him I didn't know."

Nar nodded. "Good answer."

"Look," I said. "There's something we need to talk about."

Sister glanced up at my face now, but she wasn't looking me in the eyes. Her gaze was lower. I reached instinctively upward, but before my fingers had gotten above chin level, Sister had stepped forward, and with one crimson fingernail she flicked a crumb off my lip.

"Oh, Bro," she said, smiling. "Have you been eating brownies?"

"Yeah," I said, defensively, "what of it?"

Nar went over to the kitchen sink and saw the two empty pans.

"You're going to be one sick puppy," she said. Then she came over, kissed me on the cheek.

I was stiff now with indignation. "Is there something you'd like to tell me?"

"Yes," said Nar, heading down the hall to her bedroom.

"And what's that?"

"Stay away from liquids."

The door closed, and she was gone.

I resumed my post in the leather chair. I thought Sister would have to come out again. She'd need to use the bathroom. I picked up the Parkman, held it, but did not attempt to read.

Nor did Nar reappear. And after about fifteen minutes I gave up. I went into the bathroom myself, tried sticking a finger down my throat. I succeeded in making my eyes water. Bulimics are born, not made.

Then we lose a couple of months. Nar turned seventeen. It's early November. I didn't have a job; I hadn't had enough of my own cash to go back to school and so had let the deadline pass for registration. Elspeth urged me to take some of her, some of Uncle's money. I thanked her. "I definitely will," I said. "In the spring." Although I had my doubts. We did have a lot of money, I mean for us. But there wasn't any more coming either. Ever. The goose was dead. Yes, I tried to call Amy. I dialed her number at least three times. The line was always busy, or there was nobody home.

So I spent a lot of time alone. I did everything a person is supposed to do when grieving. I lounged about in a bathrobe and tube socks. I read children's books. I ate sweets. I took long, solitary walks. Everything but grieve.

I didn't feel sad, but then I didn't really feel anything. That's not exactly right. The sensation was of extreme dislocation. It was rather as if one of King Solomon's djinns had taken up our house and the surrounding land, given it a fearful shaking, then returned the turf and building to its original setting. Nothing was broken, but everything was slightly out of plumb. The dining room table, for instance, looked precisely as the dining room table had always looked, and yet entirely different.

There seemed to be cotton in my ears, and I had lost my sense of smell.

Uncle appeared to me almost every night. There was nothing dramatic about the dreams. He was much as he'd been in life. Death seemed to have made him a little more serious, less apt to break into laughter. But then Uncle had been mildly oracular for as long as I could remember.

It did seem to me that many of the trees were dying. Although this is not an entirely new development. The elms have been on life-support for as long as I can remember. The dogwoods have been sick for a decade.

Most of the householders around here will use hemlocks, the cheapest evergreen, to screen the edges of their property. There's a new bug that's killing the hemlocks. The horse chestnuts have also been hit, and lose their leaves before they should. Something else is killing off the ash.

It had always been my job to take the hoses in, turn off the outside faucets. This year, for the first time ever, I did the work alone. I used the wheelbarrow. It made its customary dreadful sound.

Then the frost came, the last leaves fell. The fingers of the trees went ebony in the winter air and seemed to claw at the belly of the sky. Gray roads cut through gray fields. When I walked—I walked a lot—the ground would ring like iron underfoot.

Laura kept calling. The wedding was scheduled for New Year's Day. "We can get the whole family," she explained. "He'll never forget our anniversary."

I was going to be an usher. In the meantime, I functioned as a sort of free-lance taste consultant.

"Crab cakes or shrimp?" she'd ask.

"Which costs the most?"

"Cakes."

"Have the shrimp, then. People sometimes mistake crab cakes for potatoes."

"There's one thing, "she said.

"Ummm?"

"We're having the reception at that new convention center. The Half Moon. Have you ever been there?"

I had been there.

"They have a sort of discount system for people who do some of the work themselves."

"Yeah?"

"You don't have to buy me a wedding present."

"Okay."

"You and the other ushers will be asked to stay through the reception, and then after Albert and I take off in the limousine, you're supposed to fix up the banquet room, prepare it for the next event. If you don't clean it properly, we get fined."

I didn't say anything.

"It shouldn't take that long. A couple of hours on the outside. And if you don't want to stay at the reception, you can go home, take a nap or something, and then come back."

"That's all right."

"You sure?"

"Sure."

"You're a sweetie."

"Thanks."

It might have had to do with a change in the atmosphere. It might simply have had to do with the passage of time. But slowly, surely, I began to cheer up.

Then, on one unseasonably warm morning in December, I actually woke up with a smile on my face. I'd dreamt of Uncle. He was giving me his famous "Live in the world" lecture. But then I'd heard that one before.

I went for a walk, expecting bluebirds. There were none. The sky was clear. The ground gave underfoot.

When I got back, I went into Nar's room. She was dolling herself up for a big date in the city. "I feel lucky," I told her.

"Good. Call Amy."

"I tried."

"What happened?"

"The line was busy."

"I bet you called the family number."

I nodded.

"She has her own line."

"Oh," I said, "I didn't know."

"Knock," said Nar, heading out the door, "and it shall be opened unto you."

About a half hour later, the phone rang. "It's Amy," I thought. It was Cameron.

"Nar's not here."

"I wasn't exactly calling for your sister."

There was a pause. A long pause. I thought maybe I'd been disconnected, but Cameron finally broke the silence. "It's not good news," he said.

"That's all right. I've stopped expecting good news."

"I'm a literary agent now," said Cameron.

"I know," I said. "We wanted to hire you for the last deal."

"You seem to have done a fine job of it without me."

"We did okay."

"No, I mean you."

"Me?"

"Yes, didn't you actually close the deal?"

"I answered the phone. I made some calls. Jonas made the deal. He was always in control. But you knew him. He was always in control."

"I guess," said Cameron. "It's just that I met Mrs. Smalls at a cocktail party, and she said you'd acted as agent."

"Well, it's possible Jonas said that. I mean, if she ragged him too much, he might have said that."

"In any case," said Cameron, "that's not what I'm calling about. As an agent, I sometimes get to see proposals that I'm not handling," he said, and paused.

"Yeah?"

I could hear him clearing his throat. "How to start?" he said.

"Just start," I said.

"All right. You know a guy named John Gilbert?"

"Yes."

"He's writing a book about Jonas."

"I know that. It was in the obituary."

"That's right. But this book has some surprises in it."

"Oh."

"All that time your uncle was supposed to have spent in Italy?"

"Yes?"

"Look, let me read to you. Right out of the proposal."

"Okay."

There was another pause.

"One of the problems," said Cameron, "is that I don't want to go over familiar ground. No need to rub salt in old wounds. So you'll have to tell me exactly what you do know."

"Almost nothing."

"You ever see this guy Gilbert?"

"All the time."

"He never said anything?"

"Quite a lot. At one point, he actually suggested that Jonas should have won the Nobel prize in literature. Is that what you mean?"

I guess it wasn't what Cameron had meant, because there was silence on the other end of the line.

"Are you still there?"

"Look, on second thought, I don't want to read this to you."

"Okay. I mean, why not?"

"I'd just as soon not be despised by the entire family. I'll send it. You'll have it tomorrow."

"Okay."

"Do you like this guy, Gilbert?"

"No."

"Well, that's good, at least."

"Why?"

"You won't be disappointed."

I hung up, and almost immediately the phone rang again. This time it was Laura.

"Nelson, is that you?"

"Yes."

"Your line's been busy."

"I know."

"I don't want to bother you, but he's angry. Says he's going to murder me."

"Where are you?"

"At his place. The Gold Coast Condominiums. White Plains."

"You want me to call the police?"

"No. I'll come there."

"Will he let you?"

"Yes. I just don't want to go home. I couldn't stand the idea of my mother seeing me like this. She'd make me call off the wedding."

"All right, come here. I'll make some tea."

"Fifteen minutes, then. Half an hour on the outside."

"If you're not here in forty-five minutes, I will call the police."

I shaved, took a shower, got into chinos and a red flannel shirt. By the time I'd towel-dried and combed my hair, put on the kettle, Laura was at the door. She was sobbing heavily.

I helped her in the door. She was wearing a pea jacket, a navy blue watch cap, the stone-washed jeans, and a pair of New Balance running shoes. She took off the cap, shook out her short hair. I helped her out of the jacket and got her to sit down at the kitchen table.

"You want a drink?"

She nodded. I poured us each a jelly jar of Old Smuggler. She drank off half of hers, stopped crying, then looked around the room. "Do you have any cigarettes?"

"You want one?"

Laura nodded.

There was still half a carton left on top of the refrigerator. I took a pack down, opened it. I took a glass ashtray off the dish drainer, got out a Marlboro. Laura put it in her mouth. I fished some matches out of the scissors drawer, lit her cigarette.

She inhaled deeply, let the smoke out through her nose. Then she took her right hand and swept the bangs out of her eyes.

"What happened?"

"He's crazy," she said, tapping the ash off her cigarette. "He's gotten it into his head that I'm cheating on him."

"Couldn't you convince him otherwise?"

"Not today," she said. "Not so close to the wedding." Then she looked up at me and smiled. "The idea of being cuckolded is bad enough. The idea of being cuckolded and still having to pay for the crab cakes, that's the killer."

"I thought you were having shrimp."

"His mother is allergic to shrimp."

I took a drink of scotch, pulled up a chair beside her, and sat down.

"What can I do?"

"You can't really do anything."

"You sure?"

"Quite sure."

Laura got up, went into the bathroom, and I could hear the tap running.

"How do I look?" she asked when she came back out.

"Like you've been crying."

She nodded sadly, sat back down. "Just let me stay here and drink and smoke, and I'll feel better."

"Okay," I said, and lit myself a cigarette. The kettle began to whistle. I got up, turned off the stove. "You want some tea?"

Laura shook her head, so I went back to the kitchen table, sat beside her.

Laura reached over, took my forearm in both her hands. Looked at me. "It's good to have somebody I can level with," she said.

I smiled, tried to appear fatherly. I thought my old friend looked like shit. I also noticed that I was getting an erection.

"I wish I were marrying you," she said.

"We'd have to have the shrimp," I said.

Laura grinned. "If I were marrying you," she said, "it wouldn't matter. We could hold the reception at McDonald's."

"That's about what I could afford."

Laura was nodding her head. She started to cry again. I stubbed out my cigarette, put an arm around her.

She swallowed the rest of her scotch. Looked at mine.

"You finish," she said.

I shrugged and then complied.

"Another round," she said.

I poured. Laura drank off half her jelly jar, knocked another cigarette out of the pack. I lit it.

Then I lit one for myself, leaned back in my chair. "So what happened?"

"He started hitting me again."

"And what was this about?"

"He's convinced that I slept with somebody else. That I'm going to give him AIDS or herpes or something."

I knocked my ash into the glass ashtray.

"I already had a test," she said. "If he wants, I'll have another one."

"Sounds reasonable."

Laura looked up at me. "You believe me, don't you?"

"Sure."

She finished her second drink.

"You want to see where he hit me?"

"Okay."

"Not here, though," she said.

"Where, then?"

"Your bedroom."

Laura stood, picked up the glass ashtray from the kitchen table, the package of Marlboros, swayed uncertainly. I stood as well, put an arm around her, and we made our way down the hall to my room. When we got there, I turned, closed the door. I didn't think anybody was going to come home soon. I had a deadbolt. I slid this into place. When I turned around, Laura had already settled on my bed. She was lying on her back, with her eyes closed. I sat beside her and looked down at her face. She has a pretty face. I like her chin. She has a good chin.

"So where does it hurt?"

Laura didn't open her eyes. Instead, she reached out, took my hand, rested it on the crotch of her jeans, and pulled the bottom of her shell out of the waist of her pants. Then she took my hand, pressed the palm down against her hard, flat belly, and slid it up until it cupped the bottom of her left breast.

I sat there awkwardly for a minute, looking away. The bra was made of some lacy stuff. Through it the breast was heavy, warm against the palm of my hand. I wondered if this was a mistake. I waited for her to take my hand away. She did not do so.

"You've changed a lot," I said, my throat going thick. "Since you were little."

Then I felt her other hand in my crotch. "So have you," she said.

Harold Levin would have been disappointed, as would Ernest Hemingway. There was no sound like a watermelon breaking

open. The earth didn't move either, although the bedsprings made a terrible racket. There was a lot of groping around, heavy breathing. I had a frightful time undoing her bra. I suppose we must have looked and sounded ridiculous. I mean, if one had had any distance. I didn't have any distance. I can't recall ever having had less distance.

When it was over, we found ourselves lying on our sides, face to face. Chastely, Laura pulled the sheet up to cover her breasts.

"I love you," I said.

Laura shook her head.

"I love you," I said. She put her hand over my mouth. I spoke through her fingers. "I love you," I said. "I love you, I love you." She kept my mouth covered, but she also smiled. I stopped. She took her hand away.

"You're very good looking," I said. "Especially for an old friend."

Laura smiled weakly.

"What are you thinking?"

"Oh, nothing."

"Come on, tell me."

"I'm thinking you're lucky," she said.

"Why's that?"

"Nothing to feel guilty about."

Then she turned her back to me, and I moved in, put my arm around her waist. I could feel the bottom of her breasts against the top of my forearm. "James Bond used to sleep like this with his girls," I said. "Like a couple of spoons."

Laura chuckled. "Yeah," she said. "You're a lot like James Bond."

"Fuck you," I said.

"You have," she said, and wiggled her hips.

"No Amy," I thought, "and I'll have to fight Positano. Probably I'll have to kill him. But who cares? Who the fuck cares?" Then I fell asleep. Really it was just a drunken doze. Probably it only lasted half an hour. When I woke up, Laura was already standing beside the bed. She had her bra and shell on. She was pulling up the jeans.

"I have to go now," she said.

"When will I see you?"

She came over, sat on the bed, pulled on her running shoes. Then she leaned back into me, and we kissed.

I put my arm around her, but she wriggled out of the embrace and moved away. "Greedy, greedy," she said.

I shrugged.

Laura sucked in her stomach, fastened the button at the waist of her jeans. "Soon," she said.

I got the ashtray off the bedside table, put it on my chest, lit a cigarette.

Laura came over and knelt beside the bed. She took the cigarette out of my mouth, kissed me on the lips. Then she took the ashtray off my chest, put it back on my night table, and stubbed out the cigarette.

"I worry about you," she said.

"I'm okay."

"No more smoking," she said.

"You know what?" I said, moving my back against the pillow.

"What?"

"I think I've always loved you."

Laura smiled. "I love you too," she said, "but right now, I have to go." She stopped at the door. "And remember," she said, "you don't have to buy me a wedding present. That's what I'm telling all the ushers."

Aunt and I had dinner alone that evening. Meatloaf and mashed potatoes: quite tasty. Afterward, I looked up Amy's personal number in the directory. I wrote it down on a piece of paper. It was too late to call. Nar was out. And this time I didn't wait up but fell into my snarl of sheets, exhausted, at a little before ten.

Elspeth made us breakfast Thursday and then headed off in the rented Ford. "I'm going to help Jody Rensible sort books for the fair," she explained. "Then go to the dry cleaner and the drugstore."

Nar appeared briefly, grabbed a mug of tea and one of Grape-Nuts. She was already in a skirt and blouse. By 10 A.M., she'd slipped out. Somebody picked her up at the end of the drive.

Laura called around noon. "You all right?"

"Sure."

"I was afraid your feelings were hurt."

"No," I lied. "Of course not."

"Look," said Laura, "we both know who you really love."

"What if I don't get her?" I asked.

"Jesus," said Laura, "I can't believe I'm having this conversation."

"Well, but what if I can't?"

"If you can't have her," said Laura, "then call me back," and she hung up.

When the doorbell rang that afternoon, I imagined that it might be Amy. It was Federal Express. I signed. I also checked to see that the envelope was from Cameron, but I didn't open it.

I went for a walk instead. Coming back over the last hill, in the falling light, I heard a sharp report. Then, about thirty seconds later, I heard a second bang.

The first thing I saw, when I came around the house, was Gilbert's back. He was sitting on the stone retaining wall. He was all hunched over. Nar was in the drive, about thirty feet from her lover. She had the .22. The Isuzu was parked crookedly behind her, its door still open. Gilbert was sobbing.

"So I can fire and reload before you get to me," Nar was saying, "but I don't think it will take more than one of these bullets to kill an asshole like you. To kill an asshole like yourself."

"I'm a writer," Gilbert said. "I didn't mean to hurt anybody, I just wrote down what I found out."

"You started it all, didn't you?" said Nar. "Leaked the first story to the *International Herald Tribune*?"

"That article was good for you," said Gilbert. "Without that piece, nobody outside of a couple of old ladies would ever have heard of Jonas Collingwood."

"I think," said Nar, "that for starters, I'll shoot you in the balls. Those big, fat balls of yours would make an easy target."

"Nar," I said, cutting rapidly across the ground between us, "Nar, don't shoot anybody. Please don't shoot anybody."

Sister snapped her eyes in my direction, brought the gun to her shoulder.

Gilbert began to wail.

I slowed my pace but kept walking.

"Don't touch me," she said. "You so much as lay a hand on me, Brother, and I'll shoot this sick shithead right in the eye."

"All right," I said, and stopped. "Look, Nar, I don't like this guy either, but I don't think we should kill him."

"You don't know," she said, with the gun still pointed at Gilbert's head.

"Maybe I don't know," I said, trying desperately to bring my voice down into the normal range. "We should think about it. We can always shoot him later. But if you shoot him now, we won't be able to unshoot him."

"That's my brother," said Nar, "always the philosopher."

"So here's the thing," I said. "Why don't you put my rifle down, and we can all talk."

Gilbert started to stand. The rifle barked. Gilbert let out a little grunt, fell forward into the driveway. I thought he'd been hit. He looked like he'd been hit. Nar was taking a bullet out of the hip pocket of her jeans and reloading.

Now Gilbert was screaming. "I'm shot," he said, "I'm fucking killed."

But he could stand. And as soon as he'd figured this out, he scrambled back up over the retaining wall and began to gallop off into the woods. Nar slammed the bolt home, but I was relieved to see that she didn't bring the rifle to her shoulder.

"I'm not sure I'm good enough to miss at this range," she said, and passed the weapon to me. "Want to try?"

"No," I said. We stood there, watching the biographer recede.

"Did you hit him?" I asked.

"No, stupid," said Nar. "I never got anywhere near him." Then she went into the house.

I removed the bolt, took a loose stone from the retaining wall, and beat at the metal rod until I was pretty sure it would not go back into the breach. Then I went into the house, put the bolt and gun back in the closet. Nar was at the kitchen table with a fresh half gallon of scotch and two jelly glasses.

"Aren't you glad now that you didn't kill him?" I asked.

"Read this," she said, and presented me with the document from Cameron.

A piece of the agent's stationery was stapled to the proposal.

"Sit down first," it said. "Love, Cammy."

I sat. Nar passed me a glass of Old Smuggler.

By the time Elspeth came home that evening, Sister and I were both quite drunk. There were two Jiffy Pops in the cereal cabinet. I'd burned the first one, popped the second. We'd eaten the second one; then we'd eaten the first one, even though it was burned, and had wiped the charcoal off our lips. Sister had been crying.

"You've been drinking," said Elspeth when she came in the door.

"That's right," I said, and presented her with the proposal. "Read this."

Nar brought Aunt a glass of scotch. Elspeth sat in the Rockefeller love seat. Nar settled on the floor at her feet. I pulled up the Chesterfield.

Aunt started to read, said, "Goodness me." She stopped, took a pull on her drink. "Who was Clifford Irving?" she asked.

"A writer who got paid a lot for an authorized biography of Howard Hughes," I said, "and then it turned out Howard Hughes hadn't authorized it."

"How could anyone compare you to a man like that?" she said, looking at me.

"If I'd done what he thinks I've done, I'd be a lot like Clifford Irving. A lot worse than Clifford Irving."

"What does he think you've done?"

"He thinks I forced Uncle to do the memoir, maybe even made the whole thing up myself."

"I was going to shoot him," said Nar. "I could have done it," she said. "At the very least I could have made him wish he were dead."

Then we sat in silence while Elspeth read the proposal. Finally, she put the pages beside her on the sofa, reached down, and began to run her hands through Nar's hair. She looked at me.

Nar spoke first. "Say it ain't so."

"Well, Harvard clearly isn't the school it's cracked up to be," said Elspeth. "This man's spelling and grammar are both very mediocre."

"What about Italy?" I asked.

"He's right about some of that. There was also a lot of fraternization. Italy had been a Fascist state."

"Was he there at all?" I asked.

"Your Uncle was certainly in Italy during the war. He didn't speak of it often, but that's where I met him. I think he had been out in the countryside for some time."

"Fighting?" I asked.

"He fought somebody."

"So this proposal is nonsense," I said. "The whole thing is made up."

Elspeth stood. "Not exactly. Jonas had a father who was a brute. Dr. Collingwood had trouble with the nevermind. He drank too much, and then he drank at the wrong times. Finally, he was stoned at an operation, and a child died. Whether or not he could have saved the girl had he been sober, this was not clear. But he was a society doctor. The parents were influential. When they were done, he'd been barred from practicing medicine."

Nar broke in. "I knew there was something like that."

"After that, he stayed home," said Elspeth, "and of course the drinking didn't get any better. Jonas was an odd little boy; I suppose he took the brunt of his father's rage. Finally, the child was so badly beaten that he had to be hospitalized. After that, he was sent to a Catholic boarding school. One that also took in strays, orphans. He was an outstanding student, and so they shipped him to Italy, where they operated a truly first-rate high school. Which is how he came to be there during the war."

"So Gilbert got that entirely wrong," I said, trying hard to keep the glee out of my voice.

"No," said Aunt sadly. "He didn't get it entirely wrong. The leg injury was not the result of a German rocket. That bone was broken in Baltimore."

Nar took a pull on her scotch. "What about the rest of it?" she said. "You, and Lily. What about that?"

Elspeth looked at her glass. It was almost empty. I poured her some more scotch.

Nar held up her jelly jar. I poured for her, then helped myself. "We're all going to be drunk as skunks," I said.

Elspeth stood, went into the root cellar, came back with half a package of Marlboros and the big, black, clay ashtray.

She put the ashtray down on the coffee table. We all helped ourselves to cigarettes. "Your Uncle was always in love with my sister, Lily," she said.

"Nice for you," said Nar.

Aunt shrugged. "I knew about it. Have either of you read the first draft of this last book?"

We hadn't.

"You should, then. Lily's in it. She's the beauty, Fiori, something or other. He finds her shoes with the shoes of another man and knows he's lost her. That's what really happened. He'd been dating Lily. One of his novels was about her. I forget the title. It's the one where he says that men who can't believe in God usually find a woman and believe in her.

"He was very persistent. I think she might have married him. Then she met Hamilton and fell in love. Hamilton was everything Jonas was not. He was handsome. Rich. But it wasn't just that. He was also tranquil. I think that's what Lily saw in him.

"Then, one evening, she stood Jonas up. She went for a walk with Hamilton. Jonas was walking on the beach and found their shoes.

"I guess it was the next day, he confronted Lily. They had a dreadful fight. Of course my sister denied having done anything wrong. The heart having no conscience and all that. Then she married Hamilton."

Nar spoke. "And then he married you?"

"Not right away. But within the year. I guess I was the next best thing." Elspeth sat back and sighed. "After the wedding we all spent a lot of time together."

"In Montvale?" I asked.

"No, at first we were all in the city. Then they moved to New Jersey. It turned out that Hamilton was sterile. Or as far as they could tell, he was sterile. It also turned out that he was a bore. Although I was a lot less surprised by this than Lily was."

"I thought Lily was the one who couldn't have a baby," said Nar.

"No," said Elspeth. "Lily had two babies. Two perfectly good babies. Two wonderful babies," she said, and smiled weakly. "When your father told the story, he reversed it. To protect you."

"From what?" I asked.

"From the truth."

"Why did he want to do that?"

"You must understand that an experience like he had with his father leaves the distinct impression that there's some terrible violence inherent in paternity. He never wanted to be a father. I think that if he'd been able to marry Lily, he could have convinced her not to have children. But since having children was really all he could do with her, he went ahead and did that.

"But still, he didn't really want for you and Nar to have a father. He thought you'd be better off, happier without."

"Not really his decision to make though," I said. I took a drink.

"Well," said Elspeth, "he made it anyway."

Nar spoke. "So Lily is our mother? Jonas was our father?"

Elspeth nodded.

"Shithead!" said Nar, quietly.

"But you're the one who got stuck with us," I said.

"That's not how I saw it," Elspeth said. "I didn't feel that I was stuck with you, or with Jonas for that matter. I loved you. I had wanted to be a dancer, and it didn't work out. I admired your father's work."

"That's right," said Nar. " 'They also serve who only stand and wait.' "

Elspeth smiled. "They do," she said. "They do serve."

"Jesus," said Nar. "It's so old-world."

Aunt shrugged. "People rarely marry the ones they love. And even if they do, as in the case of Lily and Hamilton, it's apt to go terribly wrong."

"He didn't like us," I said. "That's why he never acknowledged the fact that we were his children. That's why he made us out as some sort of foundlings, kept alive only by his creaky altruism. We were supposed to be thankful to him for disinheriting us."

"No," said Elspeth. "You mustn't believe that."

"Why not?"

"Because it's not true."

"What is true, then?"

"He wanted to protect you."

"From who?"

"From himself. From his memories of his own father."

"So he made me a bastard?"

Elspeth puffed on her cigarette. "You were born out of wedlock."

"Yeah, the fire-sale baby."

"That was his idea of a joke," said Elspeth.

"Some joke. What about my wild, my murderous gene? What about my auto mechanic's blood?"

Aunt stood. "He was talking about himself," she said. "When your Uncle was cruelest, he was always talking about himself."

21

The woman who is not my mother was already up and juicing oranges when I hit the kitchen Friday morning. I knew the grinder would make a terrible sound, but I clenched my teeth, operated the rotten little machine, and brewed us some of the biographer's chocolate-shop coffee. We both moved about cautiously, as if we were carrying baskets of eggs on our heads. Neither of us spoke. Nar didn't appear at all.

Sick as I was, I still felt oddly hopeful. And when the phone rang, I expected Amy. It was Joe. He'd found a short in the Falcon's generator.

"He's not certain," I told Aunt after hanging up, "but now that he's taped the wire, he thinks that for the first time in a decade, the secretary of state might be able to charge his own battery."

Elspeth smiled wanly. "Hallelujah," she said, but it was almost a whisper. "You want me to drive you down there?"

"Can't I take the Isuzu?"

"It's gone. Gilbert must have come for it last night."

"I guess you'll have to."

Aunt frowned. "I have a morning appointment at Rose's World of Beauty. To get my hair done. Then I really must go to the library. The book sale is upon us. I can take you down there a little after 2 P.M., if that's all right."

I didn't mind. "I'll read the manuscript," I said.

"Good," said Elspeth.

But I didn't read the manuscript. I don't know why, exactly, but I dreaded even going into that room. I called Laura at the *Commons*. I got her assistant. He said she'd call me back. She didn't call me back.

I don't know what happened to Nar. She never came down for breakfast, but when I finally went to her bedroom, she was gone. I had no idea where. Not a clue.

I split a little kindling. I changed my bed, washed the sheets. I thought of reading the newspaper, but when I remembered that it was still down at the end of the drive, I decided against getting it.

It wasn't until nearly 3 P.M. that Elspeth finally drove me to Tarrytown. From there she planned to go directly to ShopRite. "They're predicting snow, so I want to get supplies. I'll be home in time for dinner."

I found Joe in the office, wearing bifocals and looking as professorial as it is possible to look in a blue uniform with your name stitched over the breast pocket.

The picture of what I had been told was a hunting party was still on the corkboard. I pointed to the fat young man. "That's a woman," I said. "The one you brought to the funeral?"

Joe nodded. "Sabina."

"Have you ever looked at any of the books?" I asked. "The ones about the war?"

Joe was riffling through the papers on his desk. "I read the last one."

"*My Life as a Woman*?"

"Yes. After they mentioned it in the newspaper."

"What did you think?"

"The doctor and the baby were both made up. I don't remember any Fiori Anfiteatro either."

"Maybe you forgot?"

"A woman like that?" said Joe, and shook his head. "I'd remember."

"Was Uncle brave?"

"*Sensa paura,*" Joe said, smiling. He seemed to have found what he wanted, and he cleared the loose papers off a small electronic adding machine. "If we had listened to your Uncle, we all would have been dead. Many times. Sabina was the smart one."

I wanted to ask if they'd ever killed anybody, but I couldn't do it. I had too much respect.

I drove home, parked the car against our retaining wall. Then I walked down to Route 448 and retrieved the *Times*. Back in the kitchen, I poured myself a cup of iced tea. The stuff was dreadful.

The item was in Book Notes:

> The publishing house of Faber & Krupp will hold an auction next Tuesday for the paperback rights to a biography of Jonas Aldous Collingwood. They are said to have paid somewhere in the high six figures for domestic rights to the hardback edition of a book tentatively titled *Soldier of Fortune*. Slated for publication in January of 1993, the "warts and all" treatment is to be written by John J. Gilbert, an essayist and biographer who was a Collingwood intimate.
>
> "We're pleased, of course, to have a man with both reportorial and critical talents," noted Lucy Frawling, a Faber & Krupp vice president, "but it's the personal connection that gives this project sex appeal. It's quite unusual for a biographer to have befriended the subject. This adds value to value. Nobody who has any interest

in Collingwood can afford not to read it," she added. "Nobody who is not an ostrich."

I called the library; I spoke with Mrs. Rensible.

"Hi, Nelson. You missed her."

"No, I'm not looking for Elspeth. You know Gilbert, John Gilbert?"

"You mean that nice young man who is friends with your mother?"

"That's right. The nice young man. Is he there?"

"No. But I can tell him to call you, when he comes in."

"When he comes in, would you call me?"

"Okay."

"Jody," I said awkwardly, "would you do me a favor?"

"Sure."

"Don't tell him you're calling me."

"Why all the secrecy?"

"Nothing much. Just a little surprise."

"Where will you be?"

"At Elspeth's home number. You must have it. On your Rolodex."

"Of course."

Off the phone, I went into the kitchen, poured the tea down the sink. It wasn't yet 4 P.M., but I refilled the glass with scotch. The big, black ashtray was in the living room. I fetched it, stuck my thumb down among the charred filters. I stopped in the kitchen to empty the ashes into the aluminum garbage pail, then walked to the root cellar.

The manuscript Classic had rejected was right where I remembered it being, out on top of one of the filing cabinets. This was the original, the book Jonas had meant to write. Uncle's table is aluminum, and wobbly, so I had to pick the typewriter up in order to get it over to the side, in order to make room for the book. This done, I sat in Uncle's creaky chair, lit a cigarette, took a sip of scotch whiskey, and began to read. Or rather I began to skim.

Uncle was a rapid typist, but not a brilliant one. There were no strikeovers or cross-outs on the first page, but the next, and every other, was marred, if legible.

The opening quotation was from William Butler Yeats:

ON BEING ASKED FOR A WAR POEM

> I think it better that at times like these
> A poet's mouth be silent, . . .

Then came the preface I'd heard Whitfield complain about:

> It has been in the nature of man, at least since the Homeric legends, to dramatize his exploits on the field of battle. This largely awkward and inglorious process is willfully transformed into stories that would be completely unrecognizable to anybody with even the vaguest recollection of what actually happened.
>
> The distortion is partly the result of vanity, of course, but it is also a sensible attempt to disguise the horrors of an event that has always been a central theme in human history.

I skipped to the first chapter. This would be my father's description of my mother:

> Rare beauty is always a challenge and a provocation, but in this case it was more, it was a tragedy, the great tragedy of my war. And looking back I like to think that if God existed in anything like the form that the softhearted, the sentimental like to invoke, he would not make a woman who looked like that without first making her wise.
>
> The person of whom I'm writing was nineteen years old at the time of my story, and in the habit of wearing one of those loose peasant blouses, of the sort that were popular in this country twenty years ago and associated with incense, Indian print bedspreads, sandalwood beads, and promiscuity.

Fiori Anfiteatro was not stupid, but neither was she particularly bright.

I skipped ahead to the next chapter.

I had the opportunity, during the summer of 1943, to live in a boardinghouse with three old ladies and eight German soldiers.

During the months in which we all shared the house, seven of the Germans died of an upset stomach. I shot the other one. In the back.

I caught the unfortunate in an ambush. I'd been advised by the older partisans that it was wiser to pretend that one was not shooting a man. "Act as if it's a soup can, or an empty wine bottle."

The execution done, I buried the rifle and moved, as planned, down to the road on the other side of the hill, climbed into the back of a wagon which had been loaded with hay. The time must have been approximately 18:00 hours. I was tired, but also well pleased with myself.

After a killing, I was invariably overtaken with a strong sense of exaltation. Looking back on this from my maturity, I feel about murder the way a heroin addict must about dope: "If this is so wicked, then why does it feel so good?" The cart began to move. It rocked, and I fell into a deep, dreamless sleep.

The next sensation I recall was that of waking with hay in my face. I sat up, sneezed. Then I smelled the salt air. The Mediterranean is an inland sea, but it is a sea nevertheless. It may have been in a body of water like this that, eons ago, lightning struck. This was the miracle which, that afternoon, I had seen reversed.

I climbed out of the cart while it was still moving. The air was warm, the dawn sky gray, the street deserted. I wanted to see the woman. I wanted to know if she was carrying my baby.

I went directly to the steps that led to the castle. The Germans had told the villagers that if the Allies attacked, they should shelter in the fortress.

I had expected to find a sentry, or at least a lookout at the entrance to the fortress, but there was none.

I crossed the first field and went into the courtyard. I saw a cat, a goat, no people.

There was a kitchen building set into one of the walls, with a tin chimney from which smoke was almost always pouring. This morning there was no smoke.

I ducked through the first doorway, paused to allow my eyes to adjust to the diminished light. The barracks room was empty, and I walked through this area and into one of several enclosed stone chambers. I paused here to call out. There was no response.

The ceiling here was higher than in the barracks, and I suspected that this room had been used to stable horses. This vaulted interior was lit with four large, arched windows. These were not now, nor had they ever been, glazed. Through these windows, I caught the breeze from the sea. There was also a strong chemical presence in the air. Toward the center of the room, there was a rectangle of soil that had recently been turned and then sprinkled with a white powder.

I walked carefully around this place and to the far corner of the room. Here I found a large pile of clothes. And shoes. A pair of these had been manufactured in England: too large for a child, too small for a man.

Then I caught the sound. At first I thought somebody was out there, hurting the goat. But this was not an animal. This was the voice of a child. Crying.

I didn't get to the phone until the fourth ring.
"Nelson, this is Jody Rensible."
"Oh," I said. "Hi."
"Are you all right?"
"Sure," I said. "Why do you ask?"

"You sound like you've been crying."

"No," I said. "I'm fine."

"Your friend is here," she said. "Just arrived."

"Thanks," I said, "thanks a lot." I hung up and went back to the manuscript:

> The stone staircase from the beach at Porto Ercole ran upwards to the village, paused there, and then continued until it broached the wall of the fortress on the hill. It had been constructed so that if one took the first step chanting "Father," and repeated the Trinity, taking a word for each riser, the man or woman ascending would reach the top with the word "Ghost." There were exactly five hundred steps. Father, Son, and Holy Ghost. A word for each riser. Even the conjunction got a step.
>
> It's a long walk to salvation, and it was an equally long walk down. I suppose I could have left the baby. He, or she—no, I had not yet determined the sex—was not necessarily my child at all. It might have been, for all I knew, a Nazi in the pupa stage. And yet this angry little thing, this crippling dependence, was all I had anymore, all that was left of the woman. All that was left of love.
>
> This was the place that was all places.
>
> This was the day that was all days.
>
> This was the child that was all children.

I stopped reading, leaned back in Uncle's chair. "A Nazi in the pupa stage," I thought. And then it came to me with the force of revelation. There was no dry ice, no thunder rumbling offstage, but still it was precisely as if the old man were speaking to me. Or rather through me. And this is what I knew and didn't know:

I knew now, in a way I had not known when told, that Jonas was our biological father, and that he had hidden this. The deception seems almost to have been a sort of sadism, a way of keeping a distance between his glorious person and his less glorious offspring.

There were mitigating circumstances, of course. There were

Lily's and Hamilton's feelings to consider. Still, it does seem that Nar and I were the victims, the people with the most to lose from this elaborate con.

But there might also, as Elspeth says, have been an attempt to spare us. A man who had been so badly hurt by his own male progenitor must have been reluctant to be a father himself. He might have anticipated some violence in the very act of paternity.

Gilbert seemed to be heading toward the opposite conclusion, but there is no doubt in my mind that Jonas was a member of the resistance. It's likely that he helped hide at least one downed English pilot, brought him bread and bad wine. Whether or not Uncle ever actually shot a Nazi soldier, I do not know. Nor do I particularly care.

Either way, his stories of murder are clearly not boasts but rather an attempt to expiate some deep and imponderable sense of unworthiness.

Now I see what Gilbert has done to the man who was my father. He engineered that first story in the *International Herald Tribune*. He thrust Jonas into the world and then came, actually came to his house, ate his food, and poisoned him with false praise.

Now he wants to reverse the trick, spin on his heel and reveal Jonas Aldous Collingwood as a fraud. Having made a god, he will now point out the feet of clay.

Uncle was never a god. He was a man, that's all, another little guy, in ragged clothes, stinking of tobacco and scotch. He ordered his chinos out of a catalog, bought his underpants from the cardboard bin at the ShopRite. He rented his house, owned one spectacularly unreliable car.

True, he had a typewriter, and with this he was a magician. But magic didn't help him any more than it had helped Merlin. Because, like Merlin, he fell in love.

Certainly he cared for us. Although he was never comfortable with his paternity. It was Lily he had adored. It was Lily he had sought. What he got was children. And we were, after all is said and done, as strange to him, as unutterably strange to him, as he was ever strange to us.

258

★ ★ ★

So I drove to Caldor. The cashier was slightly bemused. "Not exactly the season for a new baseball bat," she said.

I shrugged. "Nice day, I can always hit some fungoes." It was a wooden bat. The only wooden bat they had.

By the time I got back to Pleasantville, exited the Saw Mill River Parkway at Manville Road, the light was beginning to go out of the sky, and it had begun to snow. It must already have been mid-December, because several of the smaller houses were outlined with Christmas lights.

The library lot was almost empty. But there was one car I recognized. I parked in the slot reserved for the handicapped. "Just as soon be hung for a sheep as a lamb," I thought.

I got out of the car, took off my jacket, wrapped the bat in it, tucked the jacket and weapon under my arm. This looked awkward. But not, I thought, suspicious.

Inside, Jody smiled at me over her glasses. "Feeling better?" she asked.

"Yes," I said.

"Christmas blues," she said.

I nodded.

"I get them too."

I smiled.

"He's in the back," she said. "Near the reference section. Right along the wall."

And there he was, working pretty hard for somebody born to privilege. Wearing the blue blazer, no crest, chinos, no belt. And a pair of those L. L. Bean boots that are rubber on the bottom, leather above the water line.

He hadn't heard me coming up behind him. I put my jacket down, got the bat out.

He had his enormous pen and was making notes on a yellow legal pad. The briefcase was on the floor by his feet. I stood there, quiet as an Indian. I could hear Gilbert's pen scratching paper, I could hear the thunder of my own pulse.

Finally, he sensed my presence, turned to see me, and jumped. "Oh," he said.

I smiled. "Oh indeed."

"So," he said, tentatively.

"So."

"Baseball," he said, smiling faintly.

"That's right," I said, and nodded, "the national pastime."

Three beats of silence.

"I was on your side. I was always on your side," he said.

I said I knew that.

"I have to go to the bathroom," he said.

"Yeah," I said. "I bet you do."

Afterward, I wrapped the bat back in my jacket, went out by the front desk. Jody seemed not to have heard anything. She was smiling. "Did you find him?"

"Yup."

"Was he surprised?"

"We both were," I said.

"He sure left in a hurry," she said.

"That's right," I said. "Nature called."

But no, I hadn't hit him. I let him go. I'm still not sure if this was a victory or a defeat. I guess there are some situations in which neither outcome is possible. You can hurt somebody, or you can not hurt somebody. But you can't win.

Outside, the snow was coming down in fistfuls. I trotted through it to the car, holding the jacket and bat in my arms. I opened the door, put the bat in the passenger seat, shrugged on my jacket, and got in behind the wheel.

The Falcon fired right up. I turned on the lights. Then the wipers. I put in the clutch, shifted into reverse. I had parked directly in front of the public phone. It's one of those austerity units, built to discourage vandals, just a column, without a booth or even a hood. The snow was beginning to accumulate on the metal case.

We would have a white Christmas. Der Bingle would have been pleased.

I wasn't certain that I'd ever seen that phone without somebody attached to it. Usually there's a line. The students stand, or sit on the wall, try not to look bored. And operating the instrument, there's almost always some leggy high school girl. Long, black hair and a book bag. Calling the boy with a car.

I put the Falcon back into neutral. I engaged the emergency brake. With the engine still roaring, I climbed out into the weather. I could smell the exhaust. Snow was falling into my eyes.

I moved to the front of the car, stood there, still in the yellow glow of those ancient headlights. The snowflakes were sharp, then wet against my cheeks.

There were coins in the right front pocket of my chinos. I put the quarter into the slot, dialed Amy's number from memory. I held the receiver in my left hand, used the right one to clutch at my own throat.

Knock and it shall be opened unto you. Seek and ye shall find.

Nar says it's all in the tone of voice.